Before MacGonigal knew it, his feet were off the ground. Something bright and green came from below and zipped up toward the black mass above him. Tracer fire. Spinning on the rope, MacGonigal saw lines of green tracers reaching up for them, and bright, solid, flickering bars of red as the Cobras returned fire with their miniguns.

MacGonigal never saw it coming, but suddenly something was clawing at him, pulling him off the rope, slashing at his face and body. It was gone before MacGonigal realized what it was. *A tree? The son of a bitch dragged us through a tree!*

He was spinning now, wildly, and bouncing on the rope. His right arm was numb, and his left wouldn't function at all. There were more tracers now, all different colors. Some flashed past, and some hung motionless in the sky. MacGonigal was suddenly unbearably thirsty. *I'm in shock,* he thought. *I must be hurt bad.*

*Soldier of Fortune books from Tor*

# MACGONIGAL'S RAID

## VERNON HUMPHREY

TOR

A TOM DOHERTY ASSOCIATES BOOK

MACGONIGAL'S RAID

Copyright © 1988 by Omega Group, Ltd.

First Printing: April 1988

A TOR Book

Published by Tom Doherty Associates, Inc.
49 West 24th Street
New York, NY 10010

ISBN: 0-812-51261-8
Can No.: 0-812-51262-6

Printed in the United States of America

0 9 8 7 6 5 4 3 2 1

to
the real Robbie Robbins,
who went down fighting

# I.

He could feel them crawling over him, and his flesh rippled with disgust. He tried to crane his head down, but he couldn't manage to focus his eyes. Or rather, he was unable to focus his right eye—the left one was glued shut with dried blood and serum. He could only dimly remember how that had happened, and he didn't want to think about it too hard. He might remember something that his mind wanted to hide. He forced himself to think about something else—like the maddening tickle of tiny feet all over his body.

*Cockroaches! That's what they are. They've got to be cockroaches.* It was a litany running through his head, like a song, half-remembered and going round and round in his skull. He hated cockroaches.

He could feel their feelers on his skin. They were clustering around his sores and bruises. They were on his face. He could feel them exploring his swollen left eyelid. He tried to shake his head, to scare them off, but that only brought sickening pain.

He was dimly aware of pain elsewhere. It was strange, the places where he hurt. His broken fingers, with the nails missing, were bad. The burns on the soles of his feet were agonizing. His eye wasn't all that painful, and his testicles were only a dull throb, although from what he could tell they were swollen to the size of canteloupes.

His pain and his preoccupation with the roaches caused him to miss the sound of footsteps coming down the passageway. When the wooden cell door opened, he was taken by surprise. He tried to pull himself back into the stone niche that formed his place of confinement, but hands grabbed him and dragged him out.

He tried to plead with them, *"No more! No more! I'll give you what you want! More than you want!"* but they ignored him. The roaches, which had scurried for cover when the door opened, emerged to watch as they dragged him away, leaving a trail of blood, urine and other matter on the stone floor of the passageway.

The ax rose and fell with a steady rhythm as MacGonigal split one chunk after another. Behind him was a slowly growing mountain of firewood; in front of him, a slowly diminishing hill of logs. He brought the ax down in another powerful arc, splitting a small log, then tossed the halves onto the pile behind him. He stood erect and wiped his forehead, then wiped his hands on the heavy woolen shirt. The shirt was stained with sweat, dark patches that extended all the way down and blended into the saffron of his kilt. His black hair, lightly shot with gray, and his beard—slightly more gray—were also streaked with sweat. The heavy leather belt of the kilt supported a Colt Python, strapped high up on his right side.

He put aside the ax and reached for a jug of cold water, upending it and letting it spill over him, some pouring down his throat, most of it cascading over his chest. He put the jug down and reached for the ax again, then positioned another log for splitting. As he swung the ax overhead, he heard the sound of an engine, faint and far off. He laid the ax aside and reached for the Model 99 Savage that lay across a log near at hand. He dropped the lever of the Savage a fraction of an inch and noted the gleam of brass from the chamber. He snapped the lever shut again.

Rifle in hand, he turned toward the cabin, moving with long-legged, purposeful strides, the revolver bouncing on his hip, his kilt flapping around his hairy legs.

The cabin itself was a raw but solid construction of peeled and dovetailed logs. Even as he hurried toward it, MacGonigal couldn't help feeling a thrill of pride and affection for it. He had bought the land years ago, on an offhand trip through the Arkansas

Ozarks, and it had formed the central theme of his ambitions ever since. In a dozen different countries, in jungles and deserts, he had schemed and planned, building this cabin in his mind a dozen times.

When he finally retired, he had stripped off his uniform, disdainfully refusing to attend the Army's almost obligatory retirement parade, and headed for the Ozarks.

The land was rough, remote, almost inaccessible. He had built a road, or a reasonable excuse for one, as far as Bear Pen Falls, then lugged his tools and possessions up the rough foot trail over the falls and started on the cabin. In a surprisingly short time, he had constructed a comfortable and well-laid-out home. Outbuildings, corral, barn and paddock followed.

And MacGonigal had relaxed. A little farming —gardening, really—a few cattle and horses, a lot of hunting and fishing, and a little writing made up his routine.

Until George Harris and Susan Ennis had entered the picture. That had been bad business. *I never should have listened to that dipshit George Harris*, MacGonigal thought to himself. But that wasn't quite right. George had been a foul ball from the beginning, but Sue was different. MacGonigal still had a fond place in his heart for Sue. It was Sue who had provided the money to rebuild his cabin and replace his possessions and livestock after the place burned down. Of course, Sue was the reason that the cabin had burned in the first place—in fact, she had burned it herself. And Sue was the reason that MacGonigal never went anywhere these days unarmed.

Yeah, he had been stupid to listen to George Harris, stupid to take in a girl on the run from the mob, with three-million dollars of stolen mob money. Even more stupid to shoot it out with the bastards. On the other hand, they had come on his land, had booby-trapped his cabin. They had done a lot of things a reasonable man would resent—and Francis Xavier MacGonigal was not known as a reasonable man when his blood was up. They had asked for it, dammit!

It was that asshole George Harris. He had left a back trail that a blind man could follow, and they had damn sure followed it. Still, George was dead now, probably sniveling and whining in hell, trying to strike one of his endless deals with the devil. And Sue was quite a girl . . . And there hadn't been any more unwanted visitors since he and Sue had dealt with the last bunch.

But it paid a man to keep his guard up.

MacGonigal gained the porch of the cabin in a single, fluid leap and wrenched the door open. The interior of the cabin was a mélange of overflowing bookshelves, gun racks and rough, handmade furniture. Most of the ground floor was a single room that might have been spacious in the original concept, but was now given over to an unbelievable clutter of masculine impedimenta. A huge stone fireplace engulfed one wall, and a wood stove stood across the room opposite it.

To his left, a rough set of stairs led up to the loft. MacGonigal turned and climbed them two at a time, the Savage still gripped in his hairy fist. At the head of the stairs, he finally laid the rifle aside and took up a pair of binoculars. From the loft window, he could look the length of Bear Pen Valley and see who was coming up his road.

For a long moment, all he could see was a plume of dust drifting above the trees, with an occasional flash of the vehicle itself among the fall leaves. He tracked the progress of the vehicle with his binoculars as if he were the captain of a submarine tracking a target vessel.

At last he got a good look at the intruder through a break in the foliage. The black-and-white vehicle with the lights on the roof was unmistakable.

*Harvey Siler. I wonder what the hell he wants out here?* MacGonigal mused as he slung the binoculars around his neck and picked up the rifle again. He shambled back down the stairs and outside, following the trail to the head of the falls.

He watched as the car came to a stop next to the shed that housed his pickup. The door opened and the obese sheriff oozed out of the front seat. He looked up the trail, then resignedly took off his hat, mopped his pink brow and started wheezing his way up to where MacGonigal waited.

"Dammit, Francis," the sheriff panted, "you could see it was me. Couldn't you come down, instead of making me climb up all this way?"

MacGonigal grinned. "Well, Harvey, you looked like you could use the exercise. What brings you out this way, business or just bein' friendly?"

"Business, I reckon," said the sheriff. "Let's go inside and talk and I'll let you pour me a little tot of that stuff you get from overseas."

"Why, I'm surprised at you, Harvey! Drinking on duty. And this is a dry county, too."

The sheriff entered the cabin and flopped down on one of MacGonigal's homemade chairs. Mac put the rifle on a pair of pegs driven into the wall and crossed to a cabinet, where he took out a bottle of Irish Mist and a pair of fairly clean tumblers. Filling both, he handed one to the sheriff, then seated himself and leaned back.

"Thanks, Francis. You always were a gentleman."

"And you always were a man who liked to pussyfoot around a subject. You said you were here on business. What business?"

The sheriff took another sip. "Well, Francis, you know there's been a lot of trouble hereabouts . . . I'm not sayin' you was at fault, you understand. I mean, I never thought *you* was the cause . . . but there was a lot of trouble, and them state boys was snoopin' around . . . couldn't hardly catch my breath for them state boys."

He paused for another appreciative sip. "I mean,

Francis, I know you don't go lookin' for trouble . . . but it seems that trouble comes lookin' for *you* . . . if you understand what I mean?"

"I'm not sure, Harvey. Why don't you just say what you came to say, and get it over with?"

MacGonigal remained silent, and the sheriff went on. "Well, Francis, there's a fella lookin' for you. I thought I'd better come out and talk before he finds you. *Last* time . . . I mean . . . the last fellas who come lookin' for you . . . " The sheriff's voice trailed off. The last people who had come looking for MacGonigal were Nazario's mobsters, and before that it was George Harris, ex–CIA agent, who had left New York just a jump ahead of Nazario, with a naked woman in the trunk of his car.

"How do you know he's looking for me?"

"Well, he keeps askin' folks about a crazy Irishman named Francis Xavier MacGonigal."

"Did he say what *his* name was, or why he's looking for me?"

The sheriff unbuttoned his breast pocket and fished out a small notebook. He leafed through it while MacGonigal waited. "Says his name's Robbins, Robert Robbins. I reckon that's his real name. Could be a made-up name, though."

"Robert Robbins?" said MacGonigal. "Robbie Robbins? What does he look like?"

The sheriff looked up sharply. "Tall fella. Kind of slim. Sandy hair. You know him?"

"Yeah. Robbie and I were in Nam—and a couple

of other places—together. That is, if it's the guy I'm thinking of."

"I didn't actually see him myself, you understand. Some folks said this guy was looking for you, and I had one of the deputies pull him over and give him a warning ticket." His little eyes glittered as he waited for MacGonigal to applaud his stratagem. MacGonigal nodded.

"That was pretty crafty of you, Harvey. Did the guy tell the deputy anything?"

"Well, not a lot. But the deputy—it was Paul Neighbors—got a chance to check his driver's license through the computer in Little Rock, and it come back all clear and on the up and up.

"Anyhow," the sheriff continued, "while they was talkin', the fella told Paul that he was lookin' for you—lookin' for a crazy Irishman that plays the bagpipes, that was the way he put it."

MacGonigal smiled slightly at the way the sheriff put it. He had no doubt that Harvey Siler considered him crazy—he knew that most of his neighbors did. But he got along with everybody, and nobody bothered him.

The sheriff paused a moment, looking directly at MacGonigal. "*You* wouldn't have any idea as to why this fella's lookin' for you, would you, Francis?"

"Like I said, he's an old friend. Likely enough, he's just passing through, and thought to look me up for old times' sake."

The sheriff shifted uncomfortably, then resumed

his direct, flat glare. "Francis, the last time someone came looking for you, some people hereabouts ended up dead. Just between you and me, a lot happened up here that I didn't tell the state boys about."

MacGonigal returned the sheriff's stare. His silence seemed to bother the sheriff, who paused before going on.

"Now, you listen to me, Francis. I know that a man's business is his own, and I ordinarily don't mess in too much. But I don't want no more killins in this county, understand? If this fella is bringing trouble, I want to know about it."

MacGonigal took a sip of his drink. "Well, Harvey, if there's any problem, I'll take care of it."

"No, no, Francis! I know how you take care of things. If there's a problem, *I'll* take care of it. That understood?"

MacGonigal smiled a steely, humorless smile. "I understand, Harvey. I'll let you know if there's any need for you to worry."

"Well, I guess we understand each other . . ."

MacGonigal rose. "We do, Harvey. I don't want trouble any more than you do." He moved to the door and opened it while the fat man negotiated his bulk around the table.

It was nearly dark when Robbins showed up, the sound of his vehicle and the dust raised by its passage announcing his coming well ahead of time.

MacGonigal lay in the brush on the side of the

road, just a few yards from the shed where he parked his pickup, and watched the green stationwagon approach. The driver seemed as cautious as Harvey Siler had been, barely creeping forward over the rutted, rocky road. When he reached the turnaround, he stopped, leaving the engine running, as if not sure what to do.

At last he edged the stationwagon over to the shoulder and killed the engine. MacGonigal watched as he got out, looking around as if bewildered. MacGonigal brought the Savage to his shoulder and examined the newcomer through the scope. The hairline had receded a little, and the man was heavier than he remembered, but it was Robbie.

"Can I help you, stranger?"

The man jumped as if stung, whirling around in the direction of the sound. "Jesus Christ, Mac! Don't sneak up on a man like that!"

MacGonigal rose to his feet, the rifle held casually across his body. "What's wrong, Robbie? You got a guilty conscience?"

Robbins ignored the remark. "I've been looking for you for two weeks now, Mac. Is there someplace where we can talk?"

MacGonigal pondered a moment. "What's wrong with right here? There ain't anybody around to listen in on us."

"Wait a minute, Mac," said Robbins, "we've always been friends. People told me you've turned into a hermit—some people in town claimed you'd shoot first and ask questions later if I came on your property. But we go back a long ways, and I'm damned if I'm going to stand here while you make up your mind whether that means anything to you."

MacGonigal lowered the rifle. "Come on, my cabin's up that way." He jerked his head toward the trail up the falls.

They climbed silently, Robbins following behind MacGonigal. As they reached the top of the falls, Robbins got his first view of MacGonigal's cabin. "Well, I'll be damned! They didn't exaggerate when they told me about you. You really are a hermit!"

MacGonigal grunted and led the way up to the cabin, opening the door and ushering Robbins in. Robbins' glance swept over the big, jumbled room. "Mac, this is just like you. If they'd asked me what your place would be like, this is what I'd have described."

He crossed the room to the fireplace and looked at the items scattered on the mantel. He picked up a big, strong-backed bowie knife with a brass cross guard and drew it from its heavy saddle-leather sheath. He looked at the markings on the blade, then swung around, his eyebrows raised.

"This your old Randall? The one you used to carry?"

MacGonigal returned the rifle to its pegs. "Yeah," he grunted. "That's it. Had it for years."

Robbins looked at the guns and books that lined the wall. "Everything here looks new, Mac." Robbins continued to prowl around the room. "Jesus, Mac, there must be forty- or fifty-thousand dollars' worth of guns here."

"Closer to eighty," said MacGonigal as he opened the cabinet and took out a can of coffee and a pair of stoneware mugs. He filled a kettle at the pump, after priming it with water from a bucket on the floor, then stoked up the wood stove and put the kettle on to boil while he pulled out a japanned tin coffeepot and filled its strainer with grounds.

"That's a lot of money, Mac. Where'd you get that kind of dough—especially on your retired pay?"

"I reckon, old buddy, that that's none of your damned business. But if you must know, I take a job now and then, sell some of my writing, sell a horse or cow. I get along."

"Yeah, you get along, Mac."

The kettle was whistling. "How do you take your coffee, Robbie?"

"Black, like always," said Robbins. He turned a chair around and sat straddling it. He sipped the coffee in silence while MacGonigal did the same.

"Well, aren't you even curious, Mac?"

MacGonigal turned guileless eyes on Robbins. "Curious about what, Robbie?"

"Come on, Mac. You must have some idea why I'm here. Don't you want to know the details?"

MacGonigal put his mug down. "I was wondering when you'd get around to leveling with me. You and I went through a lot together and, at first, I thought maybe you were just coming by to say hello to an old buddy. But that ain't quite it, is it, buddy?''

"No, I'm here for a reason, Mac. I've been doing some research on you lately."

"I figured that—but before we go any further, I guess I ought to tell you that I've had a few bright boys try me on before. It doesn't get them anywhere."

As MacGonigal finished speaking, there was a metallic click from under the table. Robbins' eyes widened slightly. He put his cup down carefully and laid both hands flat on the table beside it.

"I'm not armed, Mac."

"Wouldn't make a damn if you were, Robbie. This is just my subtle way of saying, 'Don't fuck with MacGonigal.'" He paused. There was another metallic noise from under the table as he let the hammer back down. Robbins seemed to sag slightly as he heard it.

"Don't get any ideas, old buddy." MacGonigal smiled. "Why don't you get on with your story . . . and I'll decide what to do about this hogleg after I've heard you out."

"Okay, Mac. I've come to feel you out about a job."

"What kind of a job?"

"The usual kind. I can't give you the details now, but it's your kind of job. The pay is good, too."

"I'm not sure I understand that business about 'my kind of job'—maybe you'd care to elucidate."

Robbins sighed. "Let's quit playing games, Mac. I'm recruiting mercenaries. I can't tell you exactly what the job is, but it'll take about six months, start to finish. We'll pay a reasonable fee. What do you say?"

"Hold it a minute, Robbie. I don't know where you got the idea I'm a hired gun, but you're off the trail on that one. When I said that I take a job now and then, I didn't mean that kind of job. I'm retired from the Army, and that's it."

Robbins' face was expressionless, his eyes like polished buttons. "Sure, Mac, sure. You rake yards, and that rebuilds your place and buys you eighty-thousand dollars' worth of guns on top of it. Sure. And you deliver the morning paper on the side."

"I don't know where you're getting your information, buddy, and I don't think I like the idea of taking this 'job' you're offering."

"Mac, you can take it or leave it. But if you *don't* take it, you're in deep kimshi, old buddy."

"It strikes me, Robbie, that you're not in any position to make threats right now."

"It's not a threat, Mac. If you don't take this job, you're going to have lots of trouble—with the IRS, with your bank, with a lot of government agencies you never heard of."

MacGonigal paused, stunned. "You son of a bitch! You really *are* trying to recruit me! You're working for the Company, aren't you?"

"Never mind who I'm working for, Mac. Let's just say I've got backing. We've got a job to do, and you're going to help—don't look at me like that! Just listen, and I think you'll *want* to come along. This job concerns an old friend of yours, Steve Nichols."

\*   \*   \*

MacGonigal could smell the leaf mold. They had crawled into a thicket and lay close to the ground while the NVA hunted them, calling and halloing to each other, and crisscrossing through the brush. MacGonigal shoved his face in the mold and lay still, cold sweat trickling from his armpits. Armstrong was on his right, as still and as sick with fear as he was.

Whitehead was on MacGonigal's left, whispering into the microphone. He was only about six feet away, but MacGonigal couldn't make out the exact words. All the same, it was too loud. *They* would hear—had to hear. An irrational rage rose up inside MacGonigal; he wanted to strangle him, stab him, smash him—anything to keep him quiet.

At the same time, he wanted him to *shout*, to do anything to get the message through. They had stumbled into the basecamp, literally stumbled. One minute they were moving slowly through the brush, intent on finding fresh tracks, any sign of human movement. Then, suddenly, there was a whiff of wood smoke.

That was what saved them, a random eddy of wind that carried the odor of the cooking fire to them. They melted into the ground, and not a half a minute later a group of NVA came up from the stream, laughing and carrying their AK-47s slung across their backs.

It was the last one, tail-end Charlie, who saw the tracks. He came stumbling up the trail, his head down, lugging two kerosene cans full of water. Suddenly he stopped dead. You could see the wheels turning in his head as he put it together: the cleated bootprints, the fact that they went off the trail, the sudden realization that they had to be right *there*. He dropped the cans with a splash, but he was dead before they hit the ground.

In the confusion that followed, they put distance between themselves and the camp and gave the NVA some wounds to lick in the process. They didn't go far, though, just to the thickest, most impenetrable patch of brush they could find. They wriggled into the middle of it and formed a tight circle, facing out.

It lasted for hours, Whitehead tirelessly whispering into the microphone, and the North Vietnamese thrashing through the bushes, looking for them.

Daylight faded and they lay there as if already dead. MacGonigal had ceased to be bothered by the insects and leeches and simply waited, his M16 in front of him, the firing device for a Claymore directional mine clutched in his right hand.

He started when Whitehead touched him, his hand contracting around the firing device—fortunately, the safety wire was still in place. Whitehead whispered something, and when MacGonigal couldn't hear, he crawled a foot or so closer.

"Check your harness. They're bringing us out on the strings."

The realization that Whitehead had got through to Chu Lai was almost painful. He reached down to check his Swiss seat, the rope harness that wound, diaperlike, around his waist and between his legs. He unclipped his snap-link and slid it down into position, clipping it to the harness in front.

Whitehead struck him sharply with the muzzle of his M16. "Pass it on, damn it! They'll be here in a few minutes."

He whispered the news to Armstrong, and heard him pass it to Nichols. Then they settled down to wait again.

This time it was different. Each second seemed to creep. The insects were torture now, clouds of them feasting on the waiting men, attracted by their sweat and the scent of their fear. The leeches couldn't be felt or heard, but they knew they were there, and there was nothing they could do about them. They waited.

When they came, it was as if the atmosphere had thickened, the throb and clatter of the helicopter blades blending with the whine of the mosquitoes and slowly overpowering the background noises.

Whitehead was talking plainly now, directing the scout ship in, giving the enemy's location and dispositions, telling them their status. Suddenly, shockingly, he switched on the strobe light. The patch of brush where they lay hidden was brilliantly lit for a fraction of a second, then plunged into absolute darkness, then bright again as the light flashed.

There was a startling *whoosh* overhead as one of the Cobra gunships salvoed rockets into the jungle ahead of them. Whitehead was up now, the light flashing right over MacGonigal. "Fire the damn Claymores!"

On his right, Armstrong fired his, and the concussion seemed to shake the jungle apart. MacGonigal squeezed his firing device, clutching it convulsively, as if to crush it in his hand. Then he remembered the safety wire, tore it out of the way, and squeezed again. This time the Claymore went off, bringing down a rain of leaves and twigs.

They were all up and running now, Whitehead carrying the flashing strobe light. In the alternating light and darkness, it was impossible to avoid running into things. MacGonigal held his rifle close to his chest, tucked his head down and tried to stay close to Armstrong.

Now the trees were bending, borne down by the blast of the rotor blades. Up above, barely seen in the flashes of the strobe, was the black hulk of the Huey. MacGonigal thought he saw the bags tumble from the door, the neatly flaked ropes inside paying out as they fell.

Suddenly MacGonigal had a rope in his hand. He slung the M16 around his neck and tried to clip the rope into the snap-link. The pilot was already lifting off, and the rope was running through his hand. He couldn't get enough slack. Frantically he ripped a dozen feet through his hand, throwing the slack ahead of him, taking his turns, and clamping his right arm behind his back.

Before MacGonigal knew it, his feet were off the

ground. Something bright and green came from below him and zipped up toward the black mass above him. Tracer fire. Spinning on the rope, MacGonigal saw lines of green tracers reaching up for them, and bright, solid, flickering bars of red as the Cobras returned fire with their miniguns.

MacGonigal never saw it coming, but suddenly something was clawing at him, pulling him off the rope, slashing at his face and body. It was gone before MacGonigal realized what it was. *A tree! The son of a bitch dragged us through a tree!*

He was spinning now, wildly, and bouncing on the rope. His right arm was numb, and his left wouldn't function at all. There were more tracers now, all different colors. Some flashed past, and some hung motionless in the sky. MacGonigal was suddenly unbearably thirsty. *I'm in shock,* he thought. *I must be hurt bad.*

MacGonigal didn't take part in the battle fought the next day, but as it was snarling and growling to a finish, another team went in to look for survivors. They found Whitehead at the base of the tree, his body almost unrecognizable. Armstrong was about seventy-five feet up, his arms wrapped around a limb, and at first they thought he was alive. They never found the others.

MacGonigal shook his head. "You'll have to do better than that, Robbie. Nichols is dead. He died that night we had to come out on the strings. The chopper pilot pulled us through a tree."

"No, no, Mac. Not dead. Missing. They never found him—at least not during the war. But he turned up alive in Cambodia. We heard rumors about him off and on, and about five years ago he walked into a refugee camp in Thailand."

"About *five years* ago? That would mean that he survived . . . let's see . . . nine years in those jungles. How the hell did he manage that?"

"He managed. He hooked up with some Montagnards . . . they found him and took care of him. He was in bad shape—really broken up. It was quite a while before he could get around, and, by then, things were falling apart in Vietnam. He never did manage to contact us, and when the Yards were driven out, he just went with them. Once over the border, he passed from tribe to tribe, got himself involved in what was going on . . . you know what was happening . . ."

"Yeah, the Yards and a whole bunch of other people were being slaughtered. And Steve was in the middle of it. So where is he now?"

"That's the problem, Mac. You understand, he was quite an asset for a while—a gold mine of intelligence. They milked him for a couple of years. I mean, he had been where *no one* had been. It was like opening a window for us."

"And when he was dry, they tossed him on the trash heap."

"No, Mac, the Company isn't like that—they found him another job."

"What kind of job—garbageman at Langley? Grounds keeper at Camp Peary?"

"Come on, Mac. Don't be so damn cynical. He was put to work in a very sensitive area."

"Like what? All he knew how to do was to live in the jungle—you're not telling me that they sent him back into Southeast Asia. I know that the Company thinks it's above the law, but even *they* must have *some* limits."

"Dammit, Mac, you've got me out on thin ice now. No, they didn't send him to Southeast Asia. They found a job for him somewhere else."

MacGonigal frowned. "What is this, a guessing game? If they gave him a job, and they used his so-called talents, and they didn't send him back into the same jungle he walked out of, then there's only one place he could be."

"I didn't tell you that. But . . ."

"But I'm right. Great. Steve Nichols is in Nicaragua, sneaking through the bushes and making the world safe for Mom and apple pie."

Robbins grimaced. "There's a little more to it than that, Mac. Steve isn't actually sneaking through the bushes—and that's where you come in."

MacGonigal blinked. "Where I come in? Wait a minute . . . Robbie, give me the straight story. You come up here threatening to have the whole U.S. Government screw up my life, telling me a wild story about a man that I thought was dead, and now you tell me that . . . Something smells here—you've got something awfully rotten up your sleeve."

"Yeah, Mac, I guess I have. You got anything to drink around here?"

"What the hell is it with you guys? People keep coming to my place and asking for drinks. What do you think I am, the goddamn county watering hole?"

He got up, went to the cabinet, and pulled out bottle and tumblers. Robbins noted with relief that the Colt had returned to its holster.

MacGonigal poured two tumblers. "*Slaint!*" Robbins looked at him uncomprehendingly. "*Slaint!*" repeated MacGonigal. "That means 'Health!' you uneducated sassenach. The reply is '*Slaint mor,*' '*Great health.*'"

"Oh," said Robbins. "Well, *Slaint mor.*"

They raised their glasses, sipped, and returned them to the table. "Well, Mac, I guess you've backed me into a corner. I *told* them I'd have to come clean with you." He took a healthy mouthful from his glass. "This is going to be a long story. You got anything to eat?"

MacGonigal pushed his chair back. "Jesus, it ain't enough they come around cadging drinks—they expect you to feed 'em, too!" He rose slowly to his feet, then turned and grinned at Robbins. "I was just going to suggest some supper, myself. How does a nice thick steak sound to you? My own beef," he added enticingly.

Robbins smiled back. "It sounds great, Mac. It sounds like you're starting to drop that bad-ass act of yours."

"It ain't an act, and you know it, me boyo," MacGonigal called from the pantry room. "Make yourself useful and set the table. Dishes over there, cutlery in the drawer."

In a surprisingly short time, MacGonigal had the steaks on the table, hot and juicy, with vegetables, toast and coffee. Robbins had watched the performance wonderingly.

"You're quite the housewife, Mac. Don't tell me you baked the bread and did the canning, too?"

"Not hardly, old buddy. Like I said, I do a little work hereabouts—help out a neighbor now and then. And when I slaughter a beeve or a hog—or kill a deer, or something like that—I give a little bit to my friends. And in return, I usually get a few jars come canning and jellying time. Every now and then, a fresh loaf of bread, some sausage, that sort of thing."

For a while, they ate silently, carving the thick steaks into manageable chunks and chewing them slowly. At last, Robbins pushed back from the table. MacGonigal rose and primed the pitcher pump, filling a large tub, which he placed on the stove.

"I'll wash. You dry."

They cleared up and put away, and MacGonigal emptied the washtub. Then he crossed the room and rummaged among the shelves, producing a leather tobacco pouch and a Peterson pipe. He charged and tamped the bowl of the crooked pipe and lit it with a splinter from the stove. He tossed the pouch to Robbins, who fished his own pipe from his jacket pocket. MacGonigal busied himself with lighting a fire in the huge fireplace, then settled down in one of his rough chairs. Robbins took his cue and sat across from him.

MacGonigal blew a cloud of fragrant blue smoke. "Well, Robbie, me boyo, it's a long story ye've to tell me."

"Yeah. One hell of a long story." He took a puff on his pipe, then continued. "Steve came out of the jungle in Thailand, like I said. You can't imagine the excitement he caused. I mean, here was *one of our own* who'd spent years wandering around in an area that's absolutely *sealed* to the rest of the world. Mac, you have no idea of how little we knew about what was going on in there—until Steve came out.

"And he'd been *everywhere*. I mean, he had contacts like you wouldn't believe! It was like finding the Rosetta stone. All of a sudden, here was an asset who could not only tell what he saw, but he could interpret it, too. And what he hadn't seen, he had heard. And he had tracked down rumors, verified reports —hell, he was running his own company toward the end there!

"We debriefed him for almost two years. It wasn't just a matter of milking him—we fed back to him everything we had, and he put it together for us. Things that had puzzled us for years—we briefed him, and he was able to make sense out of it, based on what *he* knew. And he gave us contacts—this is *absolutely top secret*, Mac. So help me, if you ever breathe a word about what I'm telling you . . ."

"I'm not known for talking out of school, Robbie. Get on with your story."

"Okay. We built a network in Southeast Asia—or rebuilt one—based on what we got from Steve. In fact, it was Steve who built the network—he just turned it over to us, vouched for us, so to speak."

"And, bingo! the Company's back in business at the old stand."

"That's overstating it, Mac. But it certainly put us back into an area where we had nothing. Anyhow, after two years, Steve had given us about all he could, without being sent back in, and even we're not stupid enough for that, for all your low opinion of us. And that left Steve on the shelf. He didn't like being benched, and he was too valuable a talent to waste. So we had to find something else for him, and fortunately, something came up."

Robbins took a pull on his pipe and went on. "We needed assets in Central America, so we gave Steve a prep and put him in. The boy's a natural. In six months, he had a network like you wouldn't believe. And he was producing high-grade HUMINT. In a year, he had assets everywhere—I won't bore you with exactly where—and he was feeding us intelligence that was almost unbelievable in both quality and quantity."

"Are you sure he was working for you?" asked MacGonigal quietly.

"Always the possibility of an agent being doubled, of course. But everything he gave us checked out —and you can believe we checked it! And this wasn't low-grade giveaways he was feeding us, either. No, Steve wasn't a double agent—not a chance in a hundred."

MacGonigal tamped his pipe again, then took another puff. It was out. He took another splinter from the stove and relit it. "This is a beautiful story you're telling me, Robbie. But where does it say 'F. X. MacGonigal enters stage right'?"

"I'm coming to that, Mac. Like you say, it's a beautiful story, but about two months ago it went sour. Steve disappeared. Gone. Vanished like a puff of smoke. Oh, his network was still operating, but it was operating blind. It took us a while to get things back into shape, but the bottom line was, they got Steve."

"*Who* got Steve?"

"Them. The opposition. The guys in badly fitted suits."

"So what's the big deal? They'll trot him out in front of the TV cameras and say, 'Look what we caught! A live CIA agent!' A few crazies will picket the White House, and everyone will forget about it. And in a few months the Company'll swap him for one of their assets."

"Are you thick, Mac? Steve's got our whole

operation—both in Central America *and* in Southeast Asia—*in his head*! He's the catch of a lifetime!"

"So? If that's what they've got, that's what they've got. I still don't see why you're sitting here in my cabin, smoking my tobacco and digesting my steak."

Robbins leaned forward. "We know where he is, Mac. And we're going to get him back. *That's* where you come in."

"Me? Hell, doesn't the government have any in-house rescue capability? I seem to recall they had somebody in that line of work."

"*Delta Force*? Don't make me laugh! Those clowns could fuck up a wet dream—and they've proved it. Several times."

"So the Company is taking on outside help for this one?"

"That's it. It's a little more complicated than that, of course. First of all, we want to be sure we get him. We can't leave him in their hands. And we need deniability, in case anything goes wrong. Delta Force has too many leaks."

"What you really mean is your tit's in the wringer, and you've got to get it out before the Congressional Oversight Committee smells a rat."

"That's a crude way of putting it."

"But accurate."

Robbins nodded, the slightest inclination of his head. "Yeah. We've got our hand stuck in the cookie jar, and we're trying to get it out before mama comes home."

"What's the pay?"

"Thirty K, plus expenses."

MacGonigal made a show of dropping his pipe. "That's good, Robbie. Funniest thing I've heard all day. Sounded like you just said 'thirty K.'"

"All right, sixty K."

"You go up fast, me boyo. Make it a hundred-and-fifty K. Plus expenses."

"Mac, I haven't got authorization to go over seventy-five."

"That's good, Robbie. That's even better than your last one. You've got a real future as a stand-up comedian. The Company's got its collective tit caught in the biggest wringer of the decade, and you can't go over seventy-five."

"Look, Mac, this is a deep operation, really *deep*. Equipment, transportation, communications, everything has to come off the bottom of the deck. You can't imagine what it's going to cost to mount this operation. And not a cent of it's recoverable. Everything has to be ditched. You understand that. You can see why I can't offer more than seventy-five."

"I can see where a hundred and fifty is a drop in the bucket—and you square it with the IRS. That hundred and fifty is take-home."

Robbins surrendered. "I'll have to get authorization tomorrow."

"Fine. Fill me in on the details and we'll shake on it."

"You'll get a full briefing at Peary. If the authorization comes through, we'll be there tomorrow." He rose and knocked out his pipe. "I'm beat, Mac. Can you put me up for the night, or do I have to drive back down that washboard you call a road?"

"I can put you up. Cost you extra, though."

"And you call *me* a comedian!"

## II.

Someone was shaking him. He tried to brush aside the hand, but it persisted. "Wake up, Robbie! We got company."

Robbins struggled to a sitting position. It was pitch-dark. He could barely make out MacGonigal's form in front of him. "What's going on, Mac?"

"Listen!"

He strained to hear. Very faintly, he could make out the growl of an engine. It sounded a long way off. "Shit, Mac. It's nothing."

"Get up." MacGonigal was moving away, toward the end of the loft.

"Look out here."

Robbins struggled to his feet and made his way across the loft, nearly tripping on something that lay on the floor. MacGonigal had opened the loft window, and the sound of the engine was louder. "I don't see anything."

"Someone's coming up the road, and he's got his lights off."

"Who . . ."

"Only one bunch of people I know of. Nazario's bunch. The mob has a long memory—especially when they get ripped off. I thought I'd seen the last of 'em, but I guess not."

Robbins felt something cold and hard against his bare thigh. He reached down to grab it. "What's this?"

"Loaded shotgun. You take it. Get dressed. I'll meet you downstairs. No lights."

Robbins was sitting on the bed, pulling on his boots, when he heard a sibilant whisper. "Hurry it up. If it's who I think it is, these guys mean business."

Robbins stumbled down the stairs. At the bottom, something hit him in the chest.

"What the hell's this?"

"Browning Hi-Power. It's loaded, too. There's an extra magazine in the pocket on the holster. I'm going out the back. You cover me with the shotgun. Once I'm out, you join me. We'll move up to the head of the trail by the falls and wait for them."

"Then what?"

"Depends . . . If I start shooting—if *anybody* starts shooting—you shoot. And shoot to kill—don't play around."

Before Robbins was fully ready, MacGonigal banged the back door open and shot through it. In the scant moonlight, Robbins got a glimpse of flying kilt, boots and a scope-sighted rifle. MacGonigal crashed into the brush a few yards away and stopped, his urgent whisper carrying across the distance. "Come on! Don't stand there!"

Robbins dashed out blindly, the shotgun at port arms across his chest, the big Browning flapping on his hip. He crashed into the brush, and MacGonigal brought him up short, almost tackling him.

"Jesus, you're clumsy, Robbie. Follow me now. Stick close."

MacGonigal was off, gliding silently through the brush. Robbins tried to emulate him, but had little success. He blushed silently as MacGonigal hissed at him each time he snapped a twig. Finally MacGonigal stopped and pressed him down. The growl of the engine could be heard plainly. From the sound of it, it was a truck or Jeep in four-wheel drive and compound low. It ground slowly on while they waited.

At last it stopped. They heard the doors open and close. Indistinct murmurs reached them. They could hear people moving around, crunching the brush. Doors opened and closed again, not exactly slamming. Someone below hissed angrily. MacGonigal's hand closed on Robbins' bicep.

"I count eight. How many do you make?"

"I can't tell."

There was a sudden crashing sound below, the breaking of glass. A voice, faint but distinct floated up.

"Asshole! What'd you do that for?"

The reply was indistinct, but the first speaker's voice was clear.

"Well, a broken windshield ain't gonna stop him, for chrissake!"

"Sounds like they just trashed your car, Robbie," whispered MacGonigal. There were more sounds. Someone was hacking away with a metal instrument. "I hope you've got insurance, old buddy. They're really doing a job on it."

There was more angry murmuring from below, then the men moved toward the trail head. There was a brief glimmer of light, followed by an angry voice.

"Put that out, asshole!"

The men began to work their way up the trail. MacGonigal shifted his position slightly, with Robbins following him. They could hear the party below floundering as they tried to make their way up the steep, slippery trail in the dark. There was some subdued cursing and the sound of something sloshing.

"I think they've got a can of gasoline, Mac. They're going to try to burn you out."

"The hell they are! These bastards aren't going to do *anything*. I'll see to that!"

The first figure came into sight. In the dim moonlight, he seemed a bulky, formless figure. There was a dull glint of metal in one hand.

"Ingram submachine gun—drug dealer's weapon. Won't do him much good tonight, though."

A second figure had appeared, and then a third. They huddled by the trail head as the rest came up, one by one. After a hurried, whispered conversation, they started for the cabin.

There was a thrashing in the brush down the trail. A straggler. MacGonigal rose silently. "Keep those other bastards covered. I'm going to intercept the man coming up the trail."

His quarry was still struggling upward, lugging a five-gallon jerry can that sloshed and gurgled with each step, pulling him off balance. He was all alone. MacGonigal watched as he reached the top of the falls and put the jerry can down, apparently to shift hands. *This is too easy*, thought MacGonigal as he stepped up behind him. Bringing the Savage up and back, he delivered a smash with the steel-shod butt. The man collapsed with a rattle and a thump. MacGonigal brought the butt down twice more, making a sound like hitting a broken melon. MacGonigal moved back to where he had left Robbins.

"Did you take care of him?"

"Permanently. Where are the others?"

"They went up that way," Robbins said, gesturing toward the cabin with the shotgun. "What do we do next?"

"Well, I count six that came up first, then the one with the gas can. That leaves one left over. He must be down by their car. I hate to leave the others to their own devices up here, but I think we'd better take out the one by the car first."

"Tell you what, you go down and get him, and I'll watch these up here."

MacGonigal considered. "Okay. But watch it. Those Ingrams aren't worth a damn in most situations, but they can put out a lot of lead. If they get a fix on you, they'll make things awful hot."

"Don't worry. I'll just watch. But if you hear any shooting, come back fast."

"All right, this is the way we'll do it. I'll go down the other side of the falls and take out the guy by the car. If you hear shooting down there, use your own judgment. I'll come back up the same way and circle around. I'll try to get one or two more without making a fuss. When the shooting starts up here, you ought to be able to locate them easily. Just come up behind 'em and grease 'em. Got it?"

"Yeah, I got it. But, Jesus Christ, I'm glad I'm a *friend* of yours."

"Anybody that pays me a hundred-and-fifty-thousand dollars is a friend of mine, old buddy," said MacGonigal as he drifted off into the darkness.

At the cabin, the first hood, obviously the boss, was giving instructions to the second. "Go see what's up with Alex. That asshole probably fell down the cliff."

"Nah, we'd have heard the racket. Shit! He's probably lost in the dark."

"Well, find him then!"

"Can I use a light?"

"For chrissake, no! Are you fuckin' crazy? That

fucker in that log cabin is *dangerous*. For all I know, he's awake and watching us right now."

The other man seemed to suppress a shudder. He stumbled off, tripping and falling almost immediately.

"For chrissake, keep it quiet, shithead!"

The other man muttered something angry and went thrashing off in the general direction of the falls, guiding on the sound.

It seemed like he was gone forever. The leader kept shifting his position and muttering. Obviously, he was impatient. After a while, another figure approached through the darkness.

"Who's that?"

"It's me, Larry. George and I were wondering what's going on."

"That asshole Alex has got himself lost. Eddie went off to find him."

At that moment, there was a shout. "Holy shit! Come over here, you guys. Alex is dead!"

MacGonigal was perhaps a hundred yards from the shed when he saw the vehicles. There was Robbins' stationwagon, and just beyond it a long-bed Toyota Landcruiser. *These boys came for an outing. It's a wonder they didn't all wear knickers and Smokey the Bear hats.*

Just then he caught a whiff of cigarette smoke. *What an asshole! Couldn't go for half an hour without a smoke. MacGonigal, me boyo, this is going to be too easy.* He crept forward, the odor growing stronger, while he watched for the tell-tale glow. In a moment he saw it. The lookout man was leaning against the Landcruiser, smoking. MacGonigal edged forward, using Robbins' stationwagon as cover.

The man was only a few feet away. MacGonigal lowered the Savage to the ground and drew the big Randall knife.

Suddenly there was a commotion from above. He could hear men shouting and thrashing in the bushes. His intended victim stepped away from the vehicle, out of easy range, and looked up, trying to peer through the darkness to fathom the reason for the noise. Suddenly a voice came floating down from the top of the bluff.

"Look out down there, Frank. The bastard is around here somewhere. He killed Alex."

Frank spun around, looking in all directions, his eyes were wide with fear and the Ingram in his fist wavering dangerously. He edged sideways nervously, but turned to call back up the bluff.

"He ain't down here—I don't see nothin' . . ."

His speech broke off in an explosive grunt as MacGonigal lunged at him, driving the seven-and-a-half-inch blade into his back with a looping blow from below. The man arched his back and stumbled forward, pulling himself off the knife blade. He turned, seeing MacGonigal at last, and grappled with him.

"What's goin' on, Frank? What the hell's happening down there?"

MacGonigal had the heel of his hand under Frank's

chin, holding him back, while he struggled to free his right wrist from the man's grip. They swayed together a moment, and MacGonigal wrenched free, sweeping the knife around in a roundhouse cut and following it with a vicious backhand. He felt the blade sink deep into muscle tissue at each stroke.

"Frank?" the voice called with a rising inflection. "What the hell's going on?"

"He's killin' me! Holy Jesus, he's killin' me!"

MacGonigal bore in, knife held low against his right side, and stiff-armed the man, knocking him off balance, then brought the knife up into the pit of the stomach. He put his weight behind it, feeling for the heart, then wrenched the blade right and left. The man went limp, as if all the stuffing had run out of him. He sagged against MacGonigal, who stepped back to let him fall.

"Dammit, Frank, what's going on down there?"

MacGonigal was covered with blood. His shirt and kilt were soaked, and his hands were slimy with it. He sheathed the knife, wiped his hands in the grass, then moved back to the Landcruiser and picked up the Savage.

There was dead silence. Frank lay in a heap, barely visible at a few yards' distance. There was a commotion on top of the bluff, and snatches of what seemed to be a heated argument drifted down. A flashlight snapped on, then went spinning.

"You damn fool! I told you, no lights! He's out here somewhere!"

"How the hell am I going to get down that cliff without a light?"

There was some more indistinct conversation, then MacGonigal heard a clear voice. "You go on down and we'll cover you from here."

Someone moved clumsily down the trail. MacGonigal could track his progress by the noise he made. Holding the Savage ready, he moved around the Landcruiser and took up a position behind the shed. He stood ready in the shelter of the structure while the man cursed, thrashed and stumbled his way down the bluff.

The door to the shed was slightly ajar, and MacGonigal slipped inside. There was an ax in the bed of the pickup. He hefted it a moment, thinking, then stepped back outside.

In a minute, his quarry reached the bottom. He stood near the end of the trail, trying to see through the darkness. MacGonigal waited for him to make the first move.

The man spoke in a hoarse stage whisper. "Hey, Frank! Are you there?"

He stood stock-still, listening for an answer. After a few moments, he moved slowly forward, his attention riveted on the Landcruiser. The strain was too much for the men on top of the bluff, apparently, and they broke the silence, calling down to him.

"Larry! Larry! Is Frank okay? What's going on down there?"

Larry exploded. "Shut up, you motherfuckers! Are you trying to tell the whole world?"

He crouched where he was, looking around, his submachine gun clutched in his fist. MacGonigal, pressed against the wall of the shed, was close enough to see that the gun had a silencer. *These boyos seem to have a thing for fancy equipment*, he mused.

At last, the man rose upright and began to move out of range. He walked at a crouch, his shoulders hunched together, every line in his body betraying his fear. MacGonigal left the shelter of the shed, circling. He held the ax across his chest, ready to deliver a blow. He crept along the side of Robbins' stationwagon, then crossed the gap between it and the Landcruiser.

"Dammit, Larry! What the hell's going on down there?"

The man jumped at the sound of the shout, then stepped backward, looking up toward the top of the bluff.

MacGonigal uncoiled himself and drove around the hood of the Landcruiser, the ax held horizontally. The man called Larry started at the sudden sound of MacGonigal's boots in the leaves and half turned, only to meet the flashing arc of the ax as MacGonigal literally threw himself into the swing. He tried to bring the submachine gun up, but it was a feeble gesture. The ax smashed aside the silencer, sent the gun flying and went on to bite deep into the man's chest.

He wrenched the ax out and brought it down again, driving it with force into the man's skull. He pulled it free again, dropped it beside the body, then turned and made his way back to the shed to collect the Savage. *That's three down, and not a shot fired yet.*

MacGonigal glanced at his watch. The men on top of the bluff must be growing nervous. He wondered what they were thinking. He wondered what Robbins was doing. *I hope old Robbie has sense enough to stay put and not start anything.*

His musings were interrupted by some low murmuring and then a shout from the top of the bluff. "Larry! Hey, Larry! You find anything down there yet?"

MacGonigal ducked behind the shed, hoping the pickup truck would shelter him if they started shooting.

There was more unintelligible babbling from the bluff top. Suddenly a burst of fire from above sent bullets cracking down through the trees. The fire was wild—the gunner obviously had no idea what he was shooting at. None of it came anywhere near MacGonigal and he relaxed slightly. Then came the deep boom of a shotgun, followed by two more booms in rapid succession.

*Holy Mary! Robbie just dealt himself in! Damn!*

Now there came a rattle of fire from the clifftop. The bastards were shooting indiscriminately in all directions. The silenced weapons made little noise themselves, but the 9mm slugs cracked through the air and whined viciously off into space. The whole thing lasted perhaps five seconds.

There was some confused shouting—MacGonigal

couldn't make out exactly what it was all about—and someone was screaming, a high, keening scream, like a saw going through bone. *I hope that's not Robbie yelling like that.*

There was another burst of fire, then MacGonigal could hear what seemed to be a scuffle on the bluff above. After a minute or two, a voice called out, "Okay, motherfucker! We've got your buddy up here. You've got one minute!"

MacGonigal waited in silence. Minutes passed, then Robbins' voice called out, "They've got me, Mac. They say they'll kill me if you don't give up."

MacGonigal permitted himself a silent, cynical laugh. *Yeah, you bastards, you'll kill your hostage. Sure, you will.* He waited for their next gambit. As long as he remained silent, they couldn't be sure that he had heard. If they carried out their threat, they'd be wasting their hostage for nothing. They couldn't possibly be that stupid. Or could they? *I guess that's a chance ol' Robbie's going to have to take, because ol' F. X. MacGonigal isn't stupid enough to play that friggin' game.*

"You've got one more minute, and by God, if you don't come out then, we're gonna castrate the son of a bitch!"

MacGonigal went into the shed and removed the distributor rotor from the pickup, then went outside and disabled the other two vehicles. As he worked, the man on the bluff repeated his threats, making them even more bloodcurdling, and once someone fired a few short bursts down through the trees. MacGonigal ignored them.

Satisfied that he had immobilized his opponents, he moved off through the woods, following a deer trail, secure in the knowledge that he had taken care of all opposition on this side of the falls.

Robbins was sick, a deep, gut-racking sickness. His left leg hurt like hell. One of the slugs that hit him must have nicked the bone. And it had all been so stupid. He had shadowed the hoods as they congregated to look at the body of their colleague with the gas can, drawn by Eddie's almost hysteric reaction when he found it.

Then, in the panic that followed the first killing down below, he had been tempted to act on his own—but remembered that he was supposed to wait for MacGonigal to return and initiate the action.

When they sent Larry down to find out what had happened to Frank, he silently applauded the dissension the decision caused. He had a bad moment when Larry switched on the flashlight, and had been tempted to fire, but Karl, who was obviously running things, had slapped it out of Larry's hand before he could sweep it around and discover Robbins crouching only yards away.

*Jesus, if I were one of these guys, I wouldn't go down there in a hundred years. You couldn't pay me enough to go down there.*

He had watched as the hoodlums' mounting apprehension escalated into near-unreasoning panic, and they had unleashed a barrage of unaimed automatic fire into the trees below. And then he had acted.

He had quickly closed the space between himself and the nearest gunmen while they were emptying their weapons into the darkness, and fired into them at point-blank range. At the first shot, one of the dark figures in front of him had simply disappeared, dropping to the ground as if yanked down by an invisible hand. Robbins fired two more quick shots, working the pump gun as rapidly as he could, then he whirled around and sprinted for cover, leaving the enemy totally disorganized behind him.

It was really bad luck that they had hit him. They had loosed a fusillade, but most of the shots had gone wild. He had covered perhaps fifty yards—out of range of a submachine gun under those conditions by anybody's rules—but a burst caught him; three red-hot baseballs striking his hip and legs. He had gone sprawling, the shotgun flying from his grasp. He was too stunned even to draw the Browning automatic when the one called Karl had come over to where he lay. The man had lifted him bodily, ripping the Browning out of its holster and shoving it into his waistband. He was a huge man, several inches taller than Robbins, and seemed immensely strong. He slapped Robbins sharply, causing lights to dance in front of his eyes, then called roughly to one of his men to search him for more weapons.

At first, he had been sure they would kill him.

George wanted to, but Karl was more businesslike. He realized that killing Robbins out of hand —especially when he was a prisoner and *hors de combat*—offered little in the way of a solution to the problem they faced.

They had trussed him with strips of cloth—and not gently—then gone on to offer aid to one of the men Robbins had shot. It appeared that Robbins had killed two of them and left a third badly wounded. George had examined the man's wounds, then come back and, very deliberately, kicked Robbins in the crotch. He had almost passed out with the pain and, from that point on, kept drifting in and out of consciousness.

When they finally roused him so that he could tell MacGonigal that they had him, he had been unable to stand. It was only his potential use as a hostage that motivated them to keep him alive. Otherwise, they would probably have left him to bleed to death.

Sick and dizzy, Robbins had called out into the darkness. There was no answer, as he had expected. They were probably going to kill him—and he realized that MacGonigal knew that. *It won't do any good. Mac will just ignore me*, he thought. Then he collapsed.

After what seemed like a long time, they roused him again. "Is that motherfucker comin', or what?"

"He's a pro—an old hand. He'll never give up."

"He better give up, you son of a bitch." Karl slapped him twice, forehand, backhand. "I swear to

God, you talk that bastard out, or you can kiss your balls good-bye!"

"Don't matter," mumbled Robbins, barely aware of what he was saying. "He won't listen. There's only one way out of here, and he's got it blocked. He'll wait for daylight. Then he'll pick you all off."

Karl threw Robbins roughly back down. Dimly he heard them talking. "I think the fucker has a sniper rifle—that's what he meant by 'pick you off.' Son of a bitch! He can do it, too! There's no way out of here."

The next time he woke, he was being hauled to his feet again and forced to move. The man he had wounded was also being brought along. He could hear him sobbing at each step as his comrades dragged him over the rough terrain.

They propped him against something rough. *It's the cabin*, he thought in mild amazement. *They're going to try to barricade themselves in Mac's cabin.* And then he fell forward.

From his position high on the hillside, MacGonigal could hear them moving toward the cabin. *Damn! The bastards are going to hole up in the house. If that goddamn Robbie hadn't screwed up and let them catch him, I'd settle things right now.* But with Robbins a prisoner, an ambush in the dark was too risky. *MacGonigal, me boyo, you're getting sentimental in your old age*, he thought, but then consoled himself with a reminder that Robbins was worth a hundred-and-fifty grand alive, and nothing at all if he was dead.

Gritting his teeth, he made his way downhill, picking his way through the underbrush and guiding on the not-inconsiderable noise they made as they struggled up the trail to the cabin. He maneuvred to within a short distance from the cabin and lay in wait for them. They passed within a few yards of him, and he counted them. Four; and two of them wounded. One of the wounded was more or less upright and leaned drunkenly on one of his companions. It looked like Robbie, but he couldn't be sure. The other wounded man seemed to be out of it, and his companion was virtually carrying him.

They finally reached the porch and laid the two wounded down. The first of the casualties stumbled and flopped sideways, as if his hands were tied. *That must be Robbie. At least they haven't killed the dumb bastard.* The other man lay as if dead, while the other two tried the door. MacGonigal could hear it swing open, and in a minute a voice called, "There's no one in here. Bring them in."

Pulling back his sleeve, MacGonigal checked his watch. Four-thirty. Dawn was a long time off. He rose, slung the rifle and made his way back up the hillside. Near the top, he followed the bluff, looking for a sheltered place where he could wait. He chose a little space formed by two leaning slabs of limestone, worming his way in and making himself comfortable. He took time to check his field of fire with the scope. The cabin could be seen, although dimly, and he had a clear shot at the doorway.

He checked the spool magazine of the Savage. It was full, as he knew it was. With one round in the chamber, that give him six shots. He unstrapped his leather sporran and checked its contents. Twenty rounds of .308s, his own handloads, 48 grains of 4895 loaded behind a 150-grain boattail. That gave him a muzzle velocity of just over 2,900 feet per second, real screamers. And the boattail bullet retained its velocity well. He estimated the range to the cabin at about four-hundred yards, give or take a dozen yards either way. That would be about a foot and a half of holdover. With any luck, he'd get a shot in the early morning, when there was no wind. It would be hard to miss.

He unbuckled the heavy leather belt of the kilt, sliding off the .357 and its little ammunition pouch, and shook the pleats out of the saffron wool. *Well, me boyo, it's one good thing about the kilt—it makes a dandy sleepin' cover when you have to rough it.*

He wrapped the dark cloth around himself and settled down. He knew that he'd rouse with his enemies' first attempt to leave the cabin, if not before.

"All right, haul that son of a bitch over here. We're gonna have a little talk, all nice and cozy."

George dragged Robbins to his feet and propelled him toward the rough divan where Karl sat. As soon as he released his grip, Robbins fell, collapsing in a heap. Karl leaned down and grabbed a handful of his shirt, pulling him around so that he could look into his face.

"Shit! He's out cold! See if you can find something to rouse him with. I don't want this bastard to die on us. Right now, he's the only hold we've got on that other bastard out there."

George felt his way across the room, not sure what he was looking for. "See if you can find something for Danny, too. I think he's gonna croak, anyway, but see what you can find."

Danny lay stretched out near the door where they had left him. Karl knelt and felt around his throat for a pulse. It was weak and rapid.

George, rummaging in the cabinet, had come upon the bottle of Irish Mist. "Here's something that might help." He made his way back with the bottle and passed it to Karl, who tried to force a little of its contents on their unconscious comrade.

"Waste of good booze. He's done for. See about a blanket, will ya?"

George blundered around among the furniture, stumbling a few times. "Lemme strike a light, Karl. I'll kill myself in here in the dark."

"A light! Are you fuckin' crazy! That motherfucker's out there with a fuckin' *sniper* rifle, for chrissake! You show one goddamn light, and he'll blow your head off."

George was silenced. He floundered around for a while, then decided to pull up the buffalo hide that served as a rug. "We can put this over Danny."

"Nah, that won't do it. It's too heavy. It'll smother him. He's barely breathin' now. Go upstairs and see what you can find."

George made his way to the stairs and climbed up into the loft. The bedding that MacGonigal and Robbins had left in disarray in their hurry to get out of the cabin was scattered over the bed and floor. He gathered an indiscriminate armful and went back downstairs, where the two of them made a sort of rough bed for Danny, putting him on top of the buffalo rug and piling blankets on top of him.

"Better do something for the other one, too. Don't want him to die on us."

Robbins was conscious now. Karl lifted him while George slipped a blanket under him, then laid him back to place another one over him.

"My hands . . . my hands are numb."

"Shut up! Be glad you still *got* hands."

"Shut up, George," said Karl. He pulled back the blankets and cut the rag bonds around Robbins' wrists. Robbins groaned and tried to massage his arms, but couldn't move them. Karl grabbed one forearm in his huge hand and began to rub the circulation back into it.

"Get some of that booze, George. It looks like our friend is coming around."

George produced the half-full bottle of Irish Mist. Karl took it and helped Robbins to a sitting position. "Here. Try some of this."

He held the bottle to Robbins' lips. Robbins managed to sip a little, then choked. The liquor ran down his chin, onto his shirt.

"Take it easy. Take it a little slower."

This time he managed to get a mouthful. Holding it in his mouth, he let it slowly trickle down his throat. It seemed to help, spreading a slowly diffusing warmth through his body. He suddenly realized how cold he was.

"C-c-cold," he stammered.

"Get these blankets around you," said Karl. "Here, George, help him." George drew the blankets around Robbins' body.

He drew his clasp knife and grasped Robbins by the hair, jerking his head back. He put the point of the blade against the corner of one eye. "Now, listen," he hissed, "you and me are gonna talk, and if you don't say what I want to hear, I'm gonna put your lights out. Understand?"

With the point of the knife pressing on the corner of his eye, Robbins could only swallow. He dared not move his head so much as a fraction of an inch.

"Now—what was it you two had cooked up?"

Robbins licked his lips. His mouth was horribly dry, and his tongue felt like a piece of wood. "I . . . we didn't have any plan . . ." He flinched as Karl applied the slightest additional pressure to the knife. "We . . . he heard your car. He got me up and we went out . . ." He paused. "I need water."

"You talk. Then maybe."

Robbins was beginning to hurt more as life came

back into his body. "We heard you pull up . . . waited while you climbed the path . . . Mac went after the guy . . . the one carrying the gas can."

"Mac? That's MacGonigal, right? He killed Alex?"

Robbins swallowed painfully. "Yeah . . . MacGonigal. He . . . I guess he killed him . . . I couldn't see . . . too dark."

"You *guess* he killed him?" broke in George. "You fuckin' well *know* he killed him! That bastard clubbed him to death. Fuckin' smashed his skull!"

"All right, all right, George. Just shut up for a while, will ya?" Karl turned back to Robbins. "All right. What happened after the bastard killed Alex?"

"He . . . he told me to stay put. He was going down . . . that's the last I saw of him. Then I heard you . . . talking and . . . about Alex . . ."

Karl shook him roughly. "Don't give me that shit! You two had a plan—now, what was it?"

"Just to work in and get close . . . and to open up when he did . . . that's all there was to it . . ."

"Where were you two supposed to meet?"

"Meet? He didn't say anything about meeting after . . . I guess he figured that by daylight, it would all be over, one way or the other . . . and then . . ."

"That was it, huh? Just slip up on us with shotguns and blast us?"

"Mac has a rifle . . . I don't know what he meant to do . . ."

"*Son* of a bitch! So he *does* have a goddamn sniper rifle!"

"Hey, Karl! *We* got sniper rifles, too. There must be two dozen of 'em in here. We could put this guy up in the window, maybe, and draw MacGonigal's fire."

Karl sat a moment, absorbed. "Maybe you're not as dumb as I thought. Get one of them rifles—get two—no, three—and bring 'em over here."

George did as he was bid, and Karl looked the rifles over in the dim light. "This one's a .30-06 . . . and this one's a 7mm magnum. Try and find some ammo for both of 'em."

"What about the other one?"

Karl snorted. "That's his rifle," he said, gesturing toward Robbins. "He won't need any ammo."

George searched the built-in drawers of one of the gun cases and returned with an armload of colored ammunition boxes. "I think there's some of what we want in here." He sorted through the boxes and quickly produced several for each rifle. He picked up one of the rifles and began to load it, then passed the weapon to Karl and loaded the other one.

"Okay, now, here's what we'll do: We'll get this guy up right in front of the window, there." Karl pointed at the big window near the door. "And we'll get ready. Then you light one of them lamps, to give him a little something to shoot by, and then . . ."

George hauled Robbins to his feet and moved him over to the window. The curtains were open, and Robbins could see across the cabin yard and up the ridge side clear to the top. He could see the girdle of stone bluffs that ringed the top of the ridge. He suddenly felt naked. *Mac's too smart to fall for this one. Christ, I hope he's too smart.*

He couldn't stand, but they propped him in position. "Now, hold this, you son of a bitch, and don't let it down," said Karl as he thrust the empty rifle into Robbins' hands.

Robbins sat there, close to the glass, cradling the rifle in his arms. Out of the corner of his eye, he could see Karl take up a position near the other window, his rifle at the ready.

"All right. Strike a light."

A match scratched and flared in the room somewhere behind him, and the light grew, making huge shadows play on the curtains and wall. He knew without turning his head that George was lighting one of the kerosene lamps.

"Don't move, you son of a bitch, and keep that rifle up where he can see it."

They waited. It seemed to Robbie that an hour or more passed. He sat propped in front of the window. At first, he had been able to see only the stark outlines of the bluff and the trees atop it. Now he could make out objects in the cabin yard. He could see the color of the leaves, could make out individual leaves on the trees. He could smell the smoky odor of the kerosene lamp behind him. From time to time, he sagged a little, and George had crawled over so that he lay on the floor directly behind him. From that position, he could prod Robbie with the barrel of his rifle.

"Keep that gun up where he can see it!"

The sun was fully up now, sending a flood of warm, gold light across the ridgetop. Somewhere up there, among those tumbled rocks and riotous autumn leaves, Robbins knew MacGonigal was waiting. Undoubtedly he had the cross hairs of his scope centered on Robbins' head right now. The thought made his skin crawl.

"How does it feel, knowing that your buddy is probably just about to blow you away, asshole?"

Robbins made no reply, but simply sat and endured. His wounds hurt, and his scrotum was painfully swollen. He forced himself to concentrate on the pain, not on the possibility that MacGonigal might have him in his sights right now. He swayed and slumped a little sideways, dropping the rifle. It slid off the chair and onto the floor with a clatter.

"You son of a bitch, you dropped it on purpose!" George retrieved the rifle and shoved it back into Robbins arms.

Karl moved away from his position by the other window. "This ain't working. He's too smart to be set up like this."

George considered this a moment. "Maybe he ain't out there."

Karl shook his head. "He's out there, all right. He's probably right up on that cliff, looking down at us right now."

George shivered ever so slightly and turned his head to look quickly up at the bluff. "Hell, Karl, he's *got* to be gone. What would he want to stay around here for? I mean, he was clear of us, and we had Asshole here to keep us busy—anybody with any sense at all would have scrammed."

"Not this guy. He's a killer, a real pro. He's out there, ready and waiting for us to make our first mistake."

Karl crawled over to where Danny lay. He put his hand under the blankets and felt at the man's throat for his pulse.

"Dead." He turned toward Robbins. "That's another one you killed. But don't get smug—you're going to pay for it." He looked over at George. "Get some rope or something to tie this motherfucker up with. And see if you can find some tape. We're getting the fuck out of here."

In a few minutes, George had found several coils of climbing rope and some electrician's tape.

"Good. Now, roll this motherfucker over and hold him down."

George did as he was bid, and Karl pulled Robbins' arms painfully back behind him, tying his hands, then wrapping rope around the elbows to keep them back at an unnatural angle. That done, he took up one of the Ingram submachine guns, loaded and cocked it, and put the muzzle against Robbins' head.

"Now, hand me that tape."

He wrapped tape around Robbins' head, then around the silencer of the Ingram, so that the gun was firmly bound in place, the muzzle against his temple. He kept wrapping until he ran out of tape.

"Now, help me stand the motherfucker up."

They got Robbins to his feet and maneuvered him over toward the door. Karl held him erect in front of the door.

"Okay. Now, open it."

George swung the door open, and Robbins stood there, supported by Karl, who was standing to one side, out of the possible line of fire, holding the pistol grip of the Ingram, his finger on the trigger. Robbins closed his eyes and gritted his teeth, waiting for a bullet, either from MacGonigal or from the Ingram. Nothing happened.

Karl leaned out a little and looked up toward the ridgetop.

"We know you're up there, you motherfucker! Now, listen good. We're walking out of here, and if you try anything, your buddy dies!"

He shoved Robbins ahead of him, so roughly that he almost fell. "You better stay on your feet—you fall, and I'll blow your head off."

Robbins, grimacing with pain, said, "You do, and he'll blow *your* head off."

Karl seemed to go pale under his tan. He called out, "Get over here, George, and stick close. And if this guy starts to fall, hold him up."

Robbins could feel the muzzle of the Ingram against his skin. Karl prodded him with it. "Move. But stay close to us."

Robbins gritted his teeth against the pain and

shifted his weight to his wounded leg. It almost collapsed under him, but George caught him and held him up. "Jeezc, Karl! If he falls, we're sitting ducks."

"Okay—you keep him on his feet. I'll hold the gun." He put his mouth close to Robbins' ear. "Remember one thing—whatever happens, *you* get it. I'll make sure of that. If he shoots me in the brain, I'll pull the trigger as I'm going down. Remember that."

They made their way down the path like some monstrous six-legged animal, the hoodlums afraid at each step that one or the other of them would expose himself too much and offer MacGonigal a target. They had to move slowly to keep together, and Robbins could feel the cold fear in the two of them mingling with his own.

At the bluff top, they faced a crisis. There was no way they could make their way down the steep path without exposing at least one of them to MacGonigal's fire.

"You take that rifle and go on down ahead of us. I'll wait with this guy until you're under cover, and then I'll come down."

George shook his head. "Unh-unh. As soon as he gets a clear shot . . ."

"Dammit, you were the one who said he'd run out. You said he was gone. What made you change your mind?"

George ignored the question. "I'm not moving away. As long as we got a hostage, we're safe—but if he can separate one of us from the hostage . . ."

He left the rest of the sentence unspoken.

"Look, you get your ass down there, or he's not gonna have to kill you. I'll do it for him."

They stood irresolutely for a long moment. At last George said, "Move him around this way, and give me some cover."

Together they shuffled around, a pivoting turn, until George stood with his back to the lower trail, and Robbins faced the cabin. George squatted down, then duck walked backward, the rifle in his hands, until he was several feet away. Then he turned and crawled down the trail as far as the first switchback.

"Okay, bring him down."

Karl maneuvered Robbins down backward until they reached George's position. They continued this way until they reached the bottom of the bluff.

"Jesus Christ! Look at that!"

Karl turned slowly, dragging Robbins with him. Lying crumpled in the leaves were two bloody bundles—both were abuzz with flies.

"*That motherfucker!*" snorted Karl. George seemed completely paralyzed by the sight.

Karl made a great effort to pull himself together. Robbins could feel a shudder pass through his massive body. He pushed George toward the Toyota.

"That's enough gawkin'. Get the engine started. Leave the back door open for us."

George looked across the open space of the turnaround that separated them from the Landcruiser.

"It's too open, Karl. Let's go across together."

They moved crabwise to the Toyota, and George opened the door on the driver's side, slid in, and pulled Robbins in with him. Karl, the pistol grip of the Ingram still firmly in his fist, slid in after him. He closed the door quickly and dug in his pocket for the keys.

"Dammit! He must have screwed with the car. Get out and see what's wrong, George."

George hesitated for a moment, obviously afraid to move too far from the shelter of their hostage, but too close now to escape to delay. He slipped out of the Toyota, saying, "Keep me covered," and lifted the hood.

"Jeeze—he's made a mess here. We'll never get this thing started, Karl."

Karl leaned out the window, his grip on the submachine gun still firm. "Try the stationwagon. Alex beat on it, but maybe it'll still run."

George glanced fearfully around him, then screwed up his courage and dashed across the few yards that separated them from Robbins' green wagon. He reached inside the shattered side window and released the hood. Maneuvering around to the front of the car, being careful to keep the green wagon in front of him and the Toyota behind him, he lifted the hood and looked into the engine compartment.

"No use, Karl. He's bitched this one up, too."

Swearing, Karl climbed out of the Toyota, dragging

Robbins with him. His eye lit on the shed where MacGonigal kept his pickup. "Go see what's in there, George."

MacGonigal woke in pitch-darkness, shivering under his kilt. He checked his watch. A good half hour before first light. He hunched his shoulders and pulled the saffron wool tighter around him, moving closer to the shelter of the rocks to avoid the drifting mist that seeped up out of the ground. *If these bastards meant to put me in a bad humor, they've succeeded. I hope they're happy with the results.*

It slowly grew lighter, the blackness of the woods turning to a dirty gray. He checked the cabin through the rifle scope several times without result, then shifted his position slightly. He remembered that he had been careful in his rebuilding of the cabin to make sure that all its exits couldn't be dominated from a single point. *It just might be, me boyo, that you've outsmarted yourself*, but he consoled himself with the knowledge that even if his enemy could escape from the cabin, they couldn't use their vehicles.

When the light appeared in the window of the cabin, MacGonigal was jerked back into alertness. He could see a figure, plainly armed, in front of the window, perfectly silhouetted by the light. He examined the figure through the scope, noting its stillness. *It has to be a trick. That's got to be Robbie they've put there, trying to draw my fire.*

For a moment, he was tempted to put a shot

through the window just above the outlined head —that would put the fear of God into them, confirm their fears that he was out here waiting for them. But then he reconsidered. *No—let 'em sweat. Let 'em wonder if I'm out here or not.*

He settled back to wait as the sun grew higher, bringing a welcome warmth to his chilled body. Unfortunately it also brought flies, attracted by the blood-caked shirt and kilt. MacGonigal endured them, but he marked this down to the account of the men down there, adding it to his store of resentment.

Then he heard the shouts from the cabin and turned his attention to the scene below. He saw the door fly open and had the cross hairs on the man who appeared framed in the doorway before the sound of the slamming door reached his position on the ridge. He recognized Robbins and tracked sideways a fraction to see the submachine gun and the beefy fist holding it. He realized the danger to Robbins and held his fire. In a moment, the three appeared, all of them visible at once. He tracked them in the scope as they made their way across the porch and down the steps, and he followed them with the cross hairs as they edged down the trail to the falls. Then he gathered up his kilt and slipped out of position.

George stood motionless next to the open hood of the station wagon.

"Go on. See what's in the shed. I'll cover you from here."

"It's too far. I'll never make it."

"All right, for chrissake. We'll all go over together." He hauled Robbins around the front end of the car and shoved him in the direction of the shed. Once there, he leaned him against the wall.

"Now, get in there and see what you can find."

George opened the door, the rifle held in front of him like a pistol as the door swung outward.

"It's a pickup. It must belong to him."

"Well, see if you can start it."

George stepped into the shed and they heard the sound of the pickup door opening, then it slammed shut. For a long moment, there was no more sound.

"Well, is the damn thing gonna start or not?"

There was the sound of some thumping and an occasional grunt from within the shed, but no real answer. They waited a few moments longer, and Karl repeated his question, louder than before.

"Yeah, it'll start."

"Well, *start* the damn thing. Let's get out of here."

"There's no hurry."

Karl was almost apoplectic with rage. "What the hell do you mean, 'no hurry'? That son of a bitch is liable to show up any minute."

"He's already here."

"What . . . what?" Karl couldn't quite assimilate the muffled but laconic reply from within the shed. "What the hell are you talking about?"

For reply, the door to the shed opened slightly, and a large, heavy object was tossed out. It landed with a soggy thud about fifteen feet away. Karl and Robbins stared at it in horror—it was a human head. It lay there, covered with bloody, matted hair, the vacant eyes staring accusingly at a point just above Karl's right shoulder, the raw stump of the neck still dripping blood.

# III.

*"Holy Christ!"* shouted Karl. *"Jesus, Mary and Joseph!"*

He took a fresh grip on Robbins' shoulder and pressed the Ingram against him. Robbins could feel his trembling through the cold metal of the gun barrel.

He took a deep, shuddering breath. "So help me, if you come near me, I'll kill him! I swear to God, I'll blow his head off!"

"And what'll ye do for an encore, me boyo?" said a voice behind him.

With an almost galvanic start, Karl whirled around. There was a thundering boom, and he was flung against Robbins, then backward. Robbins stood a moment, uncomprehending, looking down at Karl. There was a large crater in his forehead, and the back of his head was blown away entirely. Blood and gray matter mingled together on the ground.

"The top of the mornin' to ye, Robbie, me boyo."

Robbins' leg gave way, and without a word, he toppled forward and lay across Karl's body.

When he woke, he was lying on the buffalo rug in MacGonigal's cabin. His bloody clothes had been cut off, and he was wrapped in clean bandages. He seemed to have trouble seeing, but then he realized that the flickering before his eyes was actually the light of a kerosene lantern. By moving his head slightly, he could see the window where Karl had forced him to sit, and he could see that it was dark outside. *I must have been out for a long time*, he thought vaguely.

"Well, you're awake, I see. How do you feel?"

It took a great effort to turn his head enough to see the speaker. MacGonigal stood partly silhouetted by the yellow glow of the kerosene lamp. He was dressed in a rough wool sweater and a pair of faded jeans, his feet encased in a pair of worn, run-down cowboy boots. The Colt .357 was still strapped to his waist.

"I hurt, Mac. How the hell do you think I feel?"

MacGonigal grinned. "At least you're still a baritone. I was sure you were gonna be a soprano. That guy who kicked you in the balls really landed one on you. Looks like purple tennis balls between your legs."

Robbins responded with a groan.

"Hurt that bad, does it? Not surprised. You took a bad one in the leg, too. The one in the other leg and the one in the ass are just flesh wounds, but that right leg is going to take you out of commission for a while.

Can you sit up? I've got to get you to a hospital. It ain't gonna be very comfortable riding on the seat, but that'll be better than riding in the bed of my pickup."

Robbins opened his eyes again. "I think I can make it—but we haven't got time for a hospital. We've got to get to Camp Peary, Mac."

"Ol' buddy, you ain't in any condition to take a long trip. Even if you aren't ruptured, you've lost a lot of blood. You've got to get to a hospital."

Robbins gritted his teeth and tried to get to his feet. MacGonigal put a heavy but gentle hand on his shoulder, pressing him back down onto the rug. "Lie still. I'll carry you down."

"Mac," said Robbins hoarsely, "there's no way we can go to a hospital—the Company has too much at stake here. If I go into an emergency room with a gunshot wound . . . well, we can't have anyone asking questions."

MacGonigal snorted. "Don't worry about *that*, ol' buddy. There's stiffs scattered all around this place. When ol' Harvey Siler finds about what happened up here, there'll be *plenty* of questions."

Robbins' eyes opened wider. "Who's Harvey Siler?"

"The sheriff. He's gonna be fit to be tied when he finds out about *this* little donnybrook!"

"No! No sheriff! We can't have local authorities poking into this."

MacGonigal laughed shortly. "Talk sense, Robbie! We've got *eight* dead stiffs scattered around here

—*eight*. How the hell can we keep something like that secret?"

Robbins tried to get to his feet. "I've got to get to a phone—you should have never let me lie here so long."

MacGonigal pushed him back down again. "There's no phone here—we'll call whoever you want from the hospital. Or from the jail."

"Dammit, Mac! I said no hospital!" blazed Robbins. "Don't you understand that? We can't let a word get out about what happened here—the Company can't afford it."

"I don't see how the hell they can prevent it."

"Help me up—let me get to a phone, and I'll try to get a cleanup squad out here."

MacGonigal paused. "A cleanup squad? That's a *hell* of a risk. The Company must be pretty serious to even think about trying to cover up a mess like this."

"I didn't say they'd *do* it—but I'll damn sure try to talk them into it."

MacGonigal was rummaging around. He produced an unopened bottle of Irish Mist and poured a tumblerful. He passed it to Robbins, who sipped at it gratefully.

"Well, laddie boy, are you ready to go?"

Robbins was pale and drawn. "Mac, look, I know this isn't kosher, but I think you're going to have to make the contact. Have you got something to write with?"

MacGonigal looked at him. "Are you serious? You're going to put it in writing?" He produced a spiral pad and a ballpoint pen from the folding desk next to the fireplace.

Robbins took the pad and began to write. "Just call this number and give them this code number. Somebody will come on the line and ask you who you want to talk to—you just tell them you're the prospect, and you've agreed to a demonstration. If they ask you any questions, answer them—but tell them the salesman can't come to the phone." He tore off several pages from the tablet and handed them to MacGonigal. "Burn these blank pages—and burn the other one as soon as you've made the call. And don't tell anyone I ever wrote this stuff down."

MacGonigal looked at the sheaf of paper. He took the top sheet, folded it, and put it in his pocket, then crumpled the rest, opened the stove door, and threw the other sheets in.

"I'll make the call for you, laddie boy, but I'm taking you along. I'll drop you off at the hospital before I call."

"That's a nonstarter, Mac. If I'm in the hospital, then there's no way we can guarantee an airtight cleanup. The Company will never buy into it."

MacGonigal shook his head. "You're a stubborn bastard, Robbie. Always were. Not very smart, but damn stubborn. We'll do it your way, for the time being, anyway."

He helped Robbins out of the chair and back to the rug. He filled a water jug and put a thermos of soup on the floor next to him. He disappeared and came back with a stable bucket.

"Haven't got a bedpan, ol' buddy. You'll have to use this if nature calls. I'll be back in a few hours."

MacGonigal's old pickup jolted slowly over the rough excuse for a road. He was driving without lights, his .357 in his lap, ready to hand. The Savage was wedged between the seat cushion and the door on the right-hand side of the cab, so he could grab it quickly if he had to bail out. It was just possible that they hadn't yet disposed of *all* of Nazario's hit squad. Or that backup had been sent out.

He reached the end of his road without incident, and pulled out on the county road, his booted foot on the floorboards. The truck accelerated, shaking violently over the washboard road. A plume of dust rose behind him as he piloted the blacked-out vehicle onto the gravel surface, and MacGonigal leaned forward, peering through the darkness ahead of him, trying to see what was coming up.

*Sure hope I don't meet anybody coming this way*, he thought as he horsed the truck through the first of a series of hairpin curves. When he pulled out onto the highway and got the truck up to speed, he switched on the lights.

In a few miles, he was approaching the outskirts of town. He tried to think where he could make a phone call privately. He remembered there was a booth next to the laundromat just outside of the town limits. He pulled into the darkened parking lot and killed the engine. Leaving the rifle wedged between seat and door, he went over to the booth. Taking the crumpled sheet of notepaper out of his shirt pocket, he dialed the number. The call was answered on the second ring.

"Good evening. Thank you for calling Appliance Warehouse."

Squinting at the notepaper in the dim light of the laundromat parking lot, MacGonigal read off the code recognition phrase.

"Just a moment. I'll connect you with Mr. Wallace."

There was a short pause, and then a masculine voice came on the line. "Wallace speaking."

Turning the paper to catch the dim glow of a security light, MacGonigal read the second half of the code. There was a pause, and then the voice asked, "What can I do for you?"

"I'd like to arrange for a demonstration."

There was another, longer pause. "Who is this speaking, please?"

"This is the prospect."

"You'll have to arrange for any demonstrations with our salesman. If he's there, please put him on the phone."

"He's indisposed."

"Well, we can't do anything until our salesman gives us a call."

MacGonigal read off the third code phrase, the one that signified that his call was genuine, then said, "He can't do that. That's why I'm calling. I'm following his instructions."

There was a long pause, one that managed to

convey a silent message of menace. MacGonigal had no doubt that the conversation was being recorded, and that there were frantic efforts to trace the number. At last the man said, "I see. Nothing serious, I hope."

"He'll require medical attention. He had a hunting accident."

"Where is he now?"

"At my place. He's resting comfortably, but he'll require hospitalization. I'll take him to the local hospital as soon as I hang up."

"Ah. Well, if it won't put you out, we'll send someone for him. We have our own medical plan."

"So he said. I'll wait for your representative. Be sure he's equipped for that demonstration."

The man hedged. "I'm not sure we have any demonstrator models in right now. How much of a demonstration were you expecting?"

"I have eight bundles."

There was a noise on the other end of the line that suggested that "Mr. Wallace" was having trouble maintaining his attitude of detachment.

"Excuse me. I thought you said 'eight bundles.' "

"That's right. Eight. If you can't handle them, I'll have to turn them over to a local firm."

"Don't do that!" The man's voice was noticeably higher in pitch. "We'll send someone. Will tomorrow morning be too late?"

"Not if you're prepared to take care of the whole job."

"All right. We have your address."

The line went dead. MacGonigal stood a moment in the booth. He had a creepy feeling. It must be the phone trace—he didn't think that whoever sent the hoods who had attacked them could have followed him here. Nevertheless, he drew his .357 and held it in his hand as he walked back to the truck.

He had barely seated himself in the truck when he saw the beams of a slowly approaching vehicle. It was coming up the road from town, and it was obviously preparing to turn into the parking lot. The car was headed directly for him. He shielded his eyes and tried to look beyond the glare of the lights without success.

"Well, Francis, what are you doin' out here this time of night?"

MacGonigal sighed and let the hammer down on the Colt. He tucked it behind him on the seat and rolled his window down farther.

"Just came in to make a phone call, Harvey."

The fat sheriff had pulled up even with MacGonigal. He killed his engine, then reached over and turned on the squelch on his radio. "Must have been an important call, Francis. Have anything to do with that fellow that was lookin' for you?"

"In a manner of speaking. He asked me to call his home office for him. He sprained an ankle, and he won't be able to get back on time, so he asked for a couple extra days of vacation."

The sheriff thought a moment. "That's a shame, Francis. Doctor look at him?"

"No need. I can doctor a simple sprain."

"Hmm. Don't doubt you can, Francis. Don't doubt it at all." He made no move to start his engine. "Seen anybody strange around here lately?"

"What do you mean by 'strange,' Harvey?"

The sheriff shifted the toothpick in his mouth. "Some fellas from out of state was through here a couple of days ago. Bunch of 'em, drivin' one of them big Toyotas. I reckon they was hunters. They was seen goin' up toward your way."

"I haven't been off the place lately, Harvey."

"These fellas might have accidentally crossed onto your place, if they was where someone said they was seen."

"Well, I don't take kindly to trespassers, Harvey, you know that."

"Yeah, I know it, Francis. That's why I'm askin'. You see 'em?"

"If I had, I'd prosecute. You know that."

The sheriff leaned over and started the engine. "Yeah. Well, see that you do, if you catch 'em on your property." He held up a finger. "Francis, you got a temper on you—I wouldn't put it past you to do a little prosecutin' on your own. I'm tellin' you, now, if you got a problem, let the law handle it."

"I heard you before, Sheriff. And I want you to know that I take every word to heart."

The sheriff put his car in gear and eased off. "See that you do, Francis. See that you do."

The plane came at first light, passing low over the house. MacGonigal rushed outside in time to see it climb over the ridge and bank around. It was a Pilatus Porter, a long, needle-nosed, single-engine utility plane, originally designed for landing on glaciers in the Alps, and much favored by bush pilots —by them and by the Company.

MacGonigal turned back to see Robbins standing on the porch, bracing himself with MacGonigal's blackthorn walking stick.

"That your friends, Robbie?"

"Yeah. That's a Company plane."

MacGonigal returned to the cabin for his rifle. "Can't be too cautious. Last time I had visitors who came by air, they weren't too friendly."

Robbins hobbled into the cabin after him and sank down on the sofa. "No worry about this bunch. That's our plane. I've flown in it often enough to recognize it."

The plane made another pass over the pasture, its wheels almost dusting the ground, then it climbed rapidly. MacGonigal hurried to the pasture gate and stood waiting while the plane made its final approach.

The Porter made a spectacular landing, one that showed why it enjoyed such favor among pilots who have to get in and out of tight places. With its huge flaps extended, it almost stood on its nose, diving nearly straight down, flaring at the last moment, and rolling to a stop within a few yards of MacGonigal.

As soon as the plane stopped, the doors were opened. Three men tumbled out, weapons in hand.

MacGonigal stood there while they converged on him.

"Okay, buddy, where's Robbins?"

MacGonigal threw a thumb back over his shoulder in the direction of the cabin. "Back in the house. His leg's givin' him some trouble."

"What happened to him?"

"We had visitors night before last. He picked up a few bullet wounds—two flesh wounds and a fairly serious one on the leg . . . plus some bozo kicked him so hard in the balls that I'm surprised he doesn't have three Adam's apples."

One of the men reached for MacGonigal's rifle. MacGonigal tightened his grip. "You're makin' yourself free with my property, ain't you, boyo?"

"Just hold your hands out away from your sides." The leader of the group was covering him with an Uzi submachine gun. The third man had moved off to one side, his Uzi also pointed in MacGonigal's direction. The man gestured impatiently with the Uzi. "Give him the rifle. Don't make any sudden moves."

MacGonigal grinned. These guys didn't know what to do. They were afraid of starting something, and afraid of leaving him armed. He jerked the rifle away and spun on his heel.

"This way, gentlemen. Your friend is waiting."

They hesitated a moment, then trotted after him. As they approached the house, they passed the tractor shed. MacGonigal opened the door. Danny's body was lying on the dirt floor, wrapped in plastic sheeting. "Here's one of your bundles."

There was a choking noise, as if one of the men following him was having trouble with his digestive system. MacGonigal gave him a beatific smile. "There's enough of them so that you'll get used to it, laddie."

The leader spoke up. "That's enough. Let's see what Robbins says, and *then* we'll decide what to do about this."

Robbins was lying on the couch, wrapped in a blanket. He smiled, a trifle wanly, at the leader of the group. "Morning, Jerry. We've got a mess here."

Jerry snorted. "I guess you do. And I don't have to tell you that it isn't going down too well at the office. What the hell happened here?"

"I'd better let Mac tell you—he knows more about it than I do."

The man looked over at MacGonigal, his eyes hooded. He was still smarting from his man's failure to disarm and restrain MacGonigal. He didn't like the way this was developing.

"Any of you gentlemen like a drink before we get started?"

He was met with stony silence. He opened his cabinet and took out the bottle of Irish Mist and poured himself a glass. "You don't mind if I have one? Somebody has to be sociable around here." He paused. "Coffee, maybe?"

Without waiting for an answer, he filled a kettle with water and put it on the stove, then prepared the old japanned coffeepot. He took a pipe from the rack next to the stove and filled it, lighting it with a splinter from the stove. He sat back down, relaxing, and blew a cloud of smoke.

"Now, just where do you lads want me to start?"

"I don't give a damn where you start. Just tell us what happened here."

MacGonigal leaned back. "Well, Robbie here offered me a job—drove all the way out here, just for that. It was late, and he decided to spend the night. I had a little trouble here last year—I don't want to go into it too deep—but there was a lady who had run into a problem with the mob. She was staying here with me, and they came looking for her." He blew a cloud of smoke. "I couldn't let them take her, and there was a fight—my house was burned, some people got hurt, some of them badly." Night before last, eight guys showed up, all armed with those things." He pointed to where one of the Ingram submachine guns rested on the top of a cabinet. The man called Jerry got up and examined the weapon.

"Full-automatic version—with a silencer." He looked at MacGonigal with some respect. "You seem to have some serious enemies."

"You could say that. I think—don't know for sure—that these guys were sent by the partners of the guy that came up here last year, a guy named Nazario."

"His partners? Why not Nazario himself?"

"He's dead."

The man mouthed a silent "Oh," and MacGonigal went on. "These guys were pretty deep into drugs,

prostitution and pornography in New York. I understand that Nazario had connections all over the
country. Anyhow, he came after the lady, and he
didn't make it. His partners apparently have long
memories. Anyway, they came up here about mid-
night and tried to sneak up on us. One of them had a
jerry can of gas. Apparently, they meant to burn me
out.

"It wasn't Robbie's fight, and it wasn't Company
business, but he was here, and those boys didn't
intend to leave any survivors."

Jerry sat there as MacGonigal recounted the
night's events. When he was finished, MacGonigal
plunked his tumbler down on the table and got up to
run the water through the coffee strainer. He took
several stoneware mugs out of the cupboard and
poured hot, strong black coffee all around.

Jerry turned to Robbins. "I don't think the Company has an interest here. We'll load you up and get
out." He turned to MacGonigal. "Sorry, buddy, but it
looks like we're gonna have to skip the demonstration."

"Hold it a minute, Jerry. I think we'd better talk
about it."

"Robbie, I don't think this is the time or place. I've
got instructions to get you out of here. Fast. What this
guy does after we leave is his business." He turned to
MacGonigal. "Don't get any ideas about blackmail.
Robbie was never here, we were never here, and
you'll never prove any different."

MacGonigal grinned. "It hadn't crossed my mind.

But there might be some questions as to how I managed to handle *eight* professional killers all by myself." He grinned even more widely. "By the way, the local sheriff knows about Robbie. When he heard someone was looking for me, he had one of his deputies pull Robbie over for a warning ticket. Ran his driver's license and registration through the computer."

Jerry looked rapidly at Robbins. "Is that true? Can they put you here?"

"Yeah, Jerry, I'm afraid so. But there's more to it than that." He looked over to the table, where MacGonigal had left the bottle of Irish Mist.

"Can I have a little of that, Mac? I'm getting a bit tired."

MacGonigal poured him a full tumbler. "Talk to the boyos, Robbie—I don't like the way this is going."

"Don't worry, Mac. We're not going to leave you in the lurch." He took a mouthful and swallowed it slowly. "Look, aside from me being here, the local sheriff has a sort of a thing about Mac here. Very protective of him. But that's not the issue. As Mac so tastefully put it, we've got our collective tit caught in the wringer of the decade. And he's the boy who's got to get us out. We abandon him, and we're back to square one."

Jerry adopted a wary look. "I don't know what you're talking about."

"Of *course* you don't. But keep listening, anyway. I'm pretty much out of action for a while. Mac's agreed to do the job for us. Now, since he's in, he's got to know some of the details."

"You mean you've been talking out of school." He turned to MacGonigal. "Blackmail won't get you anywhere, buddy boy. We're pulling out, and if you try to say we've been here—well, don't. Nobody will believe you—I mean that."

MacGonigal grinned. "Are we friends? Because I get the feeling that you guys have something against me."

"Hold on, Mac!" Robbins turned to Jerry. "Sit down and don't make any more of an ass of yourself than you can help. I'm running this operation."

"Not anymore. You're out of it. I've got to take over."

"You've got to take over? Just who the hell do you think you are?"

"Look, Robbie, it's standard policy. You can't carry through, and that puts me in command. And I'm aborting this operation. Now." He motioned to his two companions. "Pick him up and let's get out of here."

Robbins held up a cautioning hand. "If you boys want to come out of this with your jobs, you'll stay right where you are." They hesitated, indecisive. "Just because Jerry here is having delusions of grandeur, that's no reason for you to stick your dicks into the meat grinder." The two men glanced at each other. "Look, Jerry, you guys work this out. Leave us out of it."

Jerry glared at them. "Okay, if that's the way you

want it, I'll get on the horn and see what management thinks."

"No, you won't. *I'll* get on the horn. You boys help me out to the plane."

They reluctantly helped Robbins to his feet and supported him as he hobbled out the door. Jerry looked at MacGonigal. "I'll stay here and watch this guy."

Robbins laughed shortly. "You're gonna watch *him*? If you'd had time to look around, you'd wonder if you were up to the task."

Jerry didn't reply, but watched them go. He turned to MacGonigal, the Uzi pointing almost, but not quite, at MacGonigal's midriff. "I don't know how the management will take Robbie's idea, but if it was me, I'd leave you to clean up your own mess."

MacGonigal grinned, a slow, lazy grin. "Well, me boyo, it isn't you. So why don't we make ourselves comfortable while we wait for Mr. Wallace's decision?" There was a long silence while MacGonigal drank his coffee. He put the mug down. "It's nice and hot. Want some?"

Jerry shook his head. He hadn't moved from where he stood, except to shift enough to keep MacGonigal within the arc of fire of the Uzi.

"You mind pointing that thing in some other direction?"

"Does it bother you?"

"Not near as much as it'll bother you if I have to stick it up your ass."

The muzzle of the Uzi came up sharply. Jerry's eyes

narrowed challengingly. "I'd like to see you do that."

MacGonigal grinned a wolfish grin. The stoneware mug, thrown suddenly sidearm, caught Jerry squarely on the forehead, knocking him backward. Before he could recover, MacGonigal had ripped the gun out of his hand. Jerry lay half-stunned, blood pouring from a cut in his forehead. MacGonigal stepped back and took a towel from beside the sink, throwing it to him.

"Use this, laddie-o, it'll stop the bleeding."

He released the magazine from the Uzi, pointing it up in the air to clear it, then tossed it on the sofa. Jerry, still groggy, watched it bounce on the cushion. MacGonigal laughed.

Jerry held his bleeding head. "You won't get away with this, you son of a bitch."

MacGonigal laughed. "If I were you, Jerry, I'd get out of this business. You're too dumb to last long."

Jerry glared at him, a sullen, hate-filled look. "I'm telling you, you'll never get away with this. I'll see to it personally."

"Jerry, me boyo, if I recall, you said you wanted to see me shove this sparkler of yours up your ass. Are ye still of that opinion?"

Jerry only glared. MacGonigal took another mug and poured more coffee. He handed the mug to Jerry. "Take it, laddie buck. You're in no position to refuse."

Jerry grudgingly took the mug. MacGonigal poured himself another, then came over and pried the blood-sodden towel out of Jerry's hand. He replaced the towel and took a plastic tackle box from one of the gun cabinets. He searched through its neatly arranged contents for a moment and produced a bottle of antiseptic and a butterfly bandage.

"Hold still. This'll sting."

Jerry flinched a little, but remained silent while MacGonigal cleaned the cut and applied the butterfly. He watched as MacGonigal left the room with the bloody towel, but made no move for the Uzi. MacGonigal returned and swept the room with his eyes, noting the weapon lying where he had thrown it.

"You're learnin', me boyo, you're learnin'."

He pulled a chair away from the table and swung it around to face Jerry.

"Now, there's a couple of things we need to get straight. First of all, nobody points a gun at me in my own house. And secondly, I don't take kindly to snotty-nosed bureaucrats trying to prove that they're tough guys. I don't know what your problem is, sonny, but let me give you some advice—if you ain't tough, don't act tough. I've been in this business a long time—probably longer than you've been housebroken. Now, from what Robbie says, we're going to have to work together. And you and I don't seem to have established a very sound professional relationship."

Jerry slumped in a chair, every line of his body showing a sullen resentment. There was a huge lump forming under the butterfly bandage, and it was turning a deep purple. MacGonigal gave him a beatific smile. "You don't understand this now, but you'll thank me in years to come."

He picked up the Uzi and reinserted the magazine. He passed it to Jerry. "Here's your toy. Don't point it at people."

Jerry took the weapon, still looking daggers at MacGonigal. MacGonigal pointedly turned his back. The muzzle of the weapon steadied on the small of his back.

Without turning his head, MacGonigal said, "If it ain't cocked, it won't shoot, sonny."

Jerry started, then reached for the cocking handle. His hand fell away, though, and he laid the Uzi aside. "You know something? You really are a son of a bitch."

"I am that, me boyo. That I am."

There was a scraping of boots on the porch, and the door opened. Robbins hobbled in, supported by one of the agents. He stopped short and looked at Jerry.

"What the hell's been happening in here?"

"Nothing for you to worry about, Robbie. We had a little discussion while you were gone. Just a little professional development."

Robbins looked over at Jerry. He seemed about to say something, then he shrugged. None of his business. He lowered himself into a chair.

"Here's the deal. We clean up around here, but you're in—we own you for this operation. I want to make that plain, Mac."

MacGonigal sighed. "That's not quite the way I do things, Robbie. You guys can pull out now. I don't give a shit. I'll go down and call in the TV reporters."

"Hold on, Mac. Don't make threats." He closed his eyes. His leg seemed to be causing him quite a bit of pain. "You already agreed to take the job—it's just that we want to make sure that if we help you, you help us. And you damn well know that if what happened here leaks out, you might as well forget about this idyllic life-style of yours."

MacGonigal grunted. That was true. One night of violence had changed things forever. If the Company could clean up the mess and keep it under wraps, then he would have to go along with whatever the Company wanted. But he didn't have to admit that out loud. *You're stuck—but you don't have to be stupid, MacGonigal, me boyo."*

"Okay. Now, look, Mac, things have changed since we made our deal. The Company doesn't think you're in any position to dicker about money. Seventy-five is the top offer."

MacGonigal said nothing. He knew that it wasn't money the Company was worried about. What the invisible men who controlled this operation wanted was to force MacGonigal to admit that he had to take their offer. Taking the offer would be a symbolic gesture of submission. He gritted his teeth.

Robbins was watching him closely. "Now, think about it, Mac. What we're doing here—cleaning up for you—that's worth the additional seventy-five. I mean, it's a wash. You get seventy-five cash and seventy-five in services."

There was a long, uncomfortable pause. "There's been a change in the operating mode. I was supposed to run the operation, with you and a few others as actives. Now I'm pretty much out of it." He indicated his leg. "I can't very well thrash through the jungle on this. So the upshot is that we need a new control." He took a deep breath. "That's you, Mac. You'll have to run the operation."

MacGonigal's jaw dropped. "You must be out of your head, Robbie! You want me to take a fifty-percent pay cut *and* run the operation on top of it? You're dreamin', laddie."

"No, I'm not dreaming, Mac. That's the deal they've offered. Look, I had to do some fast talking to sell this one. We—the Company—are in a bind. You know that. But you're in a bind, too. The difference is that the Company has alternatives, and you don't——not really. Anyhow, I convinced them that the fastest way to get this operation on track is to let you replace me. They bought it, but they stuck on the question of pay. And you know why. I don't have to tell you"

"Yeah, I know why. And you know why that sticks in my craw."

"I know, Mac. And I told them. But they insisted." He was almost pleading now. "Look, it doesn't really mean anything—it's like a symbol. You know that. You don't need the money, Mac. Take the deal."

MacGonigal sat as if carved out of stone. His

silence was unnerving. Robbins swallowed nervously, then went on. "I had a tough time selling this . . ." He blinked. "Look, Mac, I told you the operation needs deniability, and I convinced them that you could . . ."

MacGonigal's eyes narrowed. "I don't think I like what I'm hearing, Robbie. Why don't you just lay it out on the table?"

Robbins smiled, a sick, miserable smile. "What I told them was that the best way to mount this operation was as a private rescue mission . . . and you were the man to do that . . ."

"Hold on!" MacGonigal exploded. "You mean that you want me to pose as one of those assholes that go around raising money to find MIAs in Laos—like that asshole Buddy Rice." He was almost speechless.

"Yeah, Mac. That's the general idea."

"Jesus, Robbie, I don't think I can do it. I mean, you know Buddy . . . he's *stupid!*"

"Come on, Mac, he's not that bad."

"The hell he isn't. You remember that time in Panama? When they had that big demonstration for those South American generals?"

"I wasn't there, Mac."

"Well, *I* was. Buddy persuaded Michaelson—he was only a two-star then—that he and his Special Forces boys should put on a special show. A STABO rig. Buddy got two other dumb asses, and they rigged this thing up, all three harnesses on the same pickup. They had a big American flag, and each one of them had a smoke grenade—red, white, and violet."

"*Violet*? Why violet?"

"Because that was the closest thing to blue they could find. The idea was, they'd have the pickup line rigged on the parade field, the plane would fly by and snag them, and off they'd go, trailing an American flag and leaving a streak of red, white and blue smoke."

Robbie nodded. "Well, Buddy always was a showman."

"You don't know the half of it. Well, as I said, they were going to put on a STABO demonstration from the middle of the parade ground. They couldn't get a plane, though—the Air Force *knows* Buddy, and they're too smart to be suckered into one of his schemes. So anyway, Buddy lays on a Huey. Now, the pilot has never done a STABO extraction before —can't understand *why* he should do one from the middle of a parade field. I mean, this guy was cursed with common sense. He can't see why a helicopter has to make a STABO extraction from an open field, and he proposes to Buddy that he just *land* and pick them up. Well, Buddy finally gets it all set up. They're sitting in the middle of the parade field—all kinds of dignitaries watching—and here comes the helicopter. It snags the line and lifts them off the ground. Now, the plan is that they're gonna lift off, circle slowly around, and make a slow pass in front of the stand, trailing their American flag and their red, white and blue smoke.

"You know that gymnasium at the end of the parade ground? Well, the pilot got them high enough to clear the roof, but not high enough to clear those big sheet-metal ventilators on the roof. They hit one of those damn ventilators, and boots, helmets, flags and smoke grenades flew in all directions. The best part was, the pilot didn't *know* he'd dragged them into a ventilator, so he went on with the plan—made a big, slow circuit of the field, and flew them right past the stands, about twenty-five feet above the ground, fifteen feet away. Buddy had broken both arms, and the other two assholes were unconscious —they were hangin' out of their harnesses, half upside-down, mouths open, eyes rolled back up in their heads—and that's how they flew past the dignitaries.

"I'm telling you this was some demonstration —Michaelson beat the ambulance to the hospital, and he fired Buddy on the spot."

"I hadn't heard that story," said Robbins. "It sounds just like Buddy."

"You better believe it docs. And now you want *me* to pretend that *I'm* just like Buddy Rice, the modern-day Don Quixote, and put together a rescue operation and invade Nicaragua—all on my own."

Robbins laughed. "I wouldn't put it exactly that way, Mac—but that's the general idea."

"And if it blows up, then I'm the goat."

"Now, it's not like that, Mac . . ." he said soothingly. "Look at it this way—if it all falls apart, we can support you through diplomatic channels. I mean, if your cover's good enough, we can just tag you as a misguided citizen out to save an old buddy, and negotiate you out. But if you've got a Company label—well, I don't have to tell you what that would mean."

In spite of himself, MacGonigal thought, *The boyo's making sense.* Cautiously he said, "Go ahead. How are we going to set it up?"

"Well, we've got a few guys already recruited—all men you know, and I think you'll approve of them. Now what we have to do is arrange financing—that'll be the tricky part, because we can't leave any tracks back to the Company. Then you run it any way you want—any way within reason, I mean."

"You left out two things, old buddy: entry and exit."

"Well . . . we'll have to talk about that. I'm sure we can give you some assistance getting in and out. Maybe under cover of a military exercise . . . We'll have to work it out."

MacGonigal sat back, his hands folded across his stomach. "There's a lot we'll have to work out, old buddy. Including how much I get paid for this little job of yours. Let's get one thing straight—I'll do a fair day's work for a fair wage, but I don't kiss anybody's ass. The first order of business now is to clean up around here."

Robbins was visibly relieved. "Sure, Mac," he said brightly, "I've got that all cleared. We'll take the bodies out in the Porter—the crew is offloading the body bags now. Once they're out, they'll fly me out—Operations doesn't want to take the risk that somebody might spot you moving a man with an obvious gunshot wound. Jerry and the boys will take care of the Toyota, and you'll take my stationwagon. You'll have a reservation waiting at the airport at Little Rock, straight into Norfolk. You'll pick up a rental car there—the name is Williams, and Jerry has a driver's license and credit cards in that name. We'll take a Polaroid and put your picture on them now."

"The only thing wrong with that scenario is that your wagon isn't drivable—no windshield, among other problems."

Robbins hesitated. "Shit. We can't have you take your pickup and leave it in the parking lot. If there's any comeback, that'll be a problem. They find the truck, they find the flight you took. And they'll wonder what kind of business you had in Virginia. Tell you what—suppose one of the boys goes with you and drives it back here. How's that?"

"That's a little complex, Robbie. It's a good two, three hours into Little Rock, and the same back. And people around here know my truck. What if your boy has an accident?"

"I guess whoever it is will just have to be extra careful." He looked over at Jerry. "How about you going with Mac?"

Jerry looked apprehensively at MacGonigal, then

looked defiantly back at Robbins. "I can handle it. I'm a pro—I can work with anyone."

"How's that with you, Mac?"

MacGonigal glanced blandly at Jerry. "Fine with me. Jerry and I are old friends. We'll enjoy the trip."

One of the men was unpacking a small kit. He laid out his tools methodically on the table.

"Have you got a sheet we can use?" He indicated the book- and gun-lined walls of the room. "We need something for a backdrop."

MacGonigal got a sheet from the back-room closet, and the technician spread it over one of the bookcases, carefully smoothing out the wrinkles.

"If you'll stand over here . . ."

MacGonigal took his place, and the man took a single picture. He watched it develop for a moment, then looked up.

"Fine. Take your coat off for the next shot—we don't want the two pictures to look like they were taken at the same time."

MacGonigal complied, and the man took the second picture. While he waited for it to develop, he trimmed the first one and mounted it on the back of a two-part Virginia driver's license. He handed the document to MacGonigal, along with the second part of the document.

"Sign it right here. Be sure you get the name, Social Security number, and birthdate right."

MacGonigal looked the card over. The name was Harold Charles Williams, born in December 1946.

According to the address, he lived just outside Williamsburg—almost at Camp Peary's entrance gate. He copied the Social Security number and birthdate from the second part of the license, signed the document and handed it back to the technician, who sealed it into the little plastic pouch.

"Fill out the organ-donor card, too, if you will. Mark it 'entire body' if you don't mind."

MacGonigal hesitated slightly. "Why 'entire body'? Is there some special reason?"

The technician coughed, embarrassed. "Well, if anything happens . . . it makes things a little easier on us."

"In other words, it prevents embarrassing autopsies."

"You could say that . . . I suppose."

MacGonigal signed the document and passed it back. "Don't worry, laddie buck, I'll live to pipe you to your rest."

The technician passed him the credit card for his signature. MacGonigal signed it, and the man took it back. He produced a worn, bulging wallet, put the two documents in it, and handed it to MacGonigal. MacGonigal inspected it. It was filled with photos, business cards, receipts, and similar junk.

"I'll have to have your real wallet . . . you can keep the money, of course."

MacGonigal took out his own wallet and removed two twenties and a few ones, which he transferred, then handed it to the technician, who put it in his kit.

He passed a hand receipt over to MacGonigal, who signed it and passed it back.

Robbins braced himself and managed to get to a standing position. "Mac, if you'll show the boys where all the bodies are and point out anything you think needs special attention, they'll take it from there. Then we can put your things together—Ralph here will have to check out everything you take with you. We want you as sterile as possible for this leg of the trip."

MacGonigal led the group out of the cabin. Outside, the pilot and copilot had stacked several body bags. They had found the body in the shed, bagged it, and were in the process of carrying it to the plane.

"One of you guys had better go over the house carefully. That guy was shot down by the falls and carried into the house. There'll be plenty of blood on the trail and in the house. Better check the buffalo rug and all the furnishings, too."

The technician nodded. "We've got a lamp. Just show us the approximate route they followed, if you can."

"That's easy. They came right up the walkway here."

The technician nodded and produced a roll of white-cloth engineer tape and began staking out a search area that extended about ten feet on both sides of the path. "We'll check the whole area after dark." He looked up at MacGonigal. "Don't worry, nobody'll find anything after we've left."

He led them to the body of the first man he had killed. The corpse was stiff and swollen, the head a mass of dried blood, with splintered bone showing through the matted hair.

"Here's one." He looked around. Two others lay sprawled in the grass near the trail. "There's two more."

Jerry came up and looked down at the first body. "Jesus Christ! How'd you kill them?"

"Killed this one with a rifle butt. Robbie got the other two with a shotgun. He killed the one in the shed, too—wounded him here, and he died in the house."

They dropped three of the body bags near the corpses, and the technician staked out a wide circle around the bodies with his engineer tape. MacGonigal spotted a few 9mm cartridge cases lying nearby. He scuffed them up with the toe of his boot.

"There was quite a bit of shooting here—you'll want to collect as many cartridge cases as you can."

"Yeah. Okay. There's a metal detector in the plane. We'll get 'em."

They started down the path to the foot of the falls. Karl's body lay where he had left it, near the shed door. A few yards away lay the swollen, almost unrecognizable head.

"That one's a straight-shooting case—.308 Winchester softpoint. It probably splattered a lot of blood and tissue, so you'll need to be careful to check high up on the walls and in the brush." He pointed to the head. "The body that was attached to that is in the shed."

The technician began to stake out a wide circle. One of the other men entered the shed. He came back out, looking pale, and went around the back. In a moment, they could hear retching noises.

# IV.

MacGonigal jerked awake as the stewardess touched his shoulder.

"Put your seat in the upright position, sir. We're about to land at Norfolk."

He sat upright, pressed the button and allowed the seat to assume its fully forward position, then glanced out the window. The military installations of Tidewater, Virginia, were spread out below him: Norfolk Naval Base, headquarters of the Atlantic Fleet, almost directly below, the Naval Air Station coming up, and Fort Monroe visible across Hampton Roads. Beyond Fort Monroe, barely visible in the slight haze, was Langley Air Force Base and the NASA Research Center. Scattered here and there was a miscellany of smaller bases—Little Creek, Fort Storey, Fort Eustis, the Naval Weapons Station. *What a collection of targets*, thought MacGonigal. *It's a won-*

*der the place doesn't sink under the weight of all that hardware.*

The plane began its final approach, and he watched the streets and buildings below slide by, growing nearer and nearer, until the tires bumped on the runway and the pilot applied the brakes and thrust reversers. Across the airfield, he could see the small terminal building, virtually unchanged since his last sight of it.

He remained seated while the other passengers filled the aisle, waiting for the stewardess to open the door. As the crush cleared, he levered himself out of his seat, made his way up the aisle and collected his garment bag. It contained little more than a couple of changes of underwear, a pair of slacks and a sport coat, along with a few toilet articles picked up at a drugstore in Little Rock. There was nothing that could serve as a clue to his real identity.

"Have a nice day, sir, and thank you for flying with us."

He smiled a reply to the stewardass and started up the ramp toward the gate, following the crowd down the corridor. As he passed the security checkpoint, a young man in a three-piece suit detached himself from the knot of waiting friends and relatives and approached MacGonigal.

"Mr. Williams? I'm Charles Samuels."

He thrust out his hand, flashing MacGonigal a smile of guileless simplicity. He took the proffered hand and noticed that the grip was firm, but not so firm as to constitute a challenge. He looked the young man up and down, from his short, neatly combed brown hair to his shined shoes.

"Harry Williams. They didn't tell me anyone was meeting me here."

"We were on the same flight, sir, and I believe we're both headed for Williamsburg." The young man had already adroitly taken MacGonigal's bag and was walking him down to the ground level of the airport.

"Do you have any checked baggage, sir?"

"No. This is it. How about yourself?"

"I travel light, sir." So far as MacGonigal could see, the young man had nothing at all in the way of luggage, not even a briefcase.

"Do you have a car waiting?"

"No, sir. You have a rental car reserved. You can turn it in in Williamsburg." He smiled again. "I'll be riding with you, if you don't mind."

MacGonigal collected the keys at the rental-car desk, and he and Samuels headed through the double doors to the parking lot. MacGonigal unlocked the car and slung his bag into the back seat.

"Want me to drive?"

"No need. I know where we're headed."

He slid into the driver's seat, fastened the shoulder belt, and eased the compact Ford out into traffic. Crossing the bridge, he caught the first red light and took the opportunity to question his companion.

"Any particular reason why the boys at Peary think I needed to have a baby-sitter on the plane with me?"

Samuels seemed genuinely embarrassed. "I guess

they're worried about you, Mr. Williams. You have a rather . . . independent attitude."

MacGonigal glanced sideways at him, his attention partially occupied by the traffic as the light changed. "What do you mean by that?"

Samuels squirmed uncomfortably. "Well, I don't know any details, but they . . . there was a rumor of some unauthorized wet stuff."

"Wet stuff," a literal translation from the Russian, referred to killing, especially killing in the course of a clandestine operation. Samuels used the term self-consciously, as if not sure of its appropriateness. MacGonigal guessed that he had no real field experience. He glanced sideways again. Samuels seemed even younger than he had at first—probably hadn't been with the Company more than a year or two —and he was obviously impressed by MacGonigal's reputation.

They were approaching the ramp to Interstate 64. MacGonigal craned his neck as they approached the end of the ramp, then piloted the little Ford out into the right lane.

"What do they call you? Charlie?"

"Uh . . . Charlie is okay, sir."

"All right, then. Let's make it Harry and Charlie. That suit you?"

Samuels nodded. MacGonigal continued. "What's your role in this operation?"

"I . . . I'm not suppposed to talk business. I'm just along for the ride."

"Okay, fine," said MacGonigal. He paused a moment. "Seems like you had permission to talk about what happened at my place, though."

Samuels had the good grace to blush. "I . . . I didn't actually *talk* about it, sir. I mean . . . I had a briefing before the mission."

"What did they tell you?"

"I can't talk about that . . ." He caught himself. "Not much, sir, except that you were . . . unpredictable. And that there had been some killing. They made it sound like a massacre . . ."

"It was. Some old friends took the occasion to come calling while your man was there."

Samuels was silent for a moment. At last he said, "I guess this breaks the Agreement." His tone of voice seemed to imply that he was excited by the prospect.

"The Agreement," always spoken as if it were capitalized, was the unspoken rule that Soviet and American agents never killed in each other's homeland. The rest of the world might be a free-fire zone, but close to home there was a serious danger of provoking major retaliatory action. The Agreement was rarely broken, and by mutual understanding, all violations entailed some form of atonement. There had been no violations for years, and the two major powers policed their respective allies and client states, as well as their own clandestine organizations. An action of such a scale as to justify the term "massacre" might well bring about the collapse of the Agreement, with a resulting series of retaliation and counterretaliation. *He must be itching to mix it up with the Russians*, thought MacGonigal.

"Sorry to disappoint you, but these were home-grown hoods, in the drug, prostitution and porno businesses. They had a grudge."

"How big a grudge?"

"Pretty big. This time they sent in eight soldiers to make the hit."

"*Eight*?" he said in astonishment, "*This time*? You mean that there have been more attempts?"

"Well, it's a pretty big grudge. They think I beat them out of some money."

Samuels seemed to move away from MacGonigal, as if horrified to hear that he had been involved in something so seamy. At the same time, he seemed fascinated.

"What happened? I mean at your place—with the eight soldiers."

"Robbie Robbins and I took 'em. Robbie picked up a couple of 9mm slugs in the process."

Samuels seemed to hang, expectant, as if waiting for MacGonigal to expand on his answer. At last, unable to wait, he asked, "How many were killed? I mean . . . was it really a massacre?"

"Robbie killed three, I killed five."

"You killed them *all*? How?"

"Robbie used a 12-gauge shotgun. I used different methods."

Samuels leaned back in the seat. Finally he spoke again. "Tell me about it." His voice almost trembled as he said it.

*You really are a hot dog, me boyo,* thought MacGonigal. *Don't know if I want you in on this operation or not.* But he repeated the story for Charlie's benefit.

Then your people came in and kindly cleaned up the mess—I suppose because they want me to do a little job for them. That's about it."

The maps show only a single entrance to Camp Peary, and almost nothing beyond the entrance. In a way, they are correct. There is one, and only one, way in and out of Camp Peary. MacGonigal and Samuels approached the entrance and were halted by a uniformed security officer, who directed them into a small parking area.

"You'll have to wait here for a few minutes. Someone will come out to escort you."

MacGonigal waited for a minute or two, then twisted around in the seat, rummaging in his bag. He produced his pipe and tobacco pouch and proceeded to fill the bowl. As he did so, he caught Samuels looking doubtfully at him.

"I take it you're not a smoker, laddie?"

"No, I'm not." He paused. "I wonder if I could persuade you not to light that thing in here."

MacGonigal hesitated. "You'll have to forgive me—it's my only bad habit, unless you count cannibalism and necrophilia. But if it'll make you happy, I'll smoke outside."

He opened the door of the little Ford and crawled out, putting his back to the wind and cupping his lighter in his hand. Behind him, he heard a voice calling.

"Sir! Sir! I'll have to ask you to stay in your car."

He finished lighting the pipe and got it drawing. He took his pipe tool, retamped the tobacco, and reapplied the lighter. As he did so, the security guard put a hand on his shoulder.

"You have to stay in your car until your escort arrives, sir. It's the rules."

MacGonigal blew a cloud of smoke. "Would ye have me asphyxiate the wee lad? He's a delicate one, and his wee lungs can't stand the strain."

The security guard looked at him, perplexed. Samuels handed his identification out the window.

"I'll watch him—don't worry about him."

The guard seemed embarrassed, but was firm. "I've got instructions, sir. About both of you. You'll both have to stay here. In the car."

Samuels blanched. "Come on, Harry, get back in the car." He looked up at the guard. "There's no point in asking him to put his pipe out—do you have any objections if we leave the windows open?"

An olive-drab jeep appeared, with two uniformed marines in it. Following it was a light green U.S. Government sedan. The two vehicles braked to a stop beside the parking area. One of the marines called to the security guard, "Any trouble?"

Before the man could answer, the door on the passenger side of the sedan opened, and a short, stocky man in a rumpled suit got out.

"I'll take it from here."

MacGonigal looked at the approaching figure. The man was almost completely bald, with a fringe of graying hair just above the ears. He had bags under his eyes—pouches, really—and his fingers were tobacco-stained.

"Lemme see your ID."

It was an order, not a request. MacGonigal pulled out his wallet and passed the whole thing to him.

"The cash is mine—the rest of it's yours."

The bald man looked at the documents in the wallet, then handed it back. He turned to Samuels. "You drive. Follow me."

Samuels maneuvered himself past the center console and slid into the driver's seat.

"Give him the keys."

MacGonigal passed the keys to Samuels, then went around to the passenger side. The fat man flipped a thumb toward the waiting government sedan. "You ride with me."

MacGonigal went over to the sedan. The door was locked, and the driver made no move to unlock it. Only when the bald man put his hand on the door handle did the driver reach over and pull up the button. The bald man opened the door, pushed the front seat forward, and forced his not-inconsiderable belly past it and into the back seat.

"You ride up front, where I can watch you."

MacGonigal smiled, showing his teeth above his beard, and slid into the seat. The driver reached past him to lock the door, then started the engine and swung the car around. Looking out the side window, MacGonigal saw the marines motion Samuels to follow, then pull their jeep around to take station at the rear of the little convoy.

They followed the road for perhaps a mile, past the water tower, and turned right, along the bank of the York River. The sedan pulled up in front of a low, one-story building and stopped. The driver reached across MacGonigal again and unlocked the door. The rented Ford pulled in next to them, while the jeep merely waited in the road, its engine running.

MacGonigal got out and held the seat back while the bald man emerged. The marines watched as the man lumbered up the short walk to the front door of the building, with MacGonigal and Samuels following him. As the door closed behind them, MacGonigal heard the jeep move off.

The room they were in was decorated in the Federal Government mode, Contemporary Bureaucracy period, with gray-green walls, a nondescript carpet, two metal filing cabinets, and a word processor on a table facing the wall. There were two white pressed-wood desks, obviously products of the Federal Prison Industries, with gray swivel chairs, one of which contained a spare, dour woman with iron-gray hair. The other chair was occupied by a man in his fifties, with short, sparse hair and pale blue eyes. He looked MacGonigal up and down, then got to his feet. He was a good four inches taller than MacGonigal, but stooped, as if ashamed of his height.

"We'll be in the secure area, Miss Hogg."

Miss Hogg produced a logbook with a green cloth cover, and MacGonigal's escort began to fill out one line. He turned and handed his ballpoint pen to

MacGonigal, who inspected the log. It was one of the usual access logs, so beloved by security types. He saw that the man above him had listed his security clearance as "Top Secret," followed by a code number, and had signed his name as "William N. James." MacGonigal took the pen and signed the log, giving his cover name and listing his security clearance as "Ridiculous." Miss Hogg, reading his entry upside down, glared at him. *If you think that's outrageous, sister, try asking me my sex*, thought MacGonigal.

Miss Hogg, either unable to read his mind or unwilling to take the challenge, offered the book to Samuels, who also signed in. She closed the book, her lips compressed in a thin line, and returned it to her desk drawer. She gave MacGonigal a look of pure hatred, and he consoled himself with the thought that there were other fish in the sea. *But none colder than that bitch*, he thought.

The secure area was a room about twenty by twenty-four feet. It was heavily soundproofed, and a wooden box with colored glass inserts hung from the ceiling. The tall man threw a switch, and one of the glass inserts lighted up. It was red and bore the legend "Top Secret." A small cardboard sign hung from the box. It read, "All discussions in this room are classified. Unauthorized disclosure or discussion of anything mentioned in this room may subject the violator to penalties of appropriate federal law."

The center of the room was dominated by several folding tables formed into a horseshoe, with chairs ranged around the sides. At one end of the room was a podium. The wall at that end of the room was covered with a curtain. The tall man motioned for them to sit down, then went to the podium. He pressed a button, and a humming noise filled the room. It was possible to talk above the noise only with difficulty. A light above the podium flashed on, "Antimonitoring in effect." The man returned to the table and sat down opposite MacGonigal, his long arms and legs folding up as he lowered himself into the chair.

He looked at MacGonigal. "We went out on a limb for you, buddy. You *owe* us." He paused, his face a frozen mask of menace. "And we're going to collect —you can bet your sweet ass on that!"

MacGonigal gave him a wintry smile. "If you don't mind, I'd like to keep this on a professional basis. You have a job for me to do. Why don't we get on with it?"

The man glared at him. "I'm not sure we *do* have a job for you—not now."

"In that case," said MacGonigal, rising to his feet, "I'll send you a bill for my expenses."

"Siddown, asshole," said the fat man next to him. MacGonigal looked down at him, then back to the first speaker.

"Well, what is it? Stay or go?"

The man stood, slowly unfolding like a stork. "I don't think you understand your position here."

"I understand it, all right. *You* may be a little confused. You people approached me about a job. I'm here. If you want the job done, then we'll talk. If not, then I leave."

"That wouldn't be advisable."

"Wouldn't it? You're not in much of a position to give advice—you send a man out to recruit someone for a sensitive operation, and then you treat him like a redheaded stepchild. Now, you either get down to business or get yourself another boy."

"I told you, you owe us. Now, sit down."

MacGonigal smiled. "I thought you'd see the light."

He lowered himself into his chair, then felt in the pockets of his new tweed jacket for his pipe and tobacco pouch. "Mind if I smoke?" He went through the ritual of lighting the pipe, then settled back. "Now that we're through playing games, let's get down to business. I understand that you have to demonstrate a certain amount of control over an agent—but I'm what's called a *free* agent. And I don't take to asshole rules—understand?"

The tall man seemed about to speak, but MacGonigal held up his hand. "You boyos want me to put together a 'private' army, take it partway around the world, and invade a country where you're not supposed to meddle."

The tall man grunted something that seemed to be an affirmative.

"Good. We're beginning to understand each other. Now, let's take it one step further. Once I leave here, I'm pretty much on my own . . ."

The fat man let out a growl, half rising out of his seat. MacGonigal forestalled him. "I mean, you expect independent action—am I right?"

The cadaverous head nodded. "To a degree—but you have to be willing to accept a certain amount of direction, and you haven't proved that you can do that yet."

"I don't have to prove it. Not until *you* prove that you know how to give it, intelligently. Don't send bully boys to shove me around—and don't try to intimidate me, because I don't intimidate easily. If you want me to do something, you tell me. If it makes sense, I'll do it. If not, I won't. Understand?"

The tall man looked silently at him for a moment. "We seem to have gotten off on the wrong foot here. Let's try again." He sat back down and reached under the table, pressing a hidden button. In a moment or two, a red light began blinking over the door. It opened, and Miss Hogg came in, carrying a thick manila folder. She placed it on the table and left without speaking or looking at MacGonigal.

The tall man opened the folder. He pulled out several small envelopes and passed them to MacGonigal. "We've recruited several people—I believe you know them all—to operate with you. Robbins was to be the control, but now that he's out of it, he's recommended that you serve as team leader, and that we assign an agent to work as liaison with you—a highly irregular procedure. The question is, Do we accept his recommendation, or do we scrub the mission?"

MacGonigal took the envelopes and slit them open. He thought, *You've already made up your mind on this one, me boyo, or else you wouldn't be showing me the operations file.*

He shook out the contents of each envelope, looked at the pictures and read the brief record attached to each, and stacked them, facedown, on the table. There were five men—he knew all of them.

Ronald Evans was a big, beefy man, with arms the size of a normal man's legs. He could climb mountains, hike miles, carry the heaviest loads. He and MacGonigal had operated for six months along the Ho Chi Minh Trail, scouting NVA units, counting them, gathering intelligence, taking an occasional prisoner from the stragglers. Evans liked to stalk his enemy, ghosting silently through the jungle, an amazing feat for one of his bulk, then spring out and simply enfold his prey in his huge arms. He was a good man in a tough spot.

Willie Faith was a skinny little man. MacGonigal remembered him as a scared black kid who grew up fast under fire. He was a certified genius, a communications wizard, who worked miracles with radios. Once he had rigged a makeshift hydrogen generator, inflated a condom, and sent it aloft trailing an antenna wire from an old PRC-6 squad radio. He had made contact at a range of sixty miles, using a radio designed for less than two miles. And he had saved MacGonigal's bacon that time—along with that of five other team members.

Daniel Webster Collins, "D.W." to his friends, was a sniper, a dedicated small-arms expert. He also liked to kill. In action, he was cold as ice. He would wait patiently in ambush for days for a shot. He also was adept at constructing ingenious "mechanical ambushes"—homemade booby traps—although as a purist, he considered them unsporting, preferring to kill with a single shot from long range.

Tomás Maldonado was one of the cleverest, most insidious intelligence agents MacGonigal had ever known. He could insinuate himself into the local population wherever he was. He attracted informants and gossips like a magnet, built networks with practiced ease, and could put together a complete picture of the enemy's intentions from the skimpiest scraps of information. And he was always right. Always. It was a trait that had endeared him to MacGonigal, but not to his superiors. And he spoke fluent Spanish.

Calvin Lawrence was a West Pointer, son of a general, a man destined for a star—until he had run into a problem along the Cambodian border that even his father's influence couldn't square for him. He'd resigned from the service and immediately found a job with one of the many nameless U.S. Government activities that infested Southeast Asia. His reputation was spotted—he got results, but he lost men. Many considered him cynical, unscrupulous, and power-hungry. There was no doubt that he would willingly undertake missions that no one else would risk.

One by one, MacGonigal picked the photographs up, gave them one more survey, and replaced them in their envelopes. He handed four of the envelopes back. The fifth, Evans', he ripped in half.

"I take it you've rejected one of the men we've recruited for you?"

MacGonigal looked up at the speaker. "You've given me four very competent men—the best in their fields—and one gorilla. I don't see that one gorilla more or less is going to matter in this operation."

"No need to be sarcastic. I take it the others are acceptable?"

"For now. I'll take them, if they fit the mission. Now, who do you have in mind for my liaison agent?"

"We haven't decided if that's the way we want to go yet."

"Well, make up your mind quick. I'll take Charlie here," MacGonigal said, jerking a thumb at Samuels. The young man seemed startled, and the fat man leaned forward as if to object. The cadaverous one signaled him to remain silent, however.

"Samuels is a little too inexperienced for you. You'll need someone with more field experience."

"I'll provide the field experience—you just provide the body."

The tall man seemed to be thinking. "I don't have any basic objection—but with Robbins out of the picture, there are a lot of loose ends in this operation, principally in the areas of financing and organization. That takes a lot of experience and a lot of legwork. I'm not sure you'll have the time to train anyone."

"Why don't you fill me in, and if I think he can't cut

it, then we'll look for someone else."

The tall man passed the rest of the file across the table. "The details are in here. You'll have a place to study the operations folder at your leisure over the next couple of days. But the general situation is that, while we have a good deal of intelligence, we don't actually have an operation ready to go. We have only you and the four men you've accepted. Obviously you'll have your work cut out for you in planning and mounting this operation."

MacGonigal flipped the file open and scanned the cover sheet, then began to leaf through the contents. He pulled out a wad of neatly folded maps and aerial photographs and laid them to one side. After a while, he unfolded one of the map sheets and placed one of the photos next to it.

"Is there anyplace I can spread this stuff out?"

The tall man motioned to Samuels and rose to draw the curtain at the end of the room. Behind it was a transparent screen set up for rear projection. Several sets of sliding panels could be moved in front of the screen. One set of panels constituted a huge blackboard, while another was a cork board, randomly studded with pins. Samuels pulled the cork board into place and pinned up the maps and charts that MacGonigal handed him.

Using the maps to trace the contents of the various documents that made up the file, MacGonigal began to assimilate the outlines of the problem.

"You really *don't* have an operation here—all you have is a collection of information and a few people.

You don't even have any reliable in-country assets," he said accusingly.

The tall man looked at him with a pained expression. "We expected Robbins—and you—to put the operation together. We can't use in-country assets for two reasons. One is because they're suspect after Nichols' capture, and the other is that the operation has to have complete deniability."

"What about the Contras? They're pretty much under your control. Can't we use them?"

The tall man shook his head. "No way. You go near the Contras, and we'll chop you off at the ankles. You don't mess with them."

He gave MacGonigal a long, appraising look. "Let's make sure we understand the parameters of this operation: First of all, it's completely private. The U.S. Government has nothing to do with it. Nothing. Second, its aim is to deprive the opposition of an asset in the way of Steven Nichols. Third . . ."

He stopped as MacGonigal held up a big hand. "You mean we kill him if we can't get him out?"

The man gave MacGonigal a look like he'd found out who had stepped in dog shit. "I said we deprive them of using him as an asset. How you do it is your business." He went on. "Third, there's to be no intervention after the fact—although we'll treat you as if you were mercenaries, and try to negotiate for your release if you're caught."

"But I shouldn't hold my breath waiting for the cavalry?"

The man glared at him again. "I think you're

beginning to understand." He looked at his watch. "There's a conference scheduled here in two hours. I suggest that you take all this stuff"—he waved a hand to indicate the maps, charts, and classified documents—"and come up with some kind of workable plan."

. MacGonigal gathered up the documents and stood a moment, thinking. "There's someone else I want to bring into the operation—a very rich lady. I need her to provide the organization and funding. But you'll have to give her protection."

Wallace looked up at him. "Go ahead," he said. "Bring in anyone you like." A frosty smile played over his cadaverous features. "Because once you leave this country, you're on your own."

# V.

The phone was answered on the second ring. "United Enterprises, Ms. Bradley's office, Sharon speaking. Can I help you?"

"You can, darlin'. Tell Missus Bradley there's a broth of a boy who wants to talk to her."

There was a pause, and the voice on the other end asked uncertainly, "Who shall I say is calling?"

"Never mind, darlin', just tell her. She'll know."

"I'm not sure she's in right now. Would you like to call back?"

"She's in. Just tell her. She'll talk to me."

MacGonigal waited, hanging on the phone, while the person on the other end put him on hold. In the background, Samuels and the fat man hovered. Wallace sat across from him, wearing a pair of headphones. They had patched his call through, using secure circuits, so that, as far as telephone company records indicated, it had originated in Los Angeles.

Wallace had a switch, which he could use to break the connection if MacGonigal said anything that might betray the true origin of the call or of the background. MacGonigal knew beyond doubt that the call was being recorded, as well.

Susan Ennis came on the line. "Mac? Mac, is that you?"

"It is, big as life and twice as ugly."

"Are you in town? Can you come over? I'm dying to see you."

Wallace flashed him a warning look. He temporized. "I'll be in to see you later. Right now I've got a lot of business to take care of."

"But you will come by? You're not leaving Los Angeles without seeing me?"

"Darlin', you *know* I wouldn't do that. I called to see if you're free tomorrow night. I thought we might go out somewhere."

"I'm free, Mac. How long are you going to be here?"

"Oh, a few days. Depends on when I finish my business."

"Where are you staying? You know you can stay at my place."

"I know, beautiful. And I'm looking forward to it. But for the time being, I've got a few things to take care of. I'll see you at your place about seven o'clock tomorrow night."

"You've got my address? You know how to find it?"

"Don't worry, beautiful—I'll be there."

"I'll be waiting for you, Mac."

The relays clicked, and the line went dead. He hung up the phone.

At the airport in Ontario, California, they were met by a nondescript, informally dressed little man who approached them as they exited the security area. The man showed a card to Samuels, then handed MacGonigal a package.

"Open it in the men's room."

They went in and MacGonigal peeled back the wrapping paper. The package contained his old wallet, with his identification, driver's license, and other things. He transferred his money to the wallet and handed his forged documents to the man, who produced a receipt. MacGonigal signed for his possessions and took the proffered copy of the receipt he had signed for the Company's wallet and tucked it away.

"Wait a couple of minutes, and then you can go. There's a car reserved in your name." Without further discussion, the man left. MacGonigal and Samuels stood a moment.

"By the way, my name's MacGonigal—Francis Xavier MacGonigal. My friends call me Mac."

Samuels grinned. "My name's still Charlie Samuels. What do your enemies call you?"

"They start with 'son of a bitch,' and it goes downhill from there."

They went past the rental-car desk and collected the keys for their car, then out to the lot. The little Mazda looked clean and new, but MacGonigal was exasperated. "Can't these damn bureaucrats provide us with a decent car, for once?"

He headed out of the airfield and turned west on Highway 10, heading into Los Angeles, through the maze of small towns that sprawl across the valley. They drove for only a few minutes, until they located a motel that looked clean and turned in. MacGonigal kept the engine running while Samuels went in and checked them in, asking for adjoining rooms with a connecting door.

"Tell you what—why don't you get unpacked while I call in?"

Samuels nodded assent, gathered up his luggage, and began shaking out and hanging up his clothes. MacGonigal seated himself beside the phone and dialed. He let the phone ring several times before it was finally answered.

"Independent Insurance Adjusters. Can I help you?"

"Let me speak to Mr. Wallace, please."

There was a pause, and he could imagine the workings of the secure-phone patch system—a system that nobody trusted, and whose only advantage was that it prevented calls being recorded at their true origins. In a moment, Wallace's voice came through the instrument.

"Wallace. What can I do for you?"

"This is Harry Williams," said MacGonigal, using the same name he had used in Virginia. "I'm just calling to confirm that the premium has been paid on my policy."

"Just a minute, Mr. Williams. I'll have to check."

In a moment, Wallace came back on the line. "Yes, Mr. Williams, you're fully covered. I have confirmation from our New York office."

"Thanks, you do good work," said MacGonigal as he hung up.

Samuels came out of the other half of the double suite. "Any luck?"

"Yeah. He said that they had it all sewed up —confirmed in New York."

"That's pretty fast work—I wonder how they managed it?"

"Probably wasn't too hard," said MacGonigal. "After all, they had all the names I gave them —including several people who are still alive and operating in New York, like Teddy DeLisle. He's still operating his porno and prostitution business, and he could lead them to his partners—whoever they are."

"Yeah—but guys like that don't just roll over on their backers. It isn't conducive to a long life."

"That's true," conceded MacGonigal, "but your boys had an advantage—they didn't have to make a court case, they just had to get him to talk. And he *was* mixed up in the killing of a Company man. Even though George Harris was retired, he was a Company man one time, and it ain't good business to let hoods kill Company men."

"I suppose. But still, it couldn't have been easy to get him to talk."

"Well, they also had identifications on the bodies of the ones killed at my place. It probably wasn't too hard to get access to the National Crime Information Computer and get a fix on who it is that's been after me and my lady friend. After that, I guess it was just a matter of applying enough pressure."

Samuels was slipping into a silk shirt, a tie thrown over his shoulder. "Yeah, I guess so. Still, I'd really like to know the details—I mean, forcing an underworld group to cancel a contract, that's something that they don't teach you."

"You just have to use language they understand," said MacGonigal, drawing a finger across his throat. He hooked his jacket off the back of a chair. "Let's go, laddie. I've got a date."

MacGonigal pulled up alongside a Buick and got out, leaving the engine running. "You take it, Charlie. I'll get a ride."

"I can come back and pick you up, Mac. What time?"

MacGonigal's face split in a huge grin. "No thanks, Charlie. I might be several days."

Samuels' face showed sudden consternation, "Several *days*! We've got to report in tomorrow . . ."

MacGonigal closed the door and rapped on the roof. "Move it before you get a ticket, laddie-o." He swung around the back end of the car and gained the sidewalk with a single stride. From behind him he heard a query, "When will you be back at the motel?"

"When I'm ready to check out!" He waved and disappeared into the building.

A uniformed doorman stood in the lobby.

"Visitor for Ms. Bradley. MacGonigal's the name."

The man pressed the button for Susan's apartment. In a moment, she answered, "Let me talk to him," and the doorman passed the message.

MacGonigal stepped up to the speaker and pressed the button.

"Is that you, Mac?"

"It's me, darlin'. Are you coming down, or should I come up?"

"Come on up, Mac. We'll have a drink first."

He turned and saluted the doorkeeper, then entered the elevator.

"Mac! I love the beard. It makes you look like a big, huggy bear." She tugged him gently into the apartment. He swung the door shut behind him.

"Let me look at you, beautiful."

He pushed her away and held her at arm's length. Susan Ennis was a beautiful woman, tall and slender, with waist-length hair. She stood a moment, letting him look, and then stepped into his arms, moving like a cat. Her hands, resting on his forearms, trembled delicately.

"It's been a long time, Mac."

"Too long, darlin'." He enfolded her in his arms and pulled her toward his chest. She melted willingly against him and tilted her face up toward him.

At last they separated, and she steered him toward the couch.

"Why don't you get comfortable, Mac? Let me take your coat for you and fix you a drink—I've got some

Irish Mist, especially for you."

"That'll be fine, darlin'. I'm flattered that you remembered."

She looked at him. "Mac, you *know* I remember. I remember everything." She poured his drink and brought it to him. He watched the way she moved, and smiled to himself.

She poured one for herself and settled herself in a chair opposite him, tucking her feet up under her. There was a long, almost self-conscious silence. There was so much they had to say that neither of them could think how to begin. They sat and sipped their drinks. MacGonigal looked around the apartment, searching for something to start a conversation.

"This is a beautiful place you've got here, Sue."

"I'm glad you like it, Mac. Would you like some music—or maybe a fire? We could curl up and watch the flames, like we used to in your place."

"Little hot for a fire, isn't it?"

"I can turn on the air conditioner."

He looked at her over the rim of his glass. "That's a little expensive, isn't it?"

"I'm a rich girl, Mac. I can afford it."

He nodded. "I'm fairly well off, myself, thanks to you."

"You don't owe me any thanks, Mac. I owe you. If it wasn't for you, I wouldn't be alive today."

He waved a hand, dismissing it all, and put down his glass. "Well, tell you what—let me take you out to dinner, and we'll call it even. How's that? But you'll have to provide the transportation—I don't have any wheels."

She rose and picked up his glass. "Why don't we just forget about that and let me fix something for us to eat here."

He nodded, and she poured a second drink for him. "You just relax here, and I'll put something together."

She left the room while he admired her swaying buttocks. *Francis, me boyo, you've got the hots for that girl worse than ever.*

He sat for a moment, sipping at the drink, then got up and wandered around the room. It was expensively decorated, with a deep, plush carpet and severe but comfortable furnishings. He inspected some paintings on the wall and recognized them as fairly valuable originals. They fit the decor beautifully, but he thought to himself that Sue Ennis had bought them primarily for their value as investments and hedges against inflation—then he caught himself, reminding himself to think of her as Sue Bradley now, the name she had adopted to go with the identity they had created to protect her from the mob.

A large set of drapes covered the opposite wall, and he could see French doors that opened onto a terrace. He pulled aside the drapes and went out.

"How do you like the view, Mac?" she called from somewhere inside the apartment.

He looked out over the lights of the city and called

back, "Can't tell. Too many damn lights to see anything."

There was a rattling noise, as if she had put down a pan. "You're incorrigible, Mac. I had hopes of civilizing you."

"You wouldn't like me if I was civilized."

"I guess you're right. You wouldn't be Mac anymore."

He leaned over the railing and looked down, then went back into the apartment and picked up his drink. He could hear her moving around. "Don't come in here, Mac. I'll call you when I'm ready. Why don't you go back out on the terrace?"

He wandered back out. Sue Ennis—Bradley, he reminded himself again—was one hell of a woman. He'd probably never get her out of his system. Hell, he didn't want to! He leaned over the rail and thought about her.

"Mac? Are you really hungry?"

"Not really. Why?"

"Come in here."

He turned away from the railing. She was standing there, framed by the French doors, wearing a pair of high-heeled shoes and a *very* inviting smile.

Later on, she raised herself up on one elbow and looked down at him. She traced a design in the hair of his chest with one forefinger.

"You know something, Mac? You really are an animal."

He ran a hand up through the curtain of her hair, pulled her head down and kissed her. "You wouldn't have it any other way, darlin'."

"You're right," she admitted. "You're a devious bastard, too."

"Me? I thought I was pretty straightforward."

She gave him a cynical look. "You're only straightforward to a point, Mac, and once you pass that point, you're a regular Machiavelli. What is it you want?"

"I'm surprised at you, darlin'. I'd have said there was never a question about what I wanted."

"There's never doubt about *that*, but you're here for a reason—now, what is it?"

"Well, there's no fooling you, I guess. I've taken a job, and I thought I might talk you into subcontracting a part of it."

"*You've* taken a job? I didn't think you'd demean yourself."

"It's complicated. An old friend of mine came and offered me a job. And while he was there, some old friends of yours came calling."

"Oh, *no*! What happened? If there was any damage, I'll pay for it. You know I will."

He reached over and patted her bare hip. "Don't worry, darlin', it's all taken care of—permanently."

"What . . . what happened? Tell me about it."

"There were eight of 'em. They came at night. Robbie Robbins—he was the guy who offered me the job—and I heard them coming and we just went out and cleaned 'em up. Robbie picked up a couple of slugs in the process, but he's okay."

"Oh, my *God*! I'll make it up to him, Mac. If you'll tell me how to get in touch with him, I'll take care of his medical expenses—I'll pay him whatever he thinks is fair."

"He's taken care of—don't worry about it."

"Don't *worry*? The man nearly got killed, by some people who were after *me*. Mac, I can't live with something like that on my conscience. It's bad enough to know I've put *you* in danger . . ."

She stopped suddenly as the impact of her words went home to her. "My God, Mac—this means that they'll keep trying. They know where your place is, and they'll keep trying. You'll have to give up your place."

She pulled him to her, his head between her breasts. "I'm *sorry*, Mac, I'm so sorry! I know how much your place means to you, and I've ruined it all for you, haven't I?"

He gently took one of her nipples between his lips, then disengaged himself and laid her back on the pillow. He stroked her face with one hard, hairy hand. "Don't worry—there's no harm done. It's all over. There's no contract on either of us anymore."

She looked up at him for a moment. "What do you mean, no contract? Mac, they *never* cancel a contract —not one like they've got out on me. And not on you, either, not after what you've done to them."

He smiled. "Believe me, it's cancelled. Robbie had

some connections, and they cancelled it. I called in and got confirmation just before I came over here."

She put her hands flat against his chest and pushed him away. "Mac, nobody has those kinds of connections. I don't know who this Robbie is, and I don't know who his connections are, but you can't go back to your place. You can *never* go back there again. *Please* believe me. I don't want you killed."

He tried to speak, but she put a hand over his mouth. "I know you're tough, Mac, and I know you can take care of yourself, but they'll keep trying until they get you. Please, promise me that you'll never go back to your place again. I'll find you another place —in the Rockies, in Alaska, anywhere. I'll buy it for you and fix it just like you want, but don't go home again—please."

He took her small hand in his bigger hand and moved it away. "Don't worry, darlin'. Robbie works for the government. They've taken care of it. There won't be any more problems—not from Teddy DeLisle or any of his scumbag partners."

"Mac! The government can't touch him. They've tried. They can't do it. And the Federal Witness Protection Program . . . all they can do is create an identity for you, they can't make the mob stop hunting you. And they only do that *if* you testify —and neither one of us can do that."

"The *Justice* Department can't touch him—that much is true. But the boys I'm talking about don't operate under the same rules. They *can* cancel the contract. And DeLisle and Company know it."

"Mac, what the hell are you talking about? You aren't drunk, are you?"

He laughed, a deep rumbling laugh from low down in the chest. "No, darlin', I'm not drunk, and I'm not dreamin'. The boyos I'm talking about want me to do a little job *outside* the country. And in return, they're willing to do a little job for me *inside* the country."

"I think you'd better explain. I'm not sure I follow you."

"There's a friend of mine who's in trouble. And because he's in trouble, the people he works for are in trouble. So they want me to get him out. They want it in the worst way, and they aren't too particular how I do it, as long as there are no comebacks on them. They don't mind a little rough stuff—in fact, they don't mind a *lot* of rough stuff—as long as it can't be traced back to them. I agreed to it, but I need a little help—and you're in a position to provide that help. But I told them that before you could be brought into the picture, they'd have to do something about your problem with the boys in New York. So they sent some people to talk to Teddy and Company. I don't know the details, but they apparently convinced him."

"Mac," she said, "it'll take a lot more than *talk* to convince Teddy's partners to back off on us."

"These boyos *do* a lot more than talk. I expect they gave Teddy and his friends a little sample of what would happen if they bother us again."

"It would have to be quite a sample."

"It probably was. Let's put it this way: there were eight of them that came calling at my place, and these boyos made all eight of the bodies disappear. They can make live people disappear, too. And they've got too much behind them for Teddy's friends to want to take them on."

She looked doubtful. "Well . . . I still don't believe it. And I don't want you to go back home—not for a while. And when you do, I'll hire someone to go with you."

MacGonigal smiled. "Darlin', that's just what I want to talk to you about." And he proceeded to explain his plan to her and her role in it. She listened carefully, making him go over certain points again and again.

"I'll do it, Mac, but on two conditions."

"What's that?" he said, sliding a hand along the smooth length of her thigh.

"First of all, I go with you."

He stopped his stroking for a moment. "Hold on, darlin'—this isn't a vacation. You'll be getting into something that you didn't bargain for."

She sat up in the bed, the sheets falling away to her waist, revealing her small, alert breasts. To MacGonigal's eyes, she was achingly beautiful. "Now, look, Mac, it isn't as if I didn't know what it's all about. I'll help, but I go. That's final."

He tried to talk her out of it. "Sue, do you know how I'd feel if anything happened to you? I couldn't do my job if you were along."

She tugged his beard gently. "That's bullshit, Mac,

and you know it. You'll do things your way, and you won't let anything interfere with that."

"Sue, it isn't fair to ask you to take a risk like this—I can't do it."

She looked at him. "I have a right to get involved. When Nazario and his people came after me, you stepped in. And you helped me establish a new identity." She paused a moment. "You've taken all the risk—my risks—on yourself. For heaven's sake, Mac, they just tried to kill you again, and all because of me. And now you come here and . . . and now it's my turn to step in. And don't tell me that I can't —you know I can."

"It won't be like you think. It'll be hot and muggy —with lots of bugs and mud and boredom. It'll be miserable."

"Just like it was in Arkansas? There were some bad times there, too. And you never tried to back out on me. I'm going with you. That's that."

He propped himself up on his elbow and looked up at her. "You know something? I hoped you would."

She bent down and kissed his nose. "I know you did. I know you inside out, Mac. You're crazy —you're warped—but something about you attracts me."

"Good," he said, pulling her down, snuggling her head against his shoulder and cupping one breast in his hand. He gently brushed the nipple with one finger. It stood, and he spread his hand, covering both her breasts, gently arousing both nipples.

"What's your second condition, ma'am?"

She tilted her face toward him. "Kiss me, Mac."

He bent forward and kissed her, gently running his tongue along her lips, probing into her mouth. She pulled back a little, her face flushed, a little breathless. "Lower."

She guided his head down. He brushed his lips down her neck, kissing the hollow of her throat, exploring the cleft between her breasts, taking her nipples in his lips. "Lower," she said, guiding his shaggy head farther down.

He went farther, gliding down her body with his lips, murmuring gently.

Her breathing was uneven, ragged. She could hear his indistinct muttering. "What is it, Mac? What's wrong?"

He lifted his head slightly. "The things I do for my country," he said.

There was no answer to his first knock. Exasperated, MacGonigal pounded on the door with his fist, the sound booming through the corridor. Samuels opened the door, his eyes only half-open.

"Jesus, Mac, you don't have to wake everyone in the whole place."

MacGonigal pushed his way inside. "I wasn't tryin' to wake everyone, just you." He plopped himself down in a chair and reached for the phone.

"Think Wallace is awake at this hour?"

Samuels picked his watch up from the bedside

table and squinted at it. "Six o'clock. That makes it nine there. Yeah—he's been at work for a couple of hours."

MacGonigal lifted the phone and dialed, then listened as it rang the prescribed number of times. He recognized Miss Hogg's voice as she came on the line.

"Independent Insurance Adjusters. Can I help you?"

"Get me Ichabod Crane, sweetheart."

There was a shocked silence at the other end, and he could imagine her struggling to overcome her outrage. Then the line went silent as she put him on hold. He waited patiently until Wallace came on the line.

"This is Mr. Wallace. Can I help you?"

"Williams here," said MacGonigal. "I've got an estimate on the job for you."

There was a slight pause. "Is it within the limits of your policy?"

"Oh, yes. I'll have to hire some extra help, but we understood that all along."

There was another pause. "What's the hourly rate?"

"Well, you have to understand that this is California. Everything comes high here."

There was an edge to Wallace's voice now. "How much?"

"I think I can get the job done for a hundred and fifty."

The voice at the other end of the line was grim. "You're going too far."

MacGonigal's tone was smooth and bland. "You want a first-class job, don't you?"

"All right. I suppose you've already hired the other party?"

"Sure. No point in waiting around."

"Then I'll start the rest of the job. When will you be ready for the first delivery?"

MacGonigal thought a moment. "How about Tuesday morning?"

Wallace hesitated a moment. "I'll have to check the computer. Wait."

He put MacGonigal on hold for a minute, then came back on the line. "Tuesday morning at eight forty-seven. You'll meet the package?"

"I'll be there."

"Then there'll be no further need to contact this office until after delivery."

"Sure thing. Give Miss Hogg a kiss for me." He hung up.

Samuels was emerging from the bathroom, wrapped in a towel. His hair was wet, and he dripped water on the carpet. He rummaged through his bag, looking for clean underwear.

"What happened, your girlfriend throw you out?"

MacGonigal looked up and grinned. "Not even close, laddie. What do you think, I've been walking the streets all night?"

"With you, Mac, anything could happen. But did

she agree to help? Will she go along with it?"

"She's in. She wants to go along."

Samuels stopped short, one leg in his trousers, bracing himself against the bureau. "She can't do that! I hope you discouraged her."

"No, Charlie. I tried, believe me, but once Sue sets her mind on something, she's beyond stopping."

Samuels pulled his trousers on and stood upright, buckling his belt. "I can't believe that. Francis Xavier MacGonigal has finally met his match—and a girl, too!"

MacGonigal gave him a lopsided grin. "She's a lot of girl."

Samuels looked at him. "You're in love with her! I can't believe it!"

"Oh, you'll believe it when you meet her. There's nothing to compare with her."

Samuels collected his gun from under the pillow and slipped it into his waistband, then took his coat from the closet.

"Let's go get some breakfast, Mac, and then we can figure out what we're doing for the rest of the day."

"I've already had mine—I'll take a cup of coffee while you have yours." He paused a moment. "And I know what I'm doing for the rest of the day—you work out your own amusement."


At breakfast, MacGonigal outlined the main points of the agreement he had worked out with Susan.

"The money'll have to come through her laundry and dry-cleaning business. She'll set it up today, and you can start making payments in tomorrow. It'll all have to be cash, in small bills. And spread it out among the different outlets. She'll have a list of them for us this afternoon."

"A laundry? What's a laundry got to do with this?"

MacGonigal was patient. "It's the ideal setup. Laundries don't have to have an inventory, and there isn't a chain of waybills and all that paper. There's only the tickets themselves, and they're easy to make up. So nobody can ever prove that the money wasn't made legitimately."

Samuels was contrite. MacGonigal went on. "We'll set up a few more operations to provide cover and alternate sources, but we'll work that out later. The first thing is to get enough capital to work with. Now, both Sue and I are willing to kick in a little of our own—with the understanding that it'll be replaced later. That'll add to the believability of our cover story—that this is a private operation. We'll also set up someone to deal with weapons and other special gear. That'll be through a friend of mine just outside Atlanta. I'll need a guarantee of immunity for him first, though. And it'll have to be ironclad."

Samuels broke in. "I thought we'd agreed that all that was to be done out of country."

"Most of it will, but I want to do a run-through at my place, and we'll need a little equipment for that. We'll take it out with us, and ditch it at sea after we pick up our operational supplies."

"I'll have to clear that through Wallace."

"That's the reason you're here, Charlie. Now, one

more thing—we've got to be back in Arkansas by Monday night, when the first members of the group arrive. That means we have to wrap everything up between now and then. You'll have to handle the Florida end of the operation, as well as act as go-between with Wallace. Can do?"

"I can do it, all right, but I'm not sure that I know enough about what you want."

"Don't worry—just use the contacts I gave you, tell them what the specifications are, and be guided by them. Insist on a survey and tell them we'll want to take it out for a couple of days before we buy."

"How much do I pay? And where's the money coming from?"

MacGonigal leaned back. "You may have to go as high as a hundred and a half. Sue and I will set up an account for you to draw on—we'll put our money in it, say two hundred K, and you can keep track of it. That ought to make Wallace happy—his own man filing our expense account."

A waitress brought Samuels' breakfast, and MacGonigal suspended the conversation while he ate. He opened the morning paper, and the waitress came back and filled his coffee cup.

They met Sue for lunch at a place not far from her office. As they entered the place, she spotted them from a table at the back of the room and waved to them. As they approached the table, she stood, and MacGonigal felt a tiny thrill at the sight of her. Her dress was severely plain, as were her hairdo and makeup. It only served to accentuate the innate sensuality of her long, slim body.

He could tell that Samuels was as impressed as he was. He propelled him forward.

"Sue, this is Charlie Samuels. He's our contact with the Company, and he's the guy who will handle the financial end of the deal for us."

Susan held out a hand. "Hi, Charlie. Pleased to meet you. I'm Sue Bradley."

MacGonigal held Sue's chair for her as she re-seated herself, then took a chair of his own. He began to discuss the arrangements he and Samuels had made earlier in the day, but Sue spotted the waitress approaching and put a restraining hand on his arm.

"Let's order first, Mac, and we can talk business later."

MacGonigal sat silent until the waitress disappeared. "Okay, we've got to kick in a hundred thousand apiece. Charlie here needs it for up-front money. We've got to get that on track today.

"Wait a minute, Mac, we're doing the job, and *we* have to pay?"

He sighed. "I thought I explained that. We need proof that this is a *privately* sponsored operation. By bankrolling the start-up costs, we provide that proof. The Company will reimburse us later."

She was thoughtful. "Mac, you're a silver-tongued devil, but I'm not letting go of a hundred thousand until I know what it's going for."

The waitress was back with their orders, and he held his tongue while she served them.

"I want some gear to train with—a few AK-47s, some explosives, some vehicles. And don't forget about the boat—Charlie's going to pick that up for us while we're shaking down."

She reflected a moment. "Aren't AK-47s communist-made? How are you going to get them? Why do you want them, anyway?"

He was patient. "They *are* communist-made. They're also the best damn infantry weapons ever made. And that's why I want them. And I've got contacts who can get them for us. Charlie is going to handle that end of the business—aren't you, Charlie?"

Samuels nodded and MacGonigal continued. "We've got to leave tomorrow. Can you have everything set up by then?"

"You're a fine one, Mac," Sue said. "You come busting in here, demand a hundred thousand, and expect me to have everything wrapped up in two days."

"Can you do it?"

"Of course I can do it. I run a big business, and it has to be able to react fast. That's how I make my money. There's really only one thing left to do, after we set up a bank account for Charlie to draw on."

"What's that?"

"Go by your motel and pick up your things. I have plans for you."

MacGonigal grinned. "I checked out this morning, and my bag is in the car. I have plans of my own, darlin'."

"As long as *your* plans don't conflict with *mine*."

He grinned again. "The things I do for my country."

# VI.

"Mac, it's beautiful! You've made it even better!" She clasped her hands together, her face flushed, her eyes sparkling. She turned to face him.

"I love this place, Mac! I can't tell you how many times I've thought about being back here, but I was always afraid that it just wouldn't be the same."

She turned back toward the cabin, slipping an arm around him and leaning against his shoulder. "I can see why you weren't willing to leave this—I was a fool to ask you, no matter how many mobsters they send."

MacGonigal was hard-pressed to conceal his pride. He and Sue had just reached the top of the falls, catching a full view of the cabin and its outbuildings for the first time. They had flown from Los Angeles to Little Rock, rented a Jeep there, and driven up to MacGonigal's place. He had felt her anticipation build as they turned down the long dirt road that led to Bear Pen Falls, and had noticed her eagerness as they climbed up the trail from the foot of the falls. Now, as she took in the view of the place, he felt a warm glow. He remembered how it had looked the last time she saw it, the cabin a pile of smoking cinders, the twisted remains of his tractor lying where the front door had been.

"Yeah, I owe you my thanks. When you burned the place down, it gave me a chance to correct all the mistakes I made the first time I built it."

She pushed away from him. "You're not mad at me for that, are you?"

He pulled her back toward him. "Nope. You did what needed to be done—and you sure smoked Nazario and his rats out."

In his mind's eye, he could still see her, crouched over the wheel of the tractor, a five-gallon can filled with a mixture of gasoline and nitrogen fertilizer lashed to the front end. She had driven it straight up the steps, into the front door, right into the midst of Nazario and his mob. The resulting nitro-benzine explosion had demolished the cabin and ended, at least temporarily, their problems with the New York –based pornography, prostitution, and drug ring

"Come on inside—I want you to see how I've fixed it up."

She gave him a deprecating look. "I know how *you* fix things up, Mac. Your idea of interior decoration is to cover all exposed surfaces with books, guns and knives, and then scatter a little furniture around to fool people into thinking they're indoors."

Without answering, he swept her up in his arms and loped toward the house.

"Ooof! Slow down! G-g-goddammit, Mac, p-p-put m-m-me down!"

He gained the porch with a leap, almost jarring her stomach loose, and set her, flushed and disheveled, on her feet. She kicked him.

"You big, crazy, dumb Irishman. You damn near killed me!"

He swung open the door and ushered her in. She stood a moment on the threshold, looking around the big room.

"It's just like I expected—except there's no bear-skin rug."

He seemed slightly embarrassed. "Well . . . I haven't had a chance to get back to Alaska . . . I meant to go next fall . . . and I bought this rug from a friend of mine who raises buffalo in New Mexico."

She kissed him lightly. "I'm amazed at you . . . you think you have to apologize for not killing a bear hand-to-hand. This may surprise you, Mac, but it's perfectly all right to have a rug made out of *cloth*."

He returned her kiss, a trifle more passionately, and turned her around to face the room.

"Well, what do you think of it—really?"

She looked at him, her eyes half-closed. "I think it'll do." She paused a moment. "We've had a long ride. Maybe you could give me one of your famous massages?"

He put his arms around her, sliding his right arm under her thighs and lifting her. He started up the stairs to the loft. "No," she said, "not up there. Here. On the rug like last time."

He lowered her gently to the floor. She clung to him, pulling him down with her. He fumbled a moment, but managed to unfasten her jeans and work them down. She released him and allowed him to finish undressing her, then languidly rolled over and pillowed her head in her arms. He got to his feet and kicked off his boots, then stood above her, unbuttoning his shirt.

"Hurry up, Mac. You can do it faster than that."

He stood a moment, looking down at her. *My God, what a beautiful woman,* he thought. He lowered himself astride her, nestling his already erect manhood in the cleft between her gently swelling buttocks and ran his hands along the long length of her.

He began to lose himself in her, working the firm but relaxed muscles under the honey-colored skin, feeling the vibrant life glowing through her. She lay almost perfectly still as he worked his way from her shoulders down to her buttocks.

He began to massage her legs, working the muscles of her thighs, slipping his hands between them from time to time, feeling the expectant wetness of her.

At last he stretched himself full length atop her, probing for her with his aching manhood. She moved gently, subtly, to meet him, to help him, and he slowly and gently entered her.

She moved with him for a while, then brought her knees up under her, her breasts and upper body still cradled on the rug. He knelt behind her, pulling her hips against him, exalting in his strength. She rose up on her hands, so that she was on all fours before him. He reached up under her, supporting himself on one hand while he ran the other along her belly and breasts, feeling the pointed fullness of them as they hung down, filling his hand.

He could hear her, a throaty growl—almost a purr—as her nipples swelled in his fingers. He thrust himself deeper into her, clasping her to him, and they collapsed together on the rug, her body rigid and shaking, then passing into total relaxation.


She walked around the room examining the books, the huge pasteup of topographical maps, the gun racks, the simple, functional homemade furniture. She opened the pantry door and poked through the contents of the various cabinets.

"You don't seem to have any more modern conveniences than you had before."

He grinned. "Nope. I didn't need 'em. I did rearrange things a bit, made the cabin a little bigger, put in more shelves and drawers, did a few things like that." He paused for a moment. "I also made damn sure there's more than one way in and out.

She looked hard at him. "You don't seem sure that your friends have permanently cancelled the contracts on us . . . not as sure as you were in L.A."

He shook his head. "You can't be sure of anything —you ought to know that. And it doesn't cost much to provide for unwelcome company."

"You think they'll always be after us." It was a statement, not a question.

"I think that a lot of people—the wrong kind of people—know that you got a lot of money from the mob. That'll always stick in their craw. And even if the contracts are cancelled, there just may be a free-lance or two who'll try to take it away from you, no matter what deal the big boys have struck."

She looked at him glumly. "I was afraid you were going to put it that way."

He slapped her lightly on the hip. "Time enough to worry about that some other day. We've got work to do, woman. We're getting our first two team members in in the morning, and we've got to set up a place for them to stay—I plan to put them up in the stable."

They dragged out sleeping bags and bedding, and MacGonigal cleared the tack room, bundling saddles, blankets, bridles and other gear into the stalls. He took two-by-fours and knocked together some simple frame bunks. He made three sets, enough for six men, and fitted them with slats.

"I'll pick up some air mattresses tomorrow. That ought to keep the boys comfortable."

Sue swept out the room, raising a cloud of dust, then put a sleeping bag, a couple of blankets, and a pillow on each bunk. MacGonigal cleared off a workbench for a table, put a Coleman lantern on it, and dug out a few old chairs to put around it.

"There. That ought to make 'em comfortable," he said as he dumped a wooden box of firewood next to the little potbellied stove.

Sue looked around the unpainted, somewhat drafty room, with its crude furnishings. "Oh, yes. All the comforts of home."

MacGonigal was a little miffed. "Well, they won't be here long," he said defensively. "And most of the time they'll be outside." He took a last look around and shut the tack-room door. "We'd better get to bed. We've got to get up early to get to the airport on time."

She smiled and slipped her hand into his as they headed back to the cabin in the gathering dusk.

Something—an insect, an animal—was bothering her. She pushed it irritably away. MacGonigal persisted, tickling her with a lock of her hair.

"Come on, Sue. Time to get moving."

She pried her eyes open. That was no help—it was totally dark. MacGonigal disengaged her arms and heaved himself out of the bed.

"Wait a minute, sweetheart. I'll light a lamp."

She could hear him moving around in the darkness, groping for the light. In a moment, she heard the rhythmic strokes of the pump on the Coleman lantern, followed by the scratch of a match. The lantern flared into a yellow light, then settled into a piercing brightness that hurt her eyes. She shielded them with her hand. Through slitted eyelids, she could see MacGonigal standing nude next to the lamp, the harsh light bringing out in sharp contrast the black hair on white skin, so different from the leathery hide of his neck and face.

"Come on, lazybones, it's time to get up. I'll stoke up the fire and start breakfast while you get ready."

He gathered his clothes and went down the loft steps. She watched him disappear, then crawled out of bed. She pulled on a pair of jeans and a flannel shirt, then slipped her feet into a pair of boat moccasins. She could hear the hiss of another lantern downstairs and saw his shadow projected on the loft wall as he moved around.

"I hope you've got some hot water down there."

His answer floated up the steps. "Got a kettle about ready to boil. Come on down."

She came slowly down the steps, still partially asleep. He had a kettle boiling on the stove, just as he had promised. Beside it rested a frying pan, and he was cutting thick slices of bacon off a fletch. He laid them in the pan, and they began to sizzle, the aroma penetrating the cabin.

"That ought to wake you up, Sleeping Beauty."

She sniffed appreciatively. "It smells great, Mac. But what time is it?"

"About four-thirty," he said offhandedly.

"*Four-thirty!*" she yelped. "My God! No civilized person gets up at four-thirty."

He took a loaf of homemade bread and cut thick slices, which he laid on top of the stove to toast. "I'm not civilized," he reminded her, "and we've got a lot of work to do today."

She took the kettle from the stove and poured a little steaming water into a basin, then added water from the pitcher pump. While she went through her morning toilette, he cracked eggs into the skillet and poured the rest of the hot water through the strainer of the enameled coffeepot. She washed her face and hands, brushed her teeth and turned back to find him laying plates and cutlery on the table. He refilled the kettle and put it on the stove to heat water for dishwashing.

"Let's have breakfast and get on the road."

"What's on the agenda for today?"

He took a forkful of egg before replying. "We've got to pick up Cal Lawrence around eight o'clock and Charlie Samuels right after that. It's a good two-hour drive to the airport, so we'd better be on our way before six. And there's supposed to be a package waiting for us at air freight."

"What's in the package?"

"Odds and ends. A few AK-47s, some 7.62 ammo, some other things we'll need to train with before we're ready for the next phase. I had Charlie contact a fellow I know who lives near Atlanta and specializes in things like that."

"Sounds like a pretty big package."

"Ought to be just short of half a ton, by my calculations. We'll need the truck. I'll drive and you follow me with the Jeep."

He got up from the table, taking his plate and cutlery with him. She gathered up her things and elbowed him away from the sink. "You cooked. I'll wash up."

"I can't argue with that logic. I'll turn out the light in the loft and be ready to go when you are."

Calvin Lawrence was a big man, almost as big as MacGonigal himself. Fair-haired and florid, he was dressed casually but expensively in a sport coat and slacks that were obviously hand-tailored, with expensive-looking moccasins on his feet. MacGonigal and Sue met him at the gate.

"How was the trip, Cal?"

Lawrence stopped and looked closely at MacGonigal. "Francis MacGonigal, as I live and breathe! I almost didn't recognize you behind all that foliage." He thrust out a huge, scarred hand to MacGonigal. "Who's the lady, Mac? Not married, are you?"

MacGonigal took the offered hand. "Not yet, not yet, and not likely to be. This is Sue Bradley. She'll be working with us on this operation."

Lawrence looked her up and down coolly, then turned his attention to MacGonigal. "What's the deal? All I've heard is that you need me for a job somewhere—and that you're willing to pay for talent."

MacGonigal took him by the arm, steering him away from the gate, toward the baggage claim area. "We'll fill you in later. Right now, let's collect your bags and get on the road."

Once Lawrence's expensive leather suitcases were safely in the rented Jeep, MacGonigal headed away from the airport, stopping to pick up some coffee and sandwiches at a 7-Eleven. He drove to MacArthur Park and got out, the others following him, and found a fairly private area where they could talk. He passed around the coffee.

"We've got an hour to kill before the next arrival, so I might as well start filling you in. How much did they tell you about the job?"

"All I know is that it's a private deal—a rescue mission south of the border."

"Close enough. Did you know Steve Nichols?"

Lawrence thought a moment. "It doesn't ring a bell. Should I know him?"

"He and I were together in Nam for a couple of years, off and on. He disappeared on a little mission along the Cambodian border—and showed up a little later. He's been working down south, and he's in the jug. We're going to pull him out."

Lawrence sat silent a minute, digesting this information. "So who's paying the bill?"

MacGonigal waved a hand at Sue. "Sue here is his sister. She wants him out, and she's bankrolling the operation."

This was the story they had arranged between them, and Sue nodded in confirmation.

"Who else is in with us?"

"Fellow by the name of Charlie Samuels—he's our cut-out man, and he's handling most of the support chores. Willie Faith will handle commo for us—you know Willie?"

Lawrence nodded pensively. "Yeah, I've worked with Willie. I thought he was still in the Army."

"I don't know about that—Samuels ran him down for us, and he signed on. Anyhow, Tomás Maldonado will be on the team, too, and D.W. Collins. That's it."

Lawrence whistled. "That's a small team for a mighty big job. I'm not sure I like this setup."

"It'll get bigger," MacGonigal assured him. "We'll recruit some muscle in the target area."

"In the target area?" Lawrence was dubious. "That's risky. It could be suicidal." He paused a moment, as if to think out his next words, and then said slowly, "Mac, you've been out of touch for a while. Are you sure you're up to this job?"

"I'm up to it, laddie buck. Don't worry about that—and don't get antsy until you've seen how it's put together."

Lawrence grunted noncommittally. Sue flared up, "If you don't think Mac can handle the job, why don't you get back on the plane? We'll find somebody else to handle your part."

"Easy, darlin'. Cal didn't mean anything personal. It's his ass that's being risked, and he's entitled to ask all the questions he wants. And I'll answer 'em—at the proper time."

Lawrence looked steadily at MacGonigal. "And anytime I don't like the answers, Mac, I'm pulling out. That understood?"

MacGonigal returned his flat stare. "Up to a point. *That* understood?"

Lawrence nodded. "Yeah. I understand. If I go, I go all the way, and I won't do anything to jeopardize the operation—*if* I go."

MacGonigal, satisfied, said, "Eat up, and we'll go pick up Samuels and his package."

They returned to the Jeep and MacGonigal wheeled it up to the short-term parking lot and got out, leaving the engine running. Sue slid into the driver's seat while he crossed the lot and climbed into his old pickup. She waited for him at the exit to the lot, and he led her toward the air-freight office, where he parked and went inside.

Samuels was waiting for him, rather nervously it seemed to MacGonigal. As Lawrence and Sue came in, he made introductions. Samuels barely acknowledged Lawrence. He tugged at MacGonigal's sleeve. "I've got to talk to you."

MacGonigal looked at him. "We'll talk on the way home—you can ride with me," he said. "Now, have you got the stuff ready?"

"That's what I want to talk about."

"You mean you didn't get what we need?"

"I got it . . ." Samuels' voice trailed off. ". . . but we've got to talk about it."

MacGonigal sighed and led him outside. "Okay. What's all this about?"

"Jesus, Mac. That stuff is *hot*! I didn't know what all you ordered until I got there. Do you know what could happen if anybody found out about this? We could all get sent to prison! You can't *put* that kind of stuff on an airplane!"

MacGonigal shrugged. "You can't—but we did. So let's get it loaded and get the hell out of here."

"All right. Pull your truck around to the loading dock. I'll meet you there."

MacGonigal complied, and both Samuels and Lawrence were waiting for him, the latter with a heavily loaded lift cart.

"What's in here, Mac? It must weigh a ton."

Samuels shot him a warning look, but MacGonigal merely grinned. "Guns and ammunition, laddie-o. A little somethin' for the boyos back home."

"Well, it sure feels like it. What's in this one, a cannon?"

Samuels glared at Lawrence, and then at MacGonigal, who ignored him. They slid the first long box into the pickup bed and went back for the second one. In a few moments, all five boxes were loaded, and the pickup was showing the effects.

"You need new shocks on that thing, Mac."

"Yep. Need a few other things, too, but just can't seem to find the time and money to do it." He jumped off the dock and opened the door on the driver's side.

"Are you coming or not?"

Samuels jumped down, then stopped short. He opened the door and whispered frantically at MacGonigal. "My God! Your rear tires are almost *bald*! What if we have a wreck? What if the police stop us?"

MacGonigal started the engine, forced the transmission into gear, and released the brake. The old pickup lurched forward. Samuels was beside himself.

"Mac! Do you realize what we've got back there? *Eight* illegal weapons, grenades, and close to five-hundred pounds of contraband explosives. Plus sensitive documents. If they catch us, they'll put us away for twenty years!"

MacGonigal was elaborately ignoring him, concentrating on his driving. In the rearview mirror, he could see the Jeep, with Sue at the wheel and Lawrence beside her.

"Look, Mac, I know *you* thrive on this sort of thing, but it gives *me* the shits. If we have an accident or get stopped for those bald tires of yours, we're in the shit for life! If they find the papers I have in *here*"—he thumped his locked attaché case—"there'll be hell to pay."

"Relax," said MacGonigal, "this is Arkansas. There are half-a-million overage pickups with bald tires on the road. If they ticketed them all, the state's economy would collapse."

"You can relax now. We're home."

MacGonigal had turned off the pavement onto a gravel road, leaving a rooster tail of dust behind him. Samuels, however, seemed as tense as ever.

"Take it easy! That stuff is dangerous."

"Hell, Charlie, that stuff is as stable as cow shit."

MacGonigal twisted the wheel, veering around a pothole. The heavy boxes in the back of the pickup thumped and slid. The road made four hairpin turns, switching back on itself, and it was not well-maintained. In places, the fall rains had washed out parts of the road, so that there was barely room for a single vehicle to negotiate it. There were places where disaster would have been certain if they had met another truck. MacGonigal drove without concern, however, and finally they reached the valley floor. MacGonigal pulled off the road a little ways and waited for Sue with the Jeep.

When it came into view, MacGonigal pulled out onto the road in front of them. In a few-hundred yards, he turned off the county's road onto his own road and piloted the old truck down the rocky, rutted, two-track lane. The steep walls of Bear Pen Hollow began to close in on them, and he slowed to enjoy his homecoming. Samuels relaxed slightly.

At last they came to the turnaround at the end of the road. MacGonigal stopped in front of the shed and motioned to Samuels to dismount.

"Open the door for me, and we'll put her away."

Samuels looked around. "Is this where you live?"

"It's my property. But we have to walk to get to the house. Let's get the truck unloaded and I'll show you."

He killed the engine, and together they handed down the collection of boxes from the bed of the pickup. As he was backing the truck into the shed, the Jeep came into view. MacGonigal closed the shed door and waited for Sue to come up.

Lawrence got out and looked around. "So this is

your place. Sue told me all about it on the drive down. How come you decided to build your cabin at the *top* of the falls?"

"Makes it easier for me to get my exercise," said MacGonigal as he heaved one of the boxes onto his shoulder and started up the trail.

"Why don't you go on ahead of us, Sue? It'll take us a while to pack this stuff up the bluff, and we'll need some coffee—or maybe something a little stronger —when we're done."

Behind him, Lawrence shouldered another of the heavy wooden crates. Samuels watched them go, then seized a third box. It was astonishingly heavy, and it took him two tries to get it up to his shoulder. The others had disappeared by the time he got it up and balanced, and he staggered in the general direction they had gone, the box almost toppling him at every step.

The boxes varied in weight from 150 to 180 pounds, too heavy for a man to carry up such a steep trail without prior conditioning—which neither Samuels nor Lawrence had. MacGonigal himself, long used to carrying supplies up the trail from the roadhead, found it tough going, and dropped his burden at the top of the trail. He stood a moment, panting, and waited. Below him he could hear the others thrashing around, and then the sound of frightened cursing. There was a sudden crash, as if someone had fallen or dropped his load. With a sardonic smile, he started down.

Lawrence had made it halfway up the trail and

found a convenient boulder that allowed him to rest his burden without lowering it all the way to the ground. He looked beat but game. "How's it going, Cal?"

He gave MacGonigal a grimly good-humored look. "Fuck you, you crazy Irishman—if you can do it, I can do it. Just let me catch my breath."

MacGonigal slapped him on the shoulder and went on down. Samuels had somehow caught his burden in the branches of a small bush, and it had pulled him off-balance. Spinning halfway around, he had lost control of the box, just barely managing to get out from under it as it fell. He was trying to get it back on his shoulder again when MacGonigal came up.

"Need some help, Charlie?"

"Jesus, Mac, we'll never get all this shit up to the top. How far is it, anyway?"

"You've got about another three-hundred feet to go."

It didn't register. Like most city-bred men, Samuels had no idea of what three-hundred feet of climbing meant. Given his obvious exhaustion from only one-hundred feet, he wasn't likely to make it. MacGonigal squatted and heaved the box on end, leaning it back over his shoulder, then rose, using the power of his legs to bring him erect.

"I'll take it. I can carry it."

"Never said you couldn't, Charlie, but this sort of thing takes practice. I'll take this one up, and we'll team up on the last two."

When they reached the top, they found Lawrence

waiting. He looked all in. *He looks like I feel*, thought MacGonigal.

"Mac, this isn't going to cut it. There's no way I'm going to be able to pack up another one of those boxes—not today."

MacGonigal put his box down and stood a moment bent over, hands resting on his knees.

"Much as I hate to admit it, Cal, you're probably right. Let me rest a minute, and I'll rig up something to help us."

He went over to his workshop and scrounged around for a few moments. He came back with a two-by-six about twelve feet long, a length of rope and a bundle of sacking.

"This ought to do it, boys. Come on."

Reluctantly the other two followed him down the trail. He passed the rope around one of the two remaining boxes, making a huge timber hitch near one end of the box, then repeated the procedure near the other. Lashing the leftover ends of the rope around the two-by-six, he fashioned a pad of sacking and put it on his shoulder, then heaved up one end of the two-by-six.

"You want to take the other end, Cal?"

Lawrence looked at it a moment. "No, I don't *want* to, but I guess I have to."

He struggled under his end of the beam, and between them, they swayed the heavy box off the ground. Lawrence was in the lead, and he moved out at a slow, shuffling step.

"Get in front of us, Charlie. That way, if one of us

falls, we won't take you down with us. And try to keep the brush out of our way."

It took a long time to make the climb. They were nearly exhausted by now, and the steep bluff trail was taking a steady toll on them. Samuels scampered up and down the trail, holding back branches for first Lawrence, then MacGonigal, then moving past them to the next leafy obstruction. By the time they made it to the top, Susan was waiting for them. They lowered the box to the ground and collapsed on top of it.

"You boys look like you could use a cold beer."

MacGonigal looked up at her, his beard streaked with sweat. "Darlin', I do believe you've saved our lives."

He heaved himself painfully to his feet and stretched, his hands against the small of his back. The others rose with equal lack of enthusiasm and made their way to the cabin, walking like old men.

After they finally manhandled the last of the heavy boxes to the top of the bluff, MacGonigal made off in the direction of the tractor shed. He returned a few minutes later with the tractor and trailer, and pulled up beside the stack of boxes.

They loaded the trailer and towed it to the tack room, where they unloaded and stacked the boxes against one wall. MacGonigal took a small crowbar and pried one of the boxes open. With his knife he slit the brown, greasy paper and reached in, drawing out a short, ugly weapon. He passed it to Lawrence.

"An AK-47!" he murmured. "Beautiful! It's been awhile, Mac."

MacGonigal took out another of the chunky little assault rifles and passed it to Samuels. Sue stepped forward and took the next one.

"It's greasy," she said.

"Yep," said MacGonigal. "Still in the original preservative grease. We'll have to wash them down with gasoline." He racked back the bolt of the weapon and let it go forward. It moved sluggishly, retarded by the heavy grease. He laid the weapon down and set out cleaning materials on the makeshift bench while Lawrence began stripping the weapons, removing the receiver covers and pulling out the bolt assemblies. Sue watched with fascination.

"They're really simple, aren't they?"

"About as simple as you can get," Lawrence said, "for a modern assault rifle."

MacGonigal was cleaning them with gasoline and laying them out on a sheet of paper to allow the gasoline to evaporate before the next step in the cleaning process.

"What's so great about these guns, Mac?" Sue asked. "You seem in love with them."

"Well, like Cal said, they're about as simple as you can get, and that's a big plus for any piece of machinery. And they're rugged as hell. Seems like you can abuse them any way you want, and they'll still shoot."

"Are they better than American weapons?"

"Well," he temporized, "they're different. They're a lot more reliable than the first models of the M16—a hell of a lot more reliable." He handed her one of the little assault rifles. "The AK series is basically a sound design. This is the old version. They followed this with the AKM, which is a simpler, easier-to-manufacture version. The current Soviet weapon is the AK-74, which is chambered for a high-velocity 5.45mm cartridge—about .20-caliber."

He paused, shaking his head. "They'll probably be sorry for that—the M16 uses a .22-caliber round, and it isn't worth a damn. But the old AK-47 has a good cartridge, the 7.62X39. It's about the same as the old .30-30 deer cartridge, and that's a fine cartridge—don't let anybody tell you different. The Soviet 7.62 M43 cartridge only develops about 2,300 feet per second at the muzzle, and the bullet is fairly light, but it's well-shaped, and retains its velocity fairly well."

He put down the first weapon and picked up a second, pausing to put a new patch on the cleaning rod. "Of course, the AK's not perfect, not by a long shot."

"What's wrong with it, then?"

"Well, first of all, it has about the clumsiest safety that anyone's ever invented." He pointed to the big lever in the right side of the weapon. "I like a safety that you can operate with your hand on the grip and your finger in the trigger guard. This thing is awkward and hard to use—and it's noisy, too." He clacked the safety up and down. "It's also backward

—the first stop is full automatic, so if you're not careful to push it all the way down, you'll put the thing on rock and roll."

"Isn't that what you want?"

He was affronted. "Hell, no! If we get into a fracas on this operation, and I catch you firing automatic, I'll kick that cute little ass of yours right up between your shoulder blades."

Lawrence squatted down beside him and picked up another of the little rifles. "He means it, too. Old Mac used to be a terror among the newbies—he had a standard rate for automatic fire. What was it, Mac, fifty dollars?"

"You better believe it—any man in my outfit who fired full automatic had to pay for it."

He held up the AK-47 again, pointing to the gas vents on top of the barrel. "These things light up like a Christmas tree whenever you fire in the dark, and that can mess up your night vision—and you can see it doesn't have a flash hider. Those are real shortcomings."

"I never liked that short stock, either," said Lawrence. "Did you get any with the folding stock? They're a little longer, and they fit me better?"

"Sorry. I got what they had. But the short stock works pretty well for me." He brought the weapon smoothly up to his shoulder. "I hate to say it, but this little honey flows up to your shoulder like a Parker shotgun."

They finished cleaning the AKs, and MacGonigal punched a pair of holes in a can of 40-weight oil, poured some in a cloth, and began to lubricate each weapon as he reassembled it.

"Can you use that stuff on guns?" Samuels asked. "I thought you had to have a special gun oil."

"That's another reason why we're not using M16s. They're real touchy about what you lubricate them with. But these babies will work on just about any kind of oil."

"They're illegal as hell, too," said Lawrence. "If push comes to shove, gun oil on your hands *could* be incriminating under certain circumstances. But not motor oil. They can give you all the tests in the world and can't prove anything except that you change your oil regularly."

"My sentiments exactly," said MacGonigal as he opened another box. This one contained an RPD machine gun and a Dragunov sniper rifle, along with a miscellany of other gear. MacGonigal lifted the weapons out one after the other.

Lawrence looked at the RPD with distaste. "What's that for?"

"Well, it's not a bad base-of-fire weapon, and it uses the M43 cartridge, so I figured we might find it useful."

Lawrence laid the RPD aside and picked up the Dragunov. In appearance, it was a longer, heavier version of the AK-47. It had a skeletonized wooden stock, and a large telescopic sight with a rubber eye protector. He looked in the box again and took out one of the magazines for the weapon, examining the floor plate and side rail arrangement used to keep the big 7.62X54 rimmed cartridges from jamming. "Interesting—I've never used one of these before. How good are they?"

"Dunno," said MacGonigal, "but D.W. Collins will want a sniper rifle, and I had Charlie get this for us to keep him happy. We'll know how good it is when he gets here and tries it out."

He looked at the long, ungainly weapon. "It's supposed to have a maximum effective range of eight-hundred meters, same as the U.S. M21 sniper rifle. Sure doesn't look like it, though. I doubt if it's much good over six-hundred meters."

He stripped the protective cover off the scope and held the weapon to his shoulder. "Not a bad scope. As a matter of fact, it's probably pretty good for quick shooting at moderate ranges and poor light."

He took out the battery and lamp and fitted them to the rifle. "Not bad at all. Wouldn't mind keeping this."

"Wait a minute, Mac," said Samuels, "we've got a deal, remember? All this stuff goes over the side, once you're outside the twelve-mile limit."

"What's the harm in keeping the Dragunov?"

"It has an AK-type receiver, that's what. And that makes it technically a machine gun, even if it won't fire full automatic. And that makes the boys at Alcohol, Tobacco and Firearms very uptight."

"Okay," said MacGonigal reasonably, "suppose I just keep the scope?"

Samuels looked at him, a look of complete despair.

"For once, Mac, just for once, don't jack me around. Ditch the whole thing, scope and all. Just this once, do it by the book."

MacGonigal laughed. "Okay, Charlie, no more screwing around. I'll ditch it along with the rest of this shit."

The last item out of the box was a long gray-green tube, with two pistol grips near one end and a flared breech. Along with it came a metal case containing a sight. MacGonigal fitted the sight to the weapon and shouldered it, the breech projecting back over his shoulder, his cheek against the wood-encased midsection. He lowered it to the floor, leaning it against the wall.

"That's a fine weapon, Cal."

"It sure as hell is," said Lawrence. "That son of a bitch is a real pisser. I had one shoot through an APC I was riding in—it hit the front trim vane and came out the rear ramp."

Sue looked at the ugly weapon. "What is it?"

"An RPG-7. God's gift to infantrymen. It's the best damn antitank weapon in the world—in the hand-held class, that is."

"What's so great about it?"

"Well, just like the AK-47, it's reliable. It's heavy, and it's real sensitive to wind drift, but it's accurate and powerful. It has an 85mm warhead—the U.S. M72 LAW only has a 66mm warhead—and it has a range of about five-hundred meters, compared to less than three-hundred for the LAW. So all in all, it's a pretty effective piece of ordnance."

He took up the crowbar and went to work on the third box. Once he had the cover off, he reached in and pulled out a short, thick tube, capped at one end. Lawrence drew in his breath, then reached for the tube.

"A 60mm mortar! You really *are* serious about this, aren't you, Mac?"

He put the mortar down reverently and searched in the box, pulling out a gray-green metal case. He flipped its catches open and took out the little sight, examining it carefully.

"Shit!"

"What's wrong, Cal?"

Lawrence held out the sight to MacGonigal. "Chinese—six-thousand mils. Shit!"

MacGonigal chuckled again. "You'll get used to it, Cal. It doesn't take a Ph.D. in mathematics to figure it out. For chrissakes, a Chinese *rice farmer* can learn to use the thing."

MacGonigal pulled the baseplate and bipod out of the box, passing it to Lawrence, who set the mortar up in the middle of the floor. They wiped it down and ran a wad of oily rags down its bore.

Lawrence went back to the crate and took out the rest of the accoutrements, a green canvas case containing the aiming stakes, a plotting board in a similar case, and a Chinese compass in a leather case.

He took out the compass and examined it. It had a

little metal wheel on it for measuring map distances. "Cute. But what good is it?"

"Take a look at the face of it."

He looked at the instrument. "Oh. Six-thousand mils."

"You got it." MacGonigal grinned. "Just didn't want you to repeat your old mistakes."

He laid out the equipment next to the little mortar and shook it on its mount.

"It seems pretty tight, Mac."

MacGonigal wiggled the barrel on its mount. "Not bad." He looked up at Samuels. "A lot of these little mortars are so loose that they scatter rounds all over the place. This one is almost new."

"You're not going to shoot that thing here, are you?" said Samuels.

MacGonigal looked at him as one might look at a retarded child. "Of course we are, Charlie. Why do you think I had you get me fifty rounds of ammo for it?"

Samuels shook his head. "That thing will bring police down on us. You just can't fire a thing like that and escape notice."

"Charlie," said MacGonigal kindly, "have you noticed how far back in the hills we are? Nobody is going to hear anything. And folks here mind their own business—if I blast a stump or two on my property, nobody will think anything of it." He paused, and went on more reasonably. "We have to cross-train everyone on the team on all the weapons we'll be using—with a small team, everybody has to know everyone else's duties. And this is the only training base we've got." He slapped Samuels on the shoulder. "Don't worry—everything's going to be all right." He thought a minute. "As long as we're in this country, anyway."

# VII.

ON THE AUXILIARY SAILING YACHT *TIR GRAD*
OFF THE CARIBBEAN COAST OF COSTA RICA

MacGonigal put one hand over his mask, the other over the buckle of his weight belt, and took a giant step through the lifelines. He splashed into the water, driving down into the clear gulf lining the Central American coast, then exchanged his regulator for his snorkel on the way back to the surface. He came up a few feet from the side of the boat, blew water out of the snorkel tube, and leaned back in his buoyancy jacket. He lay on his back and moved away from the side of the boat with a few powerful kicks of his flippers.

"Come on in, beautiful. The water's fine and we have some equipment to recover."

Above him, Susan approached the gap in the lifelines. Willie Faith hovered nervously at her elbow, supporting her with one hand on her arm, anxious that she would trip over her fins. Looking at him, MacGonigal thought that he had changed little since he had last seen him. Willie was small, about five-six, less than 130 pounds. In swimming trunks, his bandy legs and thin chest, with his prominent ribs, made him deceptively weak-looking. MacGonigal knew how deceptive that was. He had seen Faith in action before. He was tough, wiry, agile and able to carry his end under any circumstances.

On the fo'c'sle Daniel Webster Collins was checking the anchor and rigging the portable compressor. D.W. was a solid block of muscle, now sporting a distinct spare tire around his middle, and his fair hair was thinning a little on top. About five-ten, he weighed 200 pounds. Behind the butt of a rifle or light machine gun, he was almost immovable, a solid shooting platform. He had finished lashing down the navy-surplus air compressor, and he tugged on the starter cord, muscling the 7-horsepower engine into life.

Sue looked around at the noise, almost falling against Faith. He steadied her, and she protected her mask and weight belt as MacGonigal had, then stepped over the side. When she came to the surface, he grinned at her, then made a big okay sign to Faith, who was hovering nervously near the gap in the lifelines.

"Ready, beautiful?"

She nodded, and he led the way forward, along the

bulge of the hull, to the anchor line. Once there, he checked with her again, then switched his snorkel for his regulator. Giving the traditional thumbs-down signal, he vented air from his buoyancy jacket and slowly sank in the water. He was about eye-level when he grabbed the anchor line and pulled himself slowly downward, descending foot by foot. As he went lower, the pressure of the water worked to decrease his marginal buoyancy, and he found it easier to descend. He released the anchor line and simply drifted downward, propelling himself with his hands, and using one hand on the buoyancy control to put an occasional shot of compensating air into his jacket.

At twenty feet, he halted and waited. Sue was still above him, descending slowly, clearing her ears every foot or two. He watched her come down, then signaled to her, thumb and forefinger forming an O. She repeated the signal back to him. He checked his instrument console, noting that his timer was running, and that both pressure and depth gauges seemed to be functional. With a flick of his hand, he started himself downward again, sinking a little faster now. He thumbed the inflator button, putting a few cubic inches more air into the jacket, and continued the descent.

The water was clear—almost fifty feet of visibility—and he could see off into the distance. The bottom below him was indistinct, but as he made his way down the anchor line, it became clearer. He could see the dark shape of the wreck below, an ancient freighter that had gone down in a hurricane almost thirty years before. The anchor line led directly to its bridge deck, and he followed it all the way.

The line terminated not in the *Tir Grad*'s plow-type anchor, or in the Danforth backup, but in a grappling hook. They had located the wreck with loran, chasing the numbers on the display until they had been over the reported location, then turned on the depth finder. In a minute or so, they had seen the characteristic spike of a wreck. D.W. had been on the wheel, with MacGonigal conning from the navigator's station. Faith had dropped a buoy—just a bleach bottle with a couple of hundred feet of line wrapped around it and a lead weight.

It had taken them two more passes to hook the wreck with the grappling hook, which dragged through the sand easily. The regular anchors would have dug in immediately and stopped them short. Once hooked on, they had rigged for the dive and gone down—to all intents and purposes, just another bunch of rich Americans out for a cruise in an expensive sailboat.

The *Gulf Streamer* had broken her back, and he had a diagram of her sealed in plastic. As Sue descended beside him, he tried to get his bearings. They were on the port side, the deck sloping down and forward. He hooked a light line to the grappling hook, checked his diagram again, and motioned to Sue. She acknowledged, and he led the way across the deck and down the side of the ship, making the last thirty feet to the sandy bottom. Once there, they swam along the side of the ship, heading for the stern, the buckled side of the ship looming above them like a cliff.

The crack in the hull was just as advertised. He tied off his line and took a large underwater lantern with another reel attached to it from the bag at his waist. Motioning Sue to tend the line, he took the light in one hand and made his way around and through the tangled mess of razor-sharp steel shards that guarded the gash in the ship's side.

Once inside, he checked his instrument console. He was doing fine on air, and showing seven minutes of bottom time. The depth was just short of ninety feet, and he had planned to spend no more than twenty minutes down on this first dive. He had plenty of time. He flashed his light around the dark cavern of the ship's interior. It was crusted with marine growth, barnacles, streamers, fronds everywhere. Small fish darted away from him as he approached. He touched the surface of one bulkhead, and a cloud of dark sediment and junk filled the water. Every move seemed to stir up more, and visibility inside the ship rapidly deteriorated. Even the powerful lantern couldn't penetrate more than a few feet.

He finned his way gently down a sloping passage, reeling out the line behind him. At an intersection, he consulted his diagram again. Left. He paused a moment, turning slowly round, shining his light in all directions, looking for obstruction—"diver traps" —in the twisted piping and buckled plates.

In a few more feet, the passageway gave out, its deck plates ruptured. He shone his light out into a gaping hole. Below him he could see an orderly pile of painted olive-green steel cases, their lids fastened down with a T-handle sunk in the upper surface, under a steel carrying handle. He launched himself from the jagged steel platform where he stood and ghosted down to them. *Christ, they weren't looking to make it easy, were they?*

He counted the boxes. There were twenty of them, each about the size of those he had bought from the man outside Atlanta. They seemed intact, with no sign of leakage. He checked his instruments one more time. He had plenty of air, and had been down only thirteen minutes. For a moment he was tempted to try to wrestle one of the boxes out with him, but he resisted. He tied off the line and started back, following the slim cord with one hand circling it as he moved.

In a moment or two he emerged through the jagged gash in the ship's side. Sue was waiting where he had left her. He gave her the okay sign and she passed him the mesh bag she was carrying. He took an inflatable buoy from the bag, tied its line to a pipe jutting from the opening, and popped its $CO_2$ cartridge. The little rubber buoy barely quivered at that depth. He took it in his hand and swam upward with it until it began to tug against him, then released it. It shot upward, gathering speed as the lessening pressure allowed its gas to expand.

He turned back and joined Sue, motioning her to lead the way back to the anchor line. Together they slowly ascended. He noted the time of the start of the ascent—sixteen minutes. Not bad, still well within no-decompression limits. Still, he halted her at the ten-foot level and spent a minute there, hanging on the anchor line, a "safety stop." Then they went on upward, watching the growing patch of silvery light above them as they approached the surface.

They broke the surface, inflating their buoyancy jackets and switching from regulator to snorkle. MacGonigal could see Faith watching them anxiously from the deck. He put both hands above his head, forming a big O, one that couldn't be missed. Faith seemed relieved. MacGonigal rolled over on his back and swam lazily down the length of the hull.

At the stern, Faith and Collins had inflated the Zodiac and lashed it firmly in place by the boarding ladder. He unlatched his weight belt and lifted it into the inflatable, then rolled out of his buoyancy jacket. Sue was clinging to the lifeline that ran around the outer air chambers of the Zodiac. He dived down and took her weight belt, putting it into the Zodiac, then helped her out of the rest of her gear.

A single powerful kick brought him out of the water and almost straight into the Zodiac. He rolled over and pulled off his fins. As he did so, someone —Faith, he thought—reached down from the stern of *Tir Grad* and took them. Susan came shooting out of the water next to him. They handed up their heavy tanks and weight belts to Collins and Faith, then climbed aboard.

"Did you find it?"

MacGonigal shook water out of his ears. "Yeah. But those bastards really had fun hiding it. We'll be lucky to get out more than one or two boxes each dive. They're way back inside the wreck.''

"Did you mark them?"

"The buoy is tied off at the entrance to the wreck. There's a line from there to the boxes. All you've got to do is go down the buoy line and follow your nose."

Collins got to his feet. "Okay, Willie, let's get suited up."

"Take it easy, D.W.," said MacGonigal. "Sue and I have a four-hour surface interval before we can go down again. Let's have some coffee and talk it over before you two start down."

They went below and arranged themselves around the salon table. MacGonigal poured coffee from the pot simmering on the gimballed stove. He took the plastic-encased diagram of the *Gulf Streamer* and laid it on the table.

"The entry into the hull is here, just like it shows on the diagram. You go straight in, then turn left. A few more feet, and the whole passageway is collapsed. I think that puts us in number 3 hold —anyway, it's a big, gaping hole. Lots of twisted pipe and broken metal—plenty of stuff to snag yourself on.

"The cases are about seven feet below the passageway, and they're heavy. I could lift one, but damn sure couldn't get to the surface with it."

Faith looked over the diagram carefully. He pushed away from the table and went to the navigator's station and gathered up dividers, rulers, pencils, graph paper and calculator. He returned to the table and began to take measurements from the diagram, drawing profile sketches of various parts of the entry route into the *Gulf Streamer*.

"You're sure about the distance from the bottom of the passageway to the cases?"

"Yeah. I let everything out of my buoyancy jacket and nailed myself down so I could examine them. I could stand on the deck and reach up and easily touch the passageway deck. Can't be more than seven feet."

"How big an opening?"

MacGonigal thought a moment. "Maybe four or five feet across. Lots of tangled stuff on the overhead, though. That's what you have to watch out for, getting your tank and regulator hoses tangled in that stuff, where you can't see or reach it."

"But you could slide a box along the floor of the passageway?"

"Yeah, I guess you could. I didn't check it out that closely, but I swam along it, and I don't remember anything major in the form of an obstacle."

Faith checked his watch. "We should have a tank about full, D.W. Why don't you go and check the compressor, and Mac and I will get some equipment together."

MacGonigal drained the last of his coffee. "What have you got in mind, Willie?"

"I'm not really sure yet, Mac. But I need several snatch blocks—all you can get—and some three-quarter-inch line. A whole reel of it, if you don't mind."

"You're the man with the brains, Willie," said MacGonigal as he went forward to the bos'n's locker. He returned a few minutes later with a reel of line and a couple of dozen snatch blocks strung together. Faith had moved aside the settee and pulled up the cabin sole. He was pulling out a couple of collision boards, heavy pieces of plywood cut to clamp over *Tir Grad*'s ports in the event of a knockdown.

On deck, he began to measure out distances and lay out line, attaching snatch blocks at intervals and fastening them in position with light twine. Once done, he coiled and faked down the arrangement of lines, marking key parts of the tackle with a water-proof marking pen. He finally loaded the whole assembly into a large mesh collection bag, weighting it with extra lead weights.

Collins, who had switched the tanks on the compressor, came back and watched the whole operation, occasionally assisting as Faith directed him to bring an item or move a piece of gear. At last, Faith was satisfied. He stood up.

"The way I see it," he said, "the first problem is to get the cases up out of the hold they're lying in. Then we have to move them up the passageway to the intersection, and then around the bend to the outside of the ship. After that, it's a piece of cake to get them to the surface."

"Yeah," muttered Collins, "piece of cake."

"No, really," said Faith. "Once outside the ship, all we have to do is hook lift bags to them and hoist them aboard. The problem, as I said, is getting them out."

"Okay. So how do we do that, genius?"

"That's the idea behind this gear. We use the collision boards to make a ramp from the passageway to the hold, and align cases on the ramp. A tackle rigged from the other side of the intersection should allow us to pull the cases up to that point. I figure D.W. and I can get the whole thing rigged, and maybe move a case or two on our dive. When you and Sue go down again later, you can rig the next tackle to move the cases to the outside. Then, tomorrow, we can start moving the stuff outside. And once we get it all outside, we can start putting on the lift bags and hoisting it aboard."

Collins looked over the arrangement that Faith had sketched. "I dunno, Willie. That's a lot of work, and we can't make more than three dives a day for each team. It's gonna take a long time to get this stuff up."

"Bringing it up is later. Right now, we've got to get the gear down and rigged. Let's get suited up." He turned to MacGonigal. "Mac, I've been thinking it would be easier if we were anchored directly to the entry into the hull. If you'd break out the Danforth anchor and a cable, we'll take it down with us and make it fast."

MacGonigal thought a minute. "I'll have to lower it over the side to you, attached to a flotation bag. You can tow it over to the buoy line, vent air from the bag, and take it down that way."

Faith was already donning his gear, and just grunted. MacGonigal unscrewed the cap to the starboard chain pipe and shackled on the Danforth anchor. He attached a hundred-pound lift bag to it and laid the whole rig out on deck. As he did so, a splash from aft told him that Faith was already in the water. In a moment, he spotted him swimming along the turn of the bilge to hang on the anchor line.

"Pass it down to me. Once I get the bag filled, you can lower the anchor, then the rest of the gear. I'll take it all down at once."

MacGonigal complied, passing the lift bag through the lifelines. Faith took it and put a little air into the bag by purging his spare regulator inside it. MacGonigal slowly lowered the anchor, and Faith balanced the weight with air in the bag until the heavy yellow fabric bag floated with just its top awash. Meanwhile, Collins had made his entry and was bobbing in the water alongside Faith. MacGonigal first passed them the mesh bag of tackle, and then the collision boards. He held the anchor line in check while they lashed these items below and readjusted buoyancy, then passed them the bags with their personal gear.

The two slowly swam the ungainly mass toward the small, bobbing rubber buoy. While Collins stabilized the lift bag, Faith vented air from his vest and submerged. MacGonigal, watching from the bow of *Tir Grad*, saw the lift bag tilt, and a huge bubble broke the surface beside it. In a moment, it was completely awash. Collins vented air from his vest and disappeared.

They swam on either side of the lift bag, watching the ungainly mass of anchor, collision boards, and tackle swinging below. Using their own vests to make themselves negatively buoyant, they slowly dragged the heavy lift bag down, gingerly pulling themselves down the slim buoy line.

As they went deeper, their rate of descent increased. Additional air in their vests served to offset the squeeze of increasing pressure at first, but at twenty feet, Faith had to begin slowly releasing air from his spare regulator into the bag. At the bottom, Faith released the anchor from its lashing and firmly set it into a gash in the side of the ship. He jerked the anchor cable frantically, sending great tremors up its length, to notify MacGonigal to take up slack. He backed off and waited as the cable slowly grew taut and began to veer as *Tir Grad* came into the wind on her new anchor.

Inside the *Gulf Streamer*, the slit of MacGonigal's passage had long since dissipated, but the problems associated with maneuvering the cumbersome collision boards and bags stuffed with tackle soon turned the atmosphere impenetrable. Faith blindly followed the line MacGonigal had left, while Collins waited outside.

At the intersection of the passageways he placed a ringbolt, forcing it between two ruptured plates and holding it in place with a crosspiece. He hooked the standing part of one of the tackles to this, then groped his way down the passageway, dragging his burdens behind him. Once in the hold, he waited for the water to clear. When he could see dimly, he put the collision boards in place, lashing them with short pieces of line which he cut with his diving knife.

Satisfied at last that everything was ready, he maneuvered the first box into position, wrapping a length of line around it and hauling it up on the ramp. He got it to the top and it slid easily down the passageway under the steady pull of the tackle. He hooked up a second case, then checked his instruments. Nineteen minutes. He left the rigging in place and started up into the passage. He floated over the jagged edge and stopped. He reached up, feeling for the obstruction that held him.

Outside the *Gulf Streamer*, Collins checked his instruments. Their plan called for only twenty minutes of bottom time, and they were running close to that. No worry, though. This was their first dive of the day, and the tables gave them thirty minutes at this depth. They had plenty of time.

He was held firmly. Backing out seemed the only answer. He worked slowly back, and suddenly there was a sickening crunch. The hull seemed to reverbrate, and clouds of blackness billowed up all around him. Startled, he tried to turn around, and felt a stabbing pain in his neck. With a great effort of will, he forced himself to breathe slowly and deeply. He was sinking to the deck of the passageway, forced down by something that he couldn't see, but which pressed painfully and inexorably against his back.

"They're three minutes late!"
"Do you think they're in trouble?"

"There can't be any other reason," he said as he struggled into his gear. "I'll go down. You stay up here and be ready to call for help if we need it."

He put on the buoyancy jacket with its attached tanks, then began gathering up things he might need, a hacksaw and crowbar, a couple of wrenches, some half-inch line, a lantern. He dropped them into a mesh bag and secured them to his weight belt.

Susan began assembling her equipment. "I'm going with you." She said it determinedly, as if daring him to refuse her. He put a hand on her arm.

"No, Sue. We need someone up here to call for help if we need it. And we need your regulator —they'll have to decompress on the way up, and they haven't got enough air."

"What do you want me to do, then?" Her question was almost a defiant challenge.

"Put your regulator on a tank and lower it over the side on a line—rig it to hang just ten feet below the surface. And if I'm not back in fifteen minutes, call for help."

"Who should I call?"

"Anyone who'll answer," he said, "anyone who'll answer," and plunged into the water.

He hadn't even bothered to inflate his buoyancy jacket, and the weight of the tools he was carrying began to drag him down. He cleared his ears and swam forward, along the hull of *Tir Grad*, toward the anchor line. Once there, he started straight down it, moving so fast he had to ascend slightly a couple of times to clear his ears.

He could see the hull of the *Gulf Streamer* looming out of the dimness below him now, with the anchor line curving gracefully down to disappear into the side of the ship. As he drew closer, he looked for signs of the other two divers. There was nothing.

D.W. Collins had never been comfortable underwater. He could do what he had to, but he never submerged without a vague feeling of uneasiness. There was always a nagging doubt in the back of his mind, a doubt that he could react as he had been taught in a *real* underwater emergency. As he waited at the entrance to the wreck, he constantly checked his instruments, especially his pressure gauge and bottom timer. As the minutes passed, he became increasingly more apprehensive. So when he heard a low, rumbling sound from deep within the wreck, he was sure it portended disaster.

Collins was no coward. He knew at once that he had to go to the aid of his friend. He switched on his lantern and followed the guideline into the wreck. Once inside, the disturbed sediment drastically reduced visibility, and he felt closed in, near the edge of panic, but he continued on, following the line into the murky darkness.

At the passageway intersection, he encountered an almost active blackness. His lantern wouldn't penetrate the cloud of sediment more than an inch or so. He followed the line blindly, until he felt it suddenly terminate under a metal plate. He hesitated, unsure of what to do. As he did so, he felt a slight pulsation in the water. Feeling along the plate, he encountered an arm. Fingers gripped his forearm. He started backward, alarmed, then returned the grip.

He felt his way along the edge of the plate, feeling its extent. It appeared to be about ten feet wide, hanging from the upper part of the passageway and pinning Faith down underneath it. Collins edged his way over the plate, panic gnawing at the back of his mind with the realization that in this total blackness it would be easy to lose his orientation and simply wander helplessly inside the ship until his air ran out.

He kept contact with the plate, however, hoping to use it as a reference point. *As long as I don't lose the plate, I can always find the guideline.*

The plate was about eight feet long, with jagged edges. It seemed to be riveted to several large, heavy I-beams, apparently part of the ship's internal skeleton that had collapsed. He got his feet against the deck and heaved. It was impossibly heavy. He strained, trying with all his might to lift it enough to allow Faith to swim free. It was impossible.

MacGonigal hesitated only a minute outside the ship. He tucked up his gear bag, checked his light and air, and went into the dark interior. The pattern of swirling, drifting sediment confirmed his suspicion that someone had recently entered by the same route. He followed the guideline, feeling his way along, exploring the bulkheads of the passageway carefully, looking for breaks or new bulges that might presage a general collapse of the wreck. He found where Faith had anchored the tackle to pull out the cases, and paused a moment, feeling the arrangement, working it out in his head. He went on down the passageway until he encountered the huge metal plate. Unlike Collins, he had been inside the ship before, and knew at once that something had gone wrong. He was feeling his way along the edge of the obstacle when he suddenly collided with something soft. He gripped the object, realizing that it was another diver, and pulled him around into a face-to-face position.

So situated, with their masks just inches apart, MacGonigal's powerful lantern allowed him to recognize Collins. He brought up one hand, giving the okay signal. Collins violently shook his head, pulling him forward. In a moment, he detached MacGonigal's grip from his own arm and firmly put his hand on Faith's outstretched arm.

At first, MacGonigal's mind refused to accept what his senses told him. A trapped diver inside a wreck is a nightmare—with limited air, and with the likelihood of bends increasing every minute, a rescue depends on quick and effective action. MacGonigal forced himself to be calm. *Think, dammit, think! There's got to be something we can do.*

He grabbed Collins' instrument console and checked his air supply. Not bad—but his bottom timer showed twenty-seven minutes. Only three more minutes before decompression would be necessary. Motioning Collins to stay put, he swam back down the passageway, toward the point where Faith had anchored the tackle. He took the snatch block loose, then traced down the lines, finding where they disappeared under the plate. That done, he swam over the plate to find where they emerged. Working carefully and patiently, he cleared the tackle, cutting the lashings to the case.

Swimming blind back over the wreckage, he found a bent 1-beam that seemed sturdy, and fastened the standing end there. He groped his way along the edge of the plate until he contacted Collins again. Giving him the running end of the tackle to hold, MacGonigal tied the running snatch block to a twisted chunk of steel that projected from the plate.

Together, he and Collins heaved on the tackle. At first, the slack came out of the tackle quickly. Then, strain as they might, they could gain no more. MacGonigal motioned for Collins to hold what they had, and he slowly swam along the edge of the plate, feeling for any obstruction. Along one side of the passageway, where the bulkhead was buckled and split, the plate seemed to be binding. He inserted the tip of the crowbar and heaved. The plate seemed to slowly edge away from the bulkhead. He heaved again, and felt the crowbar slip. The plate was higher now, just by a few inches. He checked once more. It was binding against the bulkhead again. Another heave of the crowbar, another inch or two of gain. He repositioned it and heaved once more, putting all he had in it.

Suddenly it seemed to give way, throwing him over backward. He struggled to right himself, putting his hand on Faith's arm in the process. He slid his hand up the arm. There seemed to be space there. Mentally crossing himself, he pulled, and the arm came forward. He worked his way backward, brushing against Collins in the murky water. He put a hand on Collins' arm and pulled, indicating that he wanted more lift. Collins complied, and Faith's body slid free. MacGonigal worked him down the passageway, then swam back for Collins, grabbing his tank and pulling him backward.

As Collins released the tackle, the heavy steel plate collapsed, falling flat and generating a current that drove them back down the passageway. They sprawled in the intersection in a tangle of arms, legs, and hoses. Groping in the darkness, MacGonigal found Faith, and began dragging him toward the gash in the ship's skin. Collins followed, helping him maneuver the inert body around bits of twisted wreckage.

Once outside the hull, the visibility was greatly improved. MacGonigal checked Faith's body. He was breathing, and his eyes were open but unfocused. A look at his instrument console showed that he still had a little air in the twin eighty-cubic-foot tanks, but his bottom timer showed fifty-seven minutes at a depth of ninety feet. MacGonigal started up the anchor line with him, Collins trailing along behind.

Susan had watched him go down, then made her way to the navigator's station, where she switched on the radio and listened for a moment. If there was

traffic, she might have a chance of contacting someone, here off the lonely coast of Central America.
There was nothing, though. She listened a moment
more, then went back up on deck.

The surface of the water was almost flat, only a few
wind-driven ripples. There was nothing to show that
there were three men somewhere below who might
be struggling for their lives. She took up her regulator and screwed the yoke onto a fresh set of tanks,
then tied a line around the tank valve below the yoke.

There was a large inflatable buoy in the lazaret.
She got it out and attached an inflator nozzle to the
low-pressure line that dangled from her regulator,
inflating the buoy with a few shots of air. She measured off ten feet of line and tied the tanks into the
buoy, then stopped a moment. She went back to the
lazaret and produced a heavy galvanized shackle,
which she attached to the anchor line, then ran the
buoy line through it and took a couple of turns. She
shoved the tanks and buoy through the lifelines and
allowed the arrangement to slide down the anchor
line, until the buoy was short up against it. Then she
sat back and steeled herself to wait.

MacGonigal could see the dark mass of the tanks
hanging above him as he made his way up the anchor
line. Faith hung loosely in his grip, although from
time to time he made feeble attempts to help himself.
Collins hovered beside them like a nervous mother
hen.

When they reached the tanks, MacGonigal looked

at Faith's pressure gauge. Less than five-hundred pounds. *That's cutting it damn close,* he thought. He wrapped one arm around the anchor line and pulled Faith up to the tanks. Collins caught on, and swam upward, taking one of the dangling second-stage regulators and offering it to Faith. The little man made an attempt to take it, dropping his own regulator in the process. Collins grabbed his head and shoved the regulator in his mouth, hitting the purge button to clear it of water. MacGonigal watched closely, and was relieved to see Faith inhale, then expel a stream of bubbles through the exhaust ports of the regulator.

He checked the little set of dive tables dangling from his instrument console. With fifty-seven minutes of bottom time, Faith and Collins would need at least twenty-five minutes of decompression at ten feet.

He checked his own bottom timer. It hadn't been reset since his last dive, and it showed thirty-eight minutes—not as bad as the other two, especially since he had had a two-hour surface interval in the meantime, but still far beyond the no-decompression limits. He calculated his own decompression time. Seven minutes. A long time. But for Collins and Faith, it would be longer. He couldn't leave them hanging here on the anchor line alone, not after what they'd been through.

He looked over at them. Collins was supporting Faith, who was making some effort to hold on to the anchor line himself. MacGonigal checked Collins' instruments. He was almost out of air. He took the remaining second stage from Susan's regulator and offered it to Collins, who took it as if embarrassed at forgetting to check his own air supply.

They waited as the minutes ticked away. MacGonigal looked at his timer. Two minutes. They hung there on the anchor line, waiting. *Sue must be worried about us,* he thought. *Well, she'll just have to tough it out.* He looked back at his timer. Less than thirty seconds had passed. He looked closely at Faith. He seemed to be coming around. His breathing was regular, his grip on the anchor line seemed firm.

Four minutes had passed. He pulled the pencil from its clip on the side of his slate and wrote, "You have another twenty minutes." He looked at it, and added, "I'll be back." He checked his timer again and waited some more. He recited poetry to himself and looked at the timer. Six and a half minutes. He recited a few more stanzas and looked again. He reached over and grasped Faith's arm, facing him. His eyes seemed alert. He made the okay sign, and the communications expert returned it. He held up the slate so he could read the message, and then made the sign again. Faith returned it, and MacGonigal showed the slate to Collins, who gave him the "okay" and looked down, checking his own timer.

It was better now that she could see the bubbles. So many bubbles must mean that they all were still alive, and they must be near the surface. She sat down on the starboard side of the coach roof and waited, watching the bubbles come to the surface.

There was a sudden upwelling of bubbles, and she saw a head break the surface. She stood, then suddenly remembered that they might need help. She ran down the deck to get the horseshoe buoy that hung on the stern.

"Where you goin', beautiful?"

She halted in midstride. "Are you all right, Mac?"

"I'm fine—Willie's a little green around the gills, but I think he'll be all right. He's got another fifteen, twenty minutes' decompression, though. Break out the first-aid chest, will you?"

"S-sure, Mac. Will—will he be—all right?"

"Hope so, but I can't tell until we get him aboard. Did you put out a call on the radio?"

She started guiltily. "No . . . no, I didn't. I'll call now."

"Forget about it. I don't think we're going to need help—and if we do, a few minutes one way or another won't make any difference."

"Is . . . is he bad?"

"Don't know. Part of the hold collapsed, and he was caught underneath. We got him out, but he seemed to be . . . out of it. He's breathing, and seems to know where he is, so I guess he's okay." He paused a moment. "I'm going back down and wait with them—we'll be up after awhile."

She watched him go back down, and then went below to get the big first-aid chest. She brought it up on deck and left it in the cockpit, then went back down and got the little two-liter oxygen bottle and mask. She watched the bubbles a while longer, then went belowdecks again. She dragged the storm trysail, a heavy, fully roped piece of canvas, out of the sail locker and brought it topside. She rove lines through the tack, head, and clew and lowered it over the side, making the head and tack lines fast to cleats, and leading the clew line back aboard to one of the sheet winches. She had done everything she could think of, so she sat back to wait.

After what seemed like an eternity, the water began to boil as the divers ascended. She watched the three of them break the surface, Faith's smaller figure supported between MacGonigal and Collins. They inflated his jacket and towed him toward the boat.

"Over here, Mac. I'll bring him aboard in the bunt of the trysail."

They maneuvered him toward the hanging arrangement of sailcloth and line as he protested weakly. "I can climb aboard. I'm okay."

MacGonigal slid him into the bight of the sail and stripped off his jacket and weight belt, clipping them to lines Susan had let down—no point in losing equipment.

"Take it easy, Willie. No need for you to strain yourself."

He looked upward toward Susan. "Can you take a strain on this thing? Just enough to give him some support?" He turned to Collins. "Get your gear off and get aboard and help her. I'll stay here with Willie."

In a moment, he heard the clinking of the winch as Susan began to haul in line.

"Okay. That's enough. We don't want to bang him against the side of the boat."

He floated there in the water, trying to ease the swinging of the hammocklike sail against the side of the boat as *Tir Grad* rolled gently in the swells.

In a moment, Collins called to him. "I'm up, Mac. Ready to bring him aboard?"

"Heave away—but watch the swells. Let's try to get him aboard in the trough."

Collins tailed onto the winch, taking slack while the boat fell into the troughs of the swells, holding his ground when she rose. MacGonigal, his feet and knees against the turn of the bilge, held Faith away from the side of the vessel. As *Tir Grad* wallowed in the swells, they got him level with the scuppers, and as she went down into the troughs one more time, MacGonigal heaved from below while Collins and Susan pulled him aboard.

MacGonigal swam around to the Zodiac and pitched his gear aboard, then climbed up the swim ladder. He found Faith stretched out on one of the cockpit seats, a transparent oxygen mask strapped to his face, while Susan examined him for injuries.

"How is he?"

She looked up. "Bruised. And sore. Nothing broken, that I can find." She gave him a warning look.

"There may be internal injuries. We should get him to a hospital."

Faith pulled the mask off. "No hospital—we can't blow the whole mission just because I'm a little banged up." He appealed to MacGonigal, "You tell her, Mac. I'll be all right in a couple of hours, and I'll be ready to go back down."

MacGonigal shook his head. "No way, Willie. We'll give it a couple of hours, and if you seem to be okay, we'll continue to try to retrieve the gear. But there's no way you're going back down there. D.W. and I will have to do all the underwater work from now on."

As he said it, he looked across at Collins, who seemed to be a pale green. "You okay, D.W.?"

"Yeah . . . I'm okay. I just don't like the idea of going down there again." He paused. "Mac, I ain't ashamed to admit, I'm scared."

MacGonigal grunted. "Me, too, D.W. Me, too."

"That don't mean I won't do it, you understand," Collins hastened to say. "I'll do it. But I ain't gonna like it."

Susan had brought up a blanket for Faith. She tucked it around him, checked his pulse, and put a thermometer in his armpit. She turned on MacGonigal. "You don't intend to go down there again, after this has happened, do you?"

MacGonigal sighed. "There isn't any choice —unless we abort the mission. All our gear is down there—weapons, ammo, everything. But we don't have to go down until tomorrow morning, anyway —we're all maxed out on bottom time now."

She glared at him. "You're a dumb, stubborn Irish bastard, Mac. You're going to get yourself killed down there—and then what will happen to your precious mission?"

"Take it easy, Sue," he said soothingly, "we have to go down one more time, anyway. If it's safe, and we can get the stuff out, then we go on like before. If not, then we have to think of something else. It's that simple."

She glared at him. "Well, Willie isn't going back down. I won't allow it."

"Now, darlin', that's what I *said*, wasn't it? D.W. and I will do the underwater work, and you and Willie can stay topside and tend the boat."

"Oh, yes! We'll just stay up here while you two kill yourselves. And what if something happens while you're down there?"

"I guess you'll just have to use your best judgment, honey." He put a big hand on her knee. "You know I have a lot of faith in you, darlin'."

She looked at him, tears starting to show in the corners of her eyes. "You big, dumb bastard! You'll get yourself killed, and I'll spend the rest of my life thinking it's my fault."

"No, darlin'," he said. "If I get killed, it's my fault, and nobody else's. You know that—everybody knows that. What I do, I do on my own—and nobody takes the blame for it but me."

It was still twilight as MacGonigal rousted them out of their bunks. He had the gimballed kerosene stove going, and water was boiling for coffee. Susan tumbled out of her bunk and sat on the edge of the starboard settee, her hair a tangled cloud around her face.

"Damn, you love to see the sun rise, Mac!"

"Well, we've got work to do today, and only one team to do it. With a four-hour surface interval, we'll be hard-pressed to make four dives today—and it's going to take a lot of diving to get that stuff up."

She brushed a stray lock of hair out of the way. "You're determined to go on with it, aren't you? Even after what happened to Willie?"

MacGonigal had produced a frying pan and was laying strips of bacon in it. "I sure am, beautiful. But the first dive today will tell the story. If it's doable, I'll do it."

Faith emerged from the fo'c'sle, a trifle unsteady, but otherwise looking recovered from his ordeal. He sat down beside Susan and took the cup of coffee that MacGonigal offered him. "I'm ready to go down again, Mac, if you think we can do the job."

"Thanks, Willie, but I think we'll keep you up on deck from now on. You've been through enough, and we can't risk our commo man."

Collins came out of the fo'c'sle, his face a mask of suppressed emotion. "Got any more of that coffee?" he said with elaborate casualness. MacGonigal passed him a steaming mug. Susan watched him sip it, then got to her feet.

"Well, if you fools are determined to make dead heroes out of yourselves, the least you can do is let me use the head. I want to look presentable when the rescue cutter arrives and I tell them how you all died."

They watched her flounce into the head and close the slatted doors while MacGonigal lifted thick strips of bacon from the frying pan and placed them on a serving plate. He took several greased eggs from the container under the little stainless-steel sink and began to crack them into the smoking pan.

"You know I don't really want to do this, Mac."

They were hanging on the anchor line, ready to make their first descent. MacGonigal pulled the mouthpiece of the snorkel out of his mouth. "I know, D.W., but there's nothing to worry about. We'll play it safe. You stay outside, like we planned, and I'll go in and look things over."

Collins gave him a strange look. "I was on the outside *last* time—and look what happened. Mac . . . if you get in trouble in there . . ."

"Yeah, I know, D.W. And I know you. You'll be in after me."

"I know. That's what I'm afraid of."

He paused for a moment. "Well, this isn't getting us anywhere. Let's go on down and get it over with."

They exchanged snorkels for regulators and started down. The water was clear and undisturbed, showing no sign of what had happened the day before. MacGonigal led the way slowly, until the hull of the *Gulf Streamer* showed below them. He swam down the last few feet and checked the security of the

Danforth anchor. It was solid.

Collins came down beside him, and MacGonigal pointed to the tools and gear that lay scattered around the gash in the hull. He waved his hand, pointing to the mesh bag hanging from Collins' weight belt. *Pick this stuff up.*

Collins understood and began to collect the various items that lay scattered on the sand around the entrance to the hull. MacGonigal turned to the ragged gash in the steel plates and slipped inside.

The interior of the hull was much clearer than it had been, the sediment having settled out since their last dive. MacGonigal delicately adjusted his buoyancy and began to swim gently along the guideline toward the store of cased weapons buried in the vessel's hull.

The steel plate that had pinned Faith down seemed to present no obstacle. He swam over it and entered the hold. Shining his light in all directions, he inspected the entire cavernous opening in the ship's bowels. He saw where the great steel plate had come loose, and he checked the structure on either side of the gaping hole. Everything seemed solid.

Satisfied, he swam back down to the cached weapons. One of the boxes was knocked aside, lying at an angle to the others. Otherwise, they seemed undisturbed.

The collapsed steel plate formed a natural ramp, he noticed. He lifted the first box and maneuvered it into position on the ramp, then swam up and detached the tackle that he and Collins had used to free

Faith. He swam back down the passageway and hooked it to the original ringbolt, then paid it out down the passageway.

It was ridiculously easy. The box obediently slid up the ramp and trundled down the passageway to the intersection. He swam forward and retrieved the tackle, paying it out again, and hooked it to another box, then repeated the process.

When he had three boxes stacked in the intersection, it seemed a little crowded. He looked at his bottom timer. Twelve minutes. Plenty of time. He seized one of the boxes and half dragged, half carried it to the gash in the hull, raising clouds of sediment in the process. He could barely see the opening, and encumbered with the box, he couldn't maneuver his light properly. He shoved the box through the gaping steel plates and followed it through the hole.

As he swam through the gash in the hull, he saw Collins already fashioning a bridle of half-inch line around the case. The limp yellow form of a two-hundred-pound lift bag lay nearby on the sand. MacGonigal clipped it to the bridle Collins was tying, and pulled his auxiliary second-stage regulator from its pocket in his buoyancy jacket. Thrusting the regulator inside the bag, he pressed the purge button, and the bag began to fill. When it lifted itself off the sand and hovered above the case, he stopped purging and looked toward Collins, who gave him first the okay signal and then the thumbs-up.

MacGonigal shot more air into the bag while Collins watched the case. In a moment, the bag was straining, the bridle lines to the case taut. Collins lifted the box. It came up easily. He shot a little air into his jacket and began to rise, thrusting powerfully with his fins as he came off the bottom.

MacGonigal rose beside him, swimming slowly upward, allowing his increasing buoyancy to take him up as he controlled the bag. Below him, Collins shepherded the case, keeping it from swinging or tilting and falling out of the harness of half-inch line.

MacGonigal checked his instruments. Only seventeen minutes. Not bad at all. They continued to rise slowly, with MacGonigal venting air from the bag from time to time, while Collins clung to the case, his fins projecting stiffly outward to provide drag, should their prize get away from them.

Susan paced the deck nervously after they went down. Faith, wearing a heavy wool sweater, despite the growing warmth of a day that promised to reach ninety, sat more quietly beside the hammering compressor, filling the tanks that they had exhausted the day before.

"They'll be all right. You'll see."

She rounded on him. "They better be all right. If they're not up in twenty minutes, I'm going down after them."

Faith shrugged. "If they're late coming up, we'll both go after them."

She started to reply, then bit her tongue, realizing how effectively he had checkmated her. If she went, he went. And she couldn't allow that. She still wasn't sure that Faith was recovered. She had stumbled across the DAN *Underwater Diving Accident Manual* in the first-aid box, and had morbidly read through it. Its twenty pages of text had scared her more than she wanted to admit, and she feared that Faith might have some permanent injury as a result of his experience.

"All right, Willie, we'll both stay topside—but we'll get on that radio and start calling just as soon as they're overdue."

They sat quietly for a few more minutes, Susan occasionally glancing at her watch as the minutes passed. Suddenly Faith nudged her and pointed. Bubbles were breaking the surface, welling up out of the depths. She stood and gripped the lifelines, looking down into the clear water. She could see shapes slowly rising into view. At last a yellow mass broke the surface.

"Willie, they've brought something up!"

Faith got to his feet as the divers themselves broke the surface. "We've got the first one. Rig the main boom, and we'll get it aboard."

The two divers swam the ponderous bag, its top just awash, toward the port quarter of the boat while Faith and Susan unlashed the main boom from its position in the boom crutch. Faith dug into the lazaret and produced a handy billy, usually used for hoisting a rigid dinghy aboard, and clipped it to the bail at the end of the boom. Then the two of them swung the heavy spar outboard. Faith went forward and rigged a preventer, to hold the boom in position, while Susan ran the end of the tackle down until it touched the water.

While MacGonigal steadied the bag, Collins vented air from his jacket and took the end of the tackle down and fastened it to the harness of line that swathed the case. He yanked vigorously on the tackle and watched as the slack came out of it. Slowly the case began to rise in the water, the bridle line between it and the lifting bag going slack.

"You've got it, haul away."

The two men in the water watched as both Faith and Susan heaved on the tackle, straining to lift the heavy case to the surface. As it broke the surface, the waves just washing over it, MacGonigal called, "Hold off. Belay the line, and one of us will come up to help."

He turned to Collins. "You watch it from here, and I'll go aboard and help them get it on deck."

As Collins steadied the case in the water, keeping it away from *Tir Grad*'s topsides as she rolled in the swell, MacGonigal stripped off his gear and clambered aboard.

"Okay, haul away." The case rose out of the water, penduluming just above the surface of the sea as *Tir Grad* responded to the swell.

"Willie, you man the topping lift. Sue, get ready to slack off that preventer."

They took stations as MacGonigal watched the swaying weight. "Okay, Willie, heave up."

As Faith cranked the mast-mounted winch, taking

up on the topping lift and raising the end of the boom, the case rose slowly upward. MacGonigal watched closely, timing his orders to the swell and the rise of the case.

"Slack off the preventer! Not too much!"

As Susan paid out line, the boom swung inboard of its own weight. Before the swell passed, MacGonigal tripped the release on the handy billy and lowered the case to the cockpit sole.

"That's got it!" He moved to the lifelines. "Come on up, D.W., and let's see what we've got."

Behind him, Faith was lowering the main boom into its notch on the boom crutch and lashing it down. Susan recovered the preventer and faked it down while Collins climbed aboard.

"Do you want to open it here in the cockpit, Mac?"

"Might as well. We'll never be able to store all this stuff belowdecks without unpacking it."

He seized the sunken T-handle of the lid of the steel case and tried to twist it. Faith passed him a short wrecking bar, and he pried against the edge of the lid, forcing the handle to turn. It gave reluctantly, and he pried again, moving it a full quarter of a turn. The lid yielded, and he pulled it off, the rubber gasket coming half away as he did. He stripped away the protective plastic and looked into the case. Six AK-47s looked back at him, packed muzzle-to-butt in the steel case.

He began to slide the weapons out of the case, passing them to Susan, who passed them down the companionway to Faith, who stowed them away. When he finished, he stood and stepped to the rail, the olive-green steel case in his arms. He heaved it over the side, open end down, and watched as water swirled in. In a moment, it sank, disappearing into the clear depths. He watched it go and threw the lid after it.

"Let's have some hot coffee. I'm ready to relax for a while."

Faith stuck his head out the companionway. "Want some whiskey in that?"

"I'd like to, but not today, thanks. We can't afford to tempt the bends with all the diving we've got to do."

Belowdecks, they clustered around the dinette table, and MacGonigal sketched the layout of the weapons cache for them.

"With that plate down, it's actually easier than it was before." He grinned at Faith. "I guess we've got you to thank for that, Willie. Brilliant move on your part."

"Thanks a lot," said Faith wryly. "It wasn't anything any other superhero couldn't have done."

"Well," MacGonigal went on, "what it amounts to is that we can move the stuff faster than I thought."

He pointed to his rough sketch. "The only problem is this damn turn in the passageway. You have to get the cases to the intersection, and then you have to get them out. If we had some way to move them smoothly, we could bring out twice as many."

Collins looked closely at him. "So what's your plan?" he asked suspiciously.

MacGonigal leaned back. "Well, I was thinkin' there's three of us fit to dive, and one who can man the boat . . ."

"Hold on, Mac, I don't think either Sue or Willie should go down."

"Speak for yourself, D.W.," said Sue. "Willie and I have agreed that we'll both stay on the surface, but if you need me . . ."

"It won't be all that hard," said MacGonigal persuasively. "It'll be fun. What I had in mind was for Sue to stay at the opening in the hull. We'd rig a tackle there, and D.W. could stay at the intersection. I'll go into the hold and hook up a crate and heave it up to D.W. When it gets to the intersection, he can unhook the tackle—I can pull it back with a messenger line—and hook it onto a tackle that runs to the entrance. Then he can pull the case all the way to the entrance. Sue can unhook it and he can pull the tackle back."

Susan looked at the diagram he had drawn. "It seems simple enough," she said. "I'm willing if the others are."

MacGonigal grinned, his teeth showing whitely through his salt-and-pepper beard. "That's my girl. I figure we can move four or five cases each dive. If luck is with us, we can be on our way by tomorrow afternoon."

Collins looked over the plan. "Okay, Mac . . . if it's

all right with everyone else, I guess I'll go along with it."

MacGonigal drained his mug. He slapped him on the shoulder. "That's the way, D.W."

He turned to Faith. "How about you, Willie?"

"I got nothing to say about it. I'll be up here, nice and comfortable, while the rest of you are down below. But it sounds good . . . I'll go along with it."

MacGonigal favored them all with a dazzling smile. "It's settled, then." He looked at his watch. "Let's get something to eat before we go down again."

# VIII.

---

*Tir Grad* floated low on her marks as she stood into the coast at Tortuguero. The low-lying, swampy coast was a smear on the horizon when MacGonigal ordered the sails dropped and hit the starter button on *Tir Grad*'s diesel engine. With Faith at the navigator's station, watching over the depth sounder and the loran, and Susan in the crosstrees, he conned the big cutter-rigged sailboat in toward the steamy shore.

The Tortuguero is a hostile coast, offering no shelter from the storms that sweep the gulf, and the beach that fronts the gulf is a narrow, treacherous strip, backed by a narrow, stinking lagoon. The jungle behind the lagoon is a nightmare of twisting, shallow, sluggish waterways, where mangrove swamps alternate with low, brush-choked hummocks. Snakes abound, fer-de-lance and bushmasters, mostly, and the air is full of bloodsucking insects of every variety. The government of Costa Rica has made the best of it, declaring the Tortuguero to be a national park, a sanctuary for the several species of marine turtles that lay their eggs on these remote beaches, and for the other varieties of wildlife that inhabit the jungle and the mangrove swamps.

Few vessels sail the waters off the Tortuguero, for as dangerous as this coast is, it is made even more hazardous by 170 miles of barrier reef paralleling the shore. At places, the waves break over the coral twenty miles out to sea. The barrier reef has claimed more than its share of unwary sailors, and even in these days of modern navigation aids, the reef is avoided by almost all traffic.

Reluctant to risk *Tir Grad* with her deep keel on this ship killer, MacGonigal had Faith steadily calling off the depth of water under the keel, while Susan watched for the telltale color change that marked the reef. With one eye on the crosstrees, and an ear cocked to hear the chanted depth readings and loran numbers, he held *Tir Grad* on her course toward shore, the diesel chugging slowly and rythmically as it pushed the heavy-bodied vessel toward the reef.

"Green water ahead, Mac."

He waved a reply. "Okay. Talk me in as close as you can." He craned his neck, looking around the dodger to the foredeck, where Collins was stationed. "Ready with the anchor, D.W."

Collins waved in reply, then turned his attention to

the water ahead of him. From the deck he could see the line where the deep blue water of the Gulf turns green as it meets the reef. Below, Faith was singing out the loan numbers, and MacGonigal, listening, realized that they were very close to where they were supposed to be. He looked up toward the crosstrees again, to see Susan looking down at him with concern.

"I think this is as far as we should go, Mac."

He nodded and cupped one hand to his mouth. "Let go the anchor, D.W."

For an answer, there came a splash as the plow anchor hit the water, followed by the rush of the double shot of chain. *Tir Grad*'s ground tackle was extra heavy—he had no desire to risk her being dashed to death on this inhospitable shore, and had provided her with extra-heavy anchors and chain.

"She's down!"

At the sound of the shout from the foredeck, he threw the prop into reverse, backing down and setting the anchor firmly in the sandy bottom. Cupping his hands around his mouth again, he called to Collins, "Let out plenty of scope—eight or nine to one won't be too much."

Once the anchor bit, he revved the engine a little, just for good luck, then shut down. "You can come down now, beautiful," he called. Fifty feet above him, Susan unfastened her safety harness and stepped gingerly into the triangular metal steps that alternated up the mast from the coach roof to the crosstrees. He watched her come down, her round bottom displayed to advantage as her small bare feet searched for each step.

Collins and Faith were already at work, rigging the compressor and breaking out the Zodiac, which they inflated with one of the half-depleted scuba tanks. With MacGonigal's help, they launched her from the stern of the boat, and lowered and attached the big 75-horse outboard. Safety buoys and lines were quickly rigged.

Susan emerged from the companionway in a revealing string bikini. MacGonigal whistled appreciatively.

"You look good, Sue."

She dangled her mask, fins and snorkel in front of him. "You'd better get ready to go in with me. No telling when some snoop is liable to fly by."

MacGonigal stripped off his old, faded canvas trousers and scooped up his own snorkeling gear. Together, he and Susan went down the swim ladder and into the warm water. They had a fairly stiff swim to the reef, and they cruised there awhile, enjoying the underwater scenery. At last MacGonigal signaled her to turn back. "Let's go back in, beautiful. We've done our bit for the audience—if there is one."

He swam strongly, his fins churning the water in powerful strokes, but he kept track of her by rolling over on his back from time to time to make sure she was keeping up with him. They arrived at the swim ladder almost out of breath and emerged dripping from the water to meet Collins and Faith already in scuba gear.

"You feel like going down so soon, Willie?"

Faith shrugged. "Got to go sometime. This is as good a place as any."

They watched the pair make their way down the ladder. Once in the water, they went through the usual gyrations of putting their fins on, and MacGonigal passed them two pole spears.

"There's lots of fish on this side of the reef. See what you can do to get supper for us."

Collins nodded as he accepted his spear, then turned to Faith and gave him the thumbs-down sign. In a moment, they were under the surface, swimming away like some sort of prehistoric monsters.

The day wore on, with no sign of human activity, except the return of the two divers. They had a string of fish that made MacGonigal groan.

"All we needed was enough for supper, for chrissake! You guys have enough fish there to feed us for a week."

Collins grinned. "Couldn't help it—they swam up and demanded to be shot."

MacGonigal groaned again and opened the lazaret, producing a pair of boards and filleting knives. He and Collins went to work on the fish while Faith washed down their gear and recharged the air tanks.

By the time they finished and sluiced the blood and scales off the deck, it was nearly dusk. Susan took charge of the fish and went below. In a short time she had a bouillabaisse bubbling on the kerosene stove.

"Better eat up, boys. There's a lot of work to do tonight."

They wrestled the second Zodiac out of the bilge, where it had lain ever since they brought it aboard, and launched it beside the first, lashing them together to form a broad raft lying under *Tir Grad*'s stern. Forming a human chain, they passed the weapons and ammunition up from belowdecks, across the cockpit, and into the two inflatables.

MacGonigal looked at the huge, plastic-wrapped masses lying on the floorboards of the Zodiacs. The rafts, for all their buoyancy, seemed to sit low in the water.

"We'd better make two trips of it."

"It's a long way," said Collins. "We can't make much time in the dark, not with all the coral heads in the water around here."

"We'll make it. It's not much more than a ten-mile round trip, and we can make that in two hours, even if we go slow and take our time unloading."

"Yeah, but we've still got to get everything across to the lagoon and under cover."

"We'll make it. Don't worry."

They started away from *Tir Grad* at slow speed, the Zodiac barely raising a ripple on the surface. MacGonigal concentrated on the boat compass lying on the floorboards in front of him while Susan watched the water in front of them for signs of sudden shoaling or of coral heads that could rip the bottom out of the heavily loaded inflatable. From time to time, she sighted back toward *Tir Grad*, using a hand-bearing compass to determine the direction to the Tilly lamp hanging from the backstay.

As they puttered slowly over the slight swell, she saw the second Zodiac pull out of the Tilly's circle of light and take station behind them, following them in to the shore. The two boats left barely any wake, and the muffled engines, running at less than a quarter throttle, made little noise.

Here and there, she could see a small white line, luminous in the darkness, the breaking of a little ripple over a treacherous coral head. She signaled MacGonigal with hoarse whispers, as if there were someone on the Tortuguero who could hear them. After each detour, she took another sighting on *Tir Grad*'s anchor light, and brought them back onto course.

In less than an hour they were within sight of the little waves breaking on the white beach. MacGonigal gunned the motor, then lifted it clear and allowed the heavily laden inflatable to carry its way up onto the beach. As the nose of the boat slid up on the sand, Sue skipped out with the painter, and made it fast to a clump of bushes.

"You'll have to hold the painter while I unload. As the boat gets lighter, it'll want to wash up onto the shore. Just let it come and give it an extra tug or two to help it along."

He spread a tarp on the other side of the beach, hard against the shore of the lagoon, weighting it down with stones to keep it fully spread. Then he returned to the Zodiac and stripped off the protective plastic sheeting from its cargo. He gathered up an armload of weapons, carrying them across the sandy beach and depositing them on the tarp, then returned for a second load.

There was a looming in the blackness, and the second Zodiac appeared, a luminous line at its bow from the little wake it made. It came ashore within a dozen yards of their boat, and Collins leaped ashore, dragging the boat up a few more feet onto the sand. Without a word, he and Faith set about moving their cargo across the narrow strip of land to the lagoon.

The second trip was as uneventful as the first, and by two o'clock in the morning, they had their entire cargo ashore. They manhandled the first Zodiac across the beach and launched it in the lagoon. They loaded it with weapons and ammo, carefully trimming it to float level. MacGonigal stepped back and eyed it critically.

"It floats awful low in the water."

"It'll be okay," said Faith. "On these sluggish backwater streams, it'll be a piece of cake."

MacGonigal looked at it again doubtfully. "I hope so. Still, it's your baby."

"Sure, Mac. Don't worry about us. We'll meet you at San Miguel in three days. No sweat."

MacGonigal wasn't satisfied. "You got everything you need, Willie? Maps, compass, rations—you got a first-aid kit?"

"I've got everything, Mac. Now, don't worry about

me and D.W. We're old hands at this sort of thing. We'll make out fine."

MacGonigal made his way back across the beach where Collins and Susan waited. The Zodiac was lying in the surge, just barely moving with the wavelets that came in now and then. He took hold of the bow and shoved her backward into the water. Susan and Collins, wading alongside, lent their efforts, until the boat was out in thigh-deep water. They clambered aboard, and MacGonigal gave her an extra shove, then tumbled in over the bow. He seized a paddle, and gave a few powerful thrusts, driving her still farther out, while Collins started the engine.

With the paddle, MacGonigal worked the bow around, fighting against a little offshore breeze, while Collins dipped the power head of the big outboard into the water and gave her a little throttle. The Zodiac swung around and headed out to sea, aiming for the bright light of the Tilly hanging from *Tir Grad*'s backstay.

It seemed a long ride over the water to the yacht, with the big outboard purring behind them. At last, *Tir Grad* was fully visible, her stern and quarter brightly lighted by the suspended Tilly, her bows dim in the faint starlight, looming over them like some kind of monster of the deep. The bow of the Zodiac kissed her stern, and MacGonigal hauled himself up the swimming ladder, pulling up on the painter to keep the boat steady for Susan as she disembarked.

As soon as she was aboard, he threw the painter

back into the boat and Collins gunned the outboard, swinging her in a wide circle, heading back toward the beach. They stood at the rail watching him until he disappeared in the darkness, then they listened to the muted sound of his engine as he bore on through the night, headed for that invisible shore.

"Have any trouble recovering the stuff?"

MacGonigal looked at Lawrence noncommittally. "The usual. It was a lot of weight to bring up."

"How about Collins and Faith? Think they'll be all right? Will they make it to the rendezvous in time?"

He shrugged. "They'll be on schedule. They've got two boats, so if one breaks down, they've got backup. How about yourself? How did you guys do?"

Lawrence seemed a little reluctant to answer directly. "There's all kinds around here. We signed on a few people, and a few more are interested."

"How many have you got? And what are they like?"

"Well, we were lucky in one way. There are a few Indians—Miskitos, mostly—who know the jungle pretty well, and are willing to do anything to get back at the Sandinistas, but . . ."

MacGonigal finished his sentence for him. "But they don't have any training or experience. No problem—they can hold up their end if they're good in the bush. How many did you sign on?"

"Seventeen. That's about all we can handle. We'll each have our hands full carrying out the technical aspects of the operation. And we won't be able to control many people if things get hot."

MacGonigal thought a minute. "Seventeen isn't enough. We'll need a few more—three at least. Preferably someone who knows something about weapons and tactics."

"I've got a line on a few of those. There are a couple of Americans down here who were working for a fellow who needed some 'security agents'—he's gone now, and they're out of work. And there's another guy who was with a group in Alabama who sent 'volunteers' to help the Contras. He's sort of stuck, and he'll do anything for passage home."

"Sounds like we don't have a lot to choose from. Anybody else?"

"Well, the situation in El Salvador and Nicaragua has attracted some professional types, mercs. There are several British types hanging around—most of them from the British forces in Belize, who took their discharges there and came down here to see what they could pick up."

"Any of them likely prospects for our operation?"

"Most of them are just hot air—like to pose as tough guys—but there are a couple that I've made arrangements to talk to tonight. I figured you'd want to meet anyone we signed on."

"What about the rest of the plan? How are we for transportation?"

"Tomás has been busy. He's lined up contacts for us, and we've got five trucks ready to go, plus a couple of jeeps. I'm not real confident about the trucks—a couple of them have seen better days, but we'll just have to deal with any breakdowns as they occur."

"What about cross-border contacts?"

Lawrence was silent for a long moment. "There aren't any. We'll have to go in blind."

MacGonigal was thoughtful. Going in blind, with no in-country assistance, is almost suicide. Very few blind insertions ever succeed, but he had known from the beginning that this was how it would bc. *Still*, he thought to himself, *it could have been a hell of a lot easier.*

"What does Tomás think of our chances?"

"You know Tomás, he's game for anything. He'd go if the devil himself were waiting for us."

The cantina was typical—MacGonigal had seen its twin a thousand times, all over the world. The tile roof held up by rough-cut poles, the plaster on the walls stained by the urine of a decade of customers, the constant buzz of flies. He stood outside a moment, sizing up the place. He felt subconsciously along his belt for the folding Buck knife and wished he had a gun.

It was dark in the bar, and the smoke in the air didn't improve things. Lawrence led them to a booth along one wall. On the other side of the room, a slatternly waitress made some joke with a patron, and there was a burst of laughter. MacGonigal looked around. Tomás Maldonado was at the bar, drooped over a glass, apparently totally uninterested in such goings-on. Charlie Samuels had yet to show up, but his instructions were the same as Maldonado's—to ignore the others, but to be on hand if needed.

The waitress, breaking free from the embrace of one of the customers, approached them and stood hipshot, her raven-black hair hanging down her back in a tangle. MacGonigal waited for Lawrence to order, then resumed his survey of the bar.

There were several characters that looked out of place—their complexions were too fair or too sunburned to be natives, and their conversation, when he could hear snatches of it over the general hubbub, was in accented English. British, ex-soldiers, as Lawrence had told him. *They must be hard-up to wind up here*, thought MacGonigal.

They waited about twenty minutes. At last a man dressed in khaki trousers and bush jacket came into the bar. He stood a moment just inside the entrance, looking through the smoky atmosphere, as if searching for someone. Lawrence lifted one hand from the sticky surface of their table and beckoned to him —the gesture was too subtle to be called a wave.

The man came over, peering into the dark corner of the booth, the better to make out MacGonigal's figure. MacGonigal could see that he was a little below middle height, with a high forehead. He wore his hair moderately long, brushed back and out over his ears, in the manner affected by upper-class British officers.

Lawrence stood, holding out his hand. "This is Harold Watson. Harry, meet my friend Francis MacGonigal."

MacGonigal got to his feet, aware that, as he did so, the conversation along the bar stopped. He stuck out his hand and received a firm grip from the man in the bush jacket. With a motion of his hand, Lawrence invited the man to sit, and snapped his fingers to attract the waitress.

They settled back, and the waitress took an order from Watson. They made small talk until she put the drink on the table and Lawrence paid for it.

"Cal tells me you've got some military experience." The man took a swallow from his glass, a locally brewed beer. "My God, that's terrible. They must have learned to brew from you Yanks."

MacGonigal made no reply, and the man went on. "I've a bit. First Seventh Gurkhas. Platoon commander."

*That would make you a captain, laddie-o*, thought MacGonigal, knowing that positions in the British Army usually called for a higher grade than similar positions in the American Army.

"What kind of bush experience?" he said aloud.

The man took another swallow and made a comical face. "Quite a bit, I should judge. Gurkhas are usually assigned to tropical areas, you know."

They fenced a bit more, the man adopting a polished but defensive posture, and MacGonigal testing his knowledge about the more esoteric aspects of jungle warfare. Watson appeared to be a competent bush soldier, albeit with a limited imagination.

Finally MacGonigal asked the key question. "Cal here says you might be interested in a job."

Watson suffered through another swallow of local beer. "Could be, old boy. What did you have in mind?"

"Hunting, picture taking. More or less a safari."

"Hmm. More? Or less?"

MacGonigal grinned. "Are you interested?"

"That would depend, old boy."

"Depend on what?" He repressed the temptation to add "old boy."

Watson looked at the bottom of his empty glass, and Lawrence signaled for the waitress again.

"I suppose it would depend on how long the job lasted, and what it paid."

"Fair enough," said MacGonigal. "It'll be about two weeks, and it pays twenty-five hundred."

The waitress brought more bottles of beer and stood by until Lawrence paid. Watson waited until she had gone, then deliberately filled his glass.

"Would that be in dollars?"

MacGonigal smiled to himself. Dropping the "old boy" seemed to be a good sign. "Dollars—U.S. If you want Canadian or British pounds, we can arrange it."

"No, no. U.S. dollars will be quite satisfactory." He paused, as if slightly embarrassed. "There is a little matter of insurance—customary, you know."

"We've arranged for coverage. Forty thousand for

the term of the job. We pay the premium."

They sat a while longer, talking in a desultory way. At last MacGonigal confronted Watson directly. "Are you in or out?"

Watson looked down in his glass. "Well, it depends on what the job is, old boy. You haven't told me much about it, after all. Twenty-five hundred U.S. dollars is a lot of money for a simple safari, you know."

"You want to know what the job is? It's a twenty-five-hundred-dollar safari—that's all you have to know for now. Now, are you in or out?"

"Ah," said Watson. "Well, if that's the way you put it. Still, one would like to know a *bit* more . . ."

"When one decides if one wants the job, one *will* learn a bit more. Until then, one has to make up one's mind."

Watson sighed. "Well, beggars can't be choosers. I suppose I'll take it."

"Fine," said MacGonigal. "Now, where's the latrine around here? My teeth are floating."

"Out the back, there." Lawrence jerked a thumb toward the depths of the smoky room. MacGonigal could see a door through the gloom.

"Use any part of the wall you fancy. Mind you don't step in anything," said Watson.

MacGonigal heaved himself out of his seat, squeezing past Lawrence, and started for the back. As he did so, he noticed that the room fell silent for the second time that evening. There were three beefy characters standing near the end of the bar. They were obviously drunk and, until a moment ago, they had been fairly rowdy. Now they paused in their boisterous activities and watched him cross the floor.

"Mind you don't piss yourself, Paddy."

MacGonigal ignored the remark and went out into the pungent darkness, stepping warily, as he had been warned. When he returned to the bar, the three stopped their conversation again and turned to watch him. He could feel their eyes on him as he passed.

"You should have warned the Irish pig not to shit himself, Jim."

He ignored the remark and returned to the booth. Watson had slid into the cracked bench seat, so he pulled a chair up to the booth and poured himself another beer.

The voice behind him was rough but clear, meant for him to hear. "No good telling a paddy not to shit himself, Bert. Taigs are all pigs. They *like* shit."

MacGonigal turned his head slightly, his expression unreadable.

"Pigs!" the man said, looking directly at him. "The Irish are scum!"

MacGonigal put his drink on the table and rose slowly from his chair. He pushed it back and crossed the floor in three strides.

"What was that you said?"

The man peered at him through the bluish haze of the barroom. "I said the Irish are scum."

His breath reeked, and he sprayed saliva as he spoke. He swayed a moment, then went on. "I've pulled my time in Northern Ireland, and those fuckin' Taigs . . ."

MacGonigal had never been good enough for the Golden Gloves, but he had a fair left hook. And the right that followed it wasn't bad, either. The first punch broke the man's nose, splattering blood over the bar, and the next punch rocked the man over backward. He fell heavily, rolling sideways off the bar. MacGonigal watched him fall, then turned away, rubbing his bruised knuckles.

He took a step and stopped, as if suddenly remembering something. He turned back. The merc was on his hands and knees, blood running from his broken nose, trying to get to his feet. MacGonigal stood a moment, watching him, thinking.

*"Erin go bragh!"* he said. His foot lashed out, and the heavy boot connected with the point of the man's jaw, snapping his head back so that it bounced off the bar with a thump. Blood flew, and several teeth along with it. The man crumpled in a sodden mess at the foot of the bar.

MacGonigal prodded him with the toe of his boot. There was no reaction. He looked at the other two. "I take it you don't share your friend's opinions?"

They stood there a moment staring at him. He returned their stares, then pointedly turned and went quietly back to his table while the other two mercenaries watched him, death in their eyes.

"Look out, Mac!"

Instinctively he hurled himself aside as a beer bottle hurtled past his head and crashed into the wall. He whirled his chair around as one of the mercenaries came charging into him, thrusting the chair into the man's groin and then bringing it up to strike hard against his chin. The man went down writhing, his hands locked into his crotch. MacGonigal stepped back, the chair held in front of him.

The third of the three mercenaries approached warily, a commando knife held out before him. He made lazy figure eights with the knife.

"Come on, Paddy. You're for it now."

MacGonigal hurled the fragments of the chair at him and kicked out. The knife went flying. Before the man could react, MacGonigal had stepped inside his reach and delivered a short, powerful punch to his midriff. The man doubled up, his hands clasped over his stomach. MacGonigal brought up his knee, at the same time slamming down on the back of the man's head with both hands. There was a sickening crunch as the man's nose collapsed.

MacGonigal stepped back. The man swayed on his feet, still doubled over, blood running from his nose and mouth. MacGonigal spun him around and smashed a clubbed fist into his back, just over his kidneys. The man went down, retching and vomitting.

There was a sudden crash of glass breaking. Out of the corner of his eye, he saw someone rise from a booth, a broken bottle in his hand. The man started toward him, but fell over Maldonado's outstretched foot. Before he could rise, Maldonado was all over him, kicking and flailing away with his own beer bottle.

Two men came around the end of the bar, headed for Maldonado. MacGonigal stopped one of them with another chair, throwing it into his path, so that he tripped spectacularly, his legs flying, his face smashing into the floor of the room. He caught the second with a flying kick to the chest, knocking him backward over the bar. He hit the floor in a crouch, hands in front of him, eyes darting in all directions.

Maldonado had finished with his now-unconscious victim. He swept up another bottle and took up a position beside MacGonigal, the bottle raised over his head like a club. The man MacGonigal had tripped with the chair was scrambling to his feet, his face a mask of blood from the glass slivers on the floor. Maldonado swung the bottle against the side of his head, and beer, foam, glass and blood sprayed over the bar. The man fell back, and Maldonado caught him squarely in the crotch with the toe of his boot. The man curled up in agony.

Lawrence and Watson were already out of their booth, almost ripping it from the floor in their haste to escape its confines. MacGonigal whirled to face Watson, but the man held up his hands.

"No fear, mate. I'm on your side."

There was the sound of a door slamming. MacGonigal jerked around in time to see the last of the other patrons of the bar leaving through the door to the backyard *pissoir*. He scanned the room. There seemed to be no one there except for his people and several bodies of men who were more or less *hors de combat*.

"What's going on in here? Are you all all right?"

They looked around to see Charlie Samuels framed in the doorway. He seemed bewildered.

MacGonigal unceremoniously pushed him back out into the street. "You're a day late and a dollar short, Charlie—we're just leaving."

The others came out behind him, their hands filled with beer bottles or other makeshift weapons.

"If I were you, mate," said Watson, "I'd get the hell out of here. Those lads have gone for their guns. And the police here won't ask any questions if someone comes across a dead Yank in the morning."

The barest trace of mist lay over the water, but if they looked ahead into the distance, the haze was thick enough to obscure everything over a hundred yards away. The inflatables moved over the water with barely a ripple, and the mutter of the two powerful outboards could barely be heard. There was just the slightest hint of a damp chill in the air. The sun was still too far down to bring warmth but, as he watched, Faith saw the first touch of morning light on the tips of the trees. They motored on in silence.

The character of the river was unchanging: flat water, hemmed in by flat, dank, densely wooded banks. The river was sluggish, brown, opaque, and laden with bits of bark, weeds and decaying vegetation. The engines labored at low speed and thrust the boats forward by sheer force. The dead weight of the equipment and supplies in the boats gave them all the maneuverability of water-soaked logs. In places, the vegetation and floating debris were so thick that they were forced to give up the use of the engines, because the propellers were constantly fouled and jammed by thick weeds and tendrils.

In the few stretches of comparatively open water, they tried to make up for lost time by opening the throttle. They learned the futility of this early on when Faith, in the lead boat, ran up on a submerged tree trunk. The overburdened Zodiac slid up the inclined, sunken log. In horror, Faith watched the bow rear up, like an enraged hippo rising from the depths, shaking tendrils of vegetation from its maw. Too paralyzed with fright to do anything about it, he allowed the engine to drive the boat farther and farther up the log, until it finally capsized, turning completely over. He had barely time to cut the engine before the mass of the Zodiac was on top of him.

Watching from just a few-dozen yards away, Collins saw the whole thing as if in slow motion. He cut the engine on his own raft and let the boat drift forward to the capsized Zodiac. He made it fast to his own raft and prepared to dive for his companion, when Faith surfaced on the other side of the raft.

"Shit! I've done it now!"

"Hang on, Willie. I'll get you out."

He managed to drag a dripping and thoroughly dispirited Faith aboard. Using their paddles, they worked the two rafts ashore, dragging the capsized inflatable as far up the muddy bank as possible. They righted it and collected the few items that remained with the raft.

"Shit! We've lost everything!" Faith slapped his forehead. "Damn! I had all the rations in there, too. We haven't got a bite to eat!"

"Take it easy, Willie. It can't be too deep out there. We can probably salvage quite a bit of stuff."

They hauled Collins' Zodiac up on shore and poled the other one out into the stream, fastening it in place with cut poles that they drove deep into the soft, oozy bottom. Hanging on to the lifeline that encircled the raft, they searched in the mud with their bare feet, trying to feel the lost cargo through the layers of silt and rotting vegetation.

From time to time, they were successful, and a growing heap of weapons, ammo boxes, cans and miscellaneous gear filled the raft by nightfall. By dark, they had recovered about half the lost gear. Despondently they built a fire, as much to drive off the clouds of insects as to dry themselves.

The next morning they took stock of their situation. They had lost a half-dozen weapons, half the mortar ammunition, all but a dozen RPG-7 rounds, and most of their rations. What they had recovered was sodden and choked with mud. They spent the morning stripping down and cleaning weapons and trying—unsuccessfully—to get the dunked outboard to run.

They finally pulled away from the bank with Collins towing Faith's raft. The water-soaked motor was clamped to the transom, its cover off, in the hope that the sun might somehow dry it enough to be useful again. Soon the vegetation closed in on them, and they were forced to abandon the use of their one remaining engine and take to paddles and poles for propulsion.

The sun was hot, and the marshy banks kept the trees back far enough to deprive them of shade most of the day. The light glancing off the water baked their faces and exposed arms. Faith could feel a nagging ache forming behind his eyes. They continually wiped sweat from their brows, and insects buzzed around them annoyingly.

The distinction between land and water was blurred. Many flat, slow-moving streams joined the main stream, and the main stream itself seemed to divide frequently, passing low, hummocky islets, mere mud bars held together by the roots of trees. The water was shallow, too, as Faith realized when his paddle dug into the soft, oozy bottom with each stroke. The river meandered maddeningly, turning back on itself in S-loops. They would make better time by walking, he thought, but as he thought it, he realized that it would be impossible to slash their way through the thick, tangled brush. And the soggy ground would not support them.

"D.W., just what are we doing here, anyway?"

Collins smiled. "You're the boss, Faith. I'm only your flunky. I follow you."

"Don't be funny. You know what I mean. Where are we going? Do you know the way?"

"No, Willie, I don't. I can read a map as well as anybody, I guess, but I don't have the slightest idea where we are, except that we're somewhere on this fuckin' river—and I'm not sure *which* river it is. I think we just have to follow the main stream, if we can, and we'll come to a sort of lake. According to the map, it's shallow and probably covered with reeds."

"Do you think Mac had any idea where we're going?"

Collins shrugged. "Who can say? He's pretty good at this stuff, but I don't know if even he could navigate this *particular* river—whatever river it is."

"But has he ever been this way before? He spoke as if he were sure of the route, at least as far as the lake."

"Beats me. If you want *my* opinion, *nobody* knows the way through this mess, 'cause nobody's ever been through here before. At least," he added, "nobody with any sense."

"Then *I* have to find the way through this mess? All by myself? *Me*, the dumb shit that turned the boat over?"

"I reckon so. If there *is* a way."

"And what comes after this swamp?"

"The mountains. They're pretty much like the mountains in Nam, I understand—steep, and with lots of deep ravines and plenty of jungle. Except that, according to the map, there are a couple of volcanoes on the route—*that's* something we didn't have to put up with in Nam.

"And we have to cross these mountains?"

"From the map, it looks like we wind around the base of a volcano before reaching the lake. Once we get there, we should find a road of some kind. With any luck, Mac will have a pickup arranged there."

Faith thought a moment. "You're right, D.W., when you say 'nobody knows.' Me, least of all. If you're smart, you'll turn back. I'll go on—I can tow the other boat, I suppose, but I can't lead you into something I don't know anything about. It doesn't seem very likely that I'll get very far, anyway."

Collins smiled. "I won't turn back, Willie. You and I are old buddies. As for not knowing what to do, or where to go, I'm not sure I could find my way back—especially if you take both boats with you, asshole!"

It was Faith's turn to smile. "I hadn't thought of it like that. I guess we're both stuck, old buddy."

Collins was serious. "I guess we are, Willie. We've been stuck ever since that fuckin' Irishman pulled up the anchor and sailed away."

The sun was now high, nearly at zenith, and Faith thrust his paddle into the water and hauled his boat around. Without speaking, Collins turned his boat and drove it into the shallows, lodging the bow in the muddy bank. He climbed out and tied the painter to a half-rotten tree that overhung the water. They gathered a few armfuls of reasonably dry wood. Collins pulled out a tarp and fashioned a place for them to sit while Faith hacked at the soft, punky wood with his bush knife until he had enough dry splinters to start a fire.

The first hesitant flames were winding their way up into the little pile of shavings, splinters, and twigs when Collins wandered down to the bank and cast out a handline. Faith watched tolerantly.

"Do you think you'll catch anything in this murk?"

"Never can tell. But I can try. Fish would be better than musty rations that have lain on the bottom of a wet boat . . . even if they are well-cooked," he added hastily, seeing Faith looking sharply in his direction.

Faith sat beside Collins and opened his map case. It was wet, and he carefully worked free the dripping map sheet and spread it out flat. "Shit! This country doesn't look anything like this damn map. I can't see anything that looks like the country we've come through."

Collins looked at the damp paper. "Hmmm. I think the problem is that these channels open and close. Islands and hummocks shift their positions. Even the lake probably changes its shape and extent from year to year. But if we bear south and follow the main stream, we're bound to come to the lake. There have to be people somewhere along the lake, probably along the south shore. Once we find people, we're bound to find some kind of link with the outside world."

"Then you should take the lead. You know your way around in this kind of shit a lot better than I do."

"Oh, no, buddy. You're the leader. You take charge —I'll follow you." He paused a moment and then added thoughtfully, "Until you turn your boat over again, that is."

They sat awhile in silence, watching the bobber of Collins' handline.

"You know, the farther we go into this damn swamp, the creepier I feel, like some disaster is overtaking us. Do you feel the same way?"

"No, Willie, not really. But I wouldn't let it worry me—we're in the middle of the fuckin' swamp, and we ain't likely to get out by worrying."

"Well," said Faith, "I can't help being apprehensive. Sometimes I think there's nothing around the next bend of this fuckin' river but another bend. And other times I think there *is* something, and that's even worse."

"Leave it, Willie," said Collins. "We've come this far, and there's no going back. Just worry about fixing lunch, and don't pry into the future."

They fell silent. Faith was clearly nervous. Collins, on the other hand, felt as if he had passed through some barrier. They had been through one disaster, and had come out of it. It somehow made a difference to have admitted aloud that the future was too frightening to face with knowledge. And if Willie *did* have some kind of premonition, Collins preferred that he keep it to himself. At last, he pulled in his line and stood up.

"I guess you're right about fish, Willie. Come to think of it, I'm not sure I'd want to eat a fish that lived in *this* water."

The noon meal was cheerless and eaten in silence. When they pushed off after eating, they were careful to keep the boats within sight of each other. They used the engine sparingly, poling their way most of the time. It was slow, agonizing work, and the insects that buzzed around them in clouds didn't make it any easier.

By evening they had reached the lake itself. They followed a channel cut in the reeds until dark, relying on compass and guesswork to pick the correct channel out of several that ran twisting through the reeds. When darkness came, they tied the boats together and set a watch. It was a long, miserable night. They lay cramped and wet in the bottoms of the boats, plagued by insects and tortured by thirst, for they dared not drink the unboiled river water. They had lost their little camp stove, and they had nowhere to build a fire.

It was an even more miserable dawn. The lake was blanketed with mist, mist that gathered in little droplets on every exposed surface, crept through their clothing, and seemed to penetrate their very consciousness. They had nothing to eat. Their fresh rations, exposed to repeated soakings and partial dryings, were moldy and unpalatable uncooked.

Cans were already so rusty that they feared to trust them, and freeze-dried rations, while still undamaged in their foil wrappers, required water to make them edible.

By late afternoon they came into sight of a collection of dirty huts. It was a lake village of some twenty Indian families. The chief of the clan was an old man with a potbelly and skinny, ulcerated legs. He emerged from his hut and cautiously approached the travelers. Children peered around the corners of the huts, but seemed afraid to come near.

Faith spoke at length with the old man, using a mixture of pidgin Spanish and sign language.

"He says there have been bandits in the swamp. His young men have encountered them. Also, there are stories about raiders coming from over the border, hunting for refugees. He's afraid and doesn't want us to enter the village."

"Does he have any food to trade?"

"He'll trade, I think, but he's afraid to admit how much he has—he seems to think that we'll rob him." Faith looked appraisingly at Collins. He was smeared with mud, and his face was lumpy with insect bites and covered with a three-day growth of stubble. His shirt and trousers were ragged, torn and filthy. The only thing clean about him was the AK-47 he had slung over his shoulder.

Faith chuckled. "Looking at you, it's no wonder! You look like a Mexican bandit! I think we should set up camp some distance away from here, and then come back in the morning to trade for food and talk about how we can get out to the nearest road."

They spent a second night on the boats, well back in the reeds. They managed to light a fire on a soggy hummock and keep it going long enough to boil water for supper, and that took the edge off their hunger. But nothing could moderate the effects of the insects. They buzzed and bit all night, and the faces of the two men were pocked and bleeding from bites the next morning.

MacGonigal looked over the sorry column of vehicles. There were two bobtailed GMCs whose factory coachwork had been replaced by a fantastically painted wooden construction that overhung the original dimensions of the vehicles by a good two feet on either side. Looking at them, MacGonigal wondered how two such behemoths could pass each other on the narrow roads he had seen. Each of them had a large name board over its windshield. He looked closely at the elaborate lettering on one of them. *Tigre Volante*, it proclaimed.

Flying Tiger, he thought. *I'll bet he's not lying, either*.

The other trucks that Maldonado had hired consisted of a Mecerdes that had obviously seen better days, an army-surplus deuce-and-a-half, and a fifth vehicle of such ancient origin that it defied identification. With no body at all, and only a few boards bolted to some structural member that seemed to serve as a frame, it was a mere skeleton of a vehicle, and it squatted behind the others, as if ashamed of itself.

The five trucks were drawn up in a rough semblance of a convoy along the edge of the road just outside of town, their proud owners standing beside them, displaying impressive sets of incisors as they extolled the virtues of their vehicles.

MacGonigal walked around the five delapidated trucks. The deuce-and-a-half was missing at least one dual on each side, and the tires that were mounted showed every sign of giving up the ghost at the first sharp rock in the road. MacGonigal laid his hand on the hood and found it warm. The engine was still ticking and cracking as it cooled down, so obviously the vehicle had just been driven up. He squatted and reached under one rear wheel well, feeling the shock absorber. It was cold. He went around the truck feeling them all. They were *all* cold.

He straightened up. Charles Samuels was watching him. "And you had the balls to talk about *my* pickup!"

Samuels goggled at him, mystified. "Come over here, Charlie, and feel *these* shocks—they're all dead."

He unhooked the hood latches and climbed up on the big six-by-six. The dipstick looked like it was welded in place. He pulled it out. There was no sign of oil on it. He thrust it back in again, twisting to make sure he got it fully home, and pulled it out. Still no oil. *Christ! What keeps the thing going?*

He replaced the dipstick and jumped down, relatching the hood. He turned to Maldonado. "Ask him when was the last time he put oil in this thing."

Maldonado spoke rapidly to the driver, a darkly villainous little man with a shock of greasy black hair falling down to his shoulders. The little man replied with much waving and gesturing, apparently reciting the life history of his truck.

"He says he puts in oil every year."

MacGonigal could feel the beginnings of a headache forming behind his eyes. "I don't suppose he has a spare tire for this thing?"

Again, Maldonado engaged in animated conversation with the driver, who punctuated his reply with theatrical gestures, dramatically kicking each tire to show its soundness.

"He had one once. That's it back there," said Maldonado, pointing to one of the rear duals. Looking closely at it, MacGonigal could see that it had only one layer of bare cord showing through where the tread had been, while all the others had two. He shook his head. His headache was getting worse.

The driver plucked his sleeve, chattering rapidly and waving violently. MacGonigal watched, dumbfounded, until Maldonado interceded for him. "He says it would be pointless to have a spare tire—the truck is too heavy for him to lift and he has no jack."

MacGonigal shook his head and went on to inspect the old Mercedes, with the driver of the deuce-and-a-half clinging to his sleeve and spraying him with saliva while he kept up a nonstop, totally unintelligible harangue on the qualities of his truck. Impatiently MacGonigal pulled away and checked the Mercedes' tires. They were in even worse condition than those of the deuce-and-a-half. He crouched to look under the truck. The differential seemed to be leaking oil. He looked more closely and saw that the drain plug was missing. In its place was a wooden plug wrapped in rags. He stood up, a feeling of hopelessness coming over him.

"Tomás, is this the best you could do?"

Maldonado's shrug was eloquent. "I'm telling you, man, this is all there is. You should have seen the dogs I *didn't* hire."

MacGonigal shook his head again. "What odds are they giving in town against us ever seeing San Miguel?"

Maldonado spread his hands, palms up. "Hey, it's not that bad, man! That's why I got five trucks. If one or two of them break down, we still got plenty!"

MacGonigal inspected the remaining trucks, discovering new wonders with each one. There were broken springs, cracked blocks, radiators plugged with rags. He turned back to Maldonado. "Look, Tomás, I'm not blaming you. If this is all you could get, well, it's all you could get. But we've got to get some tires and shocks for these old crocks. And some tools. And some oil—lots of oil."

Maldonado called the drivers around and began to explain what MacGonigal wanted. It was an animated, almost violent discussion. At first, the drivers seemed to object strenuously, until he made them understand that MacGonigal had accepted all their trucks and that he, MacGonigal, would pay for the tires, oil, and tools, and not deduct the price from their fees. When he got that across, they were incredulous at first, then deliriously happy, praising MacGonigal extravagantly. After a few moments, however, their mood began to change again.

"What's wrong now?" asked MacGonigal.

Maldonado laughed. "They say you're such an easy mark that they're sorry they didn't hit you up for twice as much."

MacGonigal looked at the crowd of unkempt, scraggly truck owners. "Tell 'em I'm keeping the new tires and tools and what's left of the oil when the trip is over."

Maldonado translated, and the drivers protested volubly, calling upon several varieties of gods, both Christian and Indian, to witness the way they were being treated. MacGonigal was adamant, and had Maldonado repeat his terms.

When the hubbub died down, he told Maldonado to take one of the trucks back into town for the tires and other needs. "And don't go anyplace the driver recommends—unless you price things somewhere else first."

Susan had observed the whole affair from the side of the road. "Mac, what's the point of taking the tires back? You won't have any use for them after the operation. And they won't bring enough to be worth your time and trouble to sell them. Besides," she said, pointing at where Samuels stood, trying to puzzle out the meaning of the negotiations, "he's paying for them."

MacGonigal kissed her on the forehead. "I don't want the damn tires, beautiful. But I damn sure don't want these guys to think I'm an easy mark. When the operation's over, I'll give 'em the tires, and anything else that's left over—but I'll *give* 'em, not be cheated out of 'em."

"What's the point? They still get the tires."

"The point is, I'm the *jefe*—and that's damned important in this part of the world. It's the difference between gaining their loyalty and having one of 'em stick a knife in your ribs when you finally have to stand up on your hind legs and put a stop to the stealing that you encouraged in the first place."

They sat beside the road, the drivers congregating into a tight knot off to one side, squatting in a circle, smoking and talking among themselves. As they waited, the sun grew hotter, and flies began to buzz around them with a vengeance. The hours passed, and the sun climbed to the zenith. Susan chafed, wondering aloud what Maldonado was doing and when he would return.

Watson opened a small ice chest and handed her a sticky sweet soft drink. "Not to worry. Everything moves slowly down here. They'll be along in a bit."

She wrinkled her nose at the drink, but drank it, anyway, balancing the risk of diarrhea against the nagging thirst generated by the hot tropical sun. They waited as noon passed and the afternoon wore on. At times a few vehicles passed them, mostly busses as colorfully decorated as *Tigre Volante*, with bodies of wood, like the *Tigre*, and crammed with people, chickens and other impedimenta. Occasionally there were a few trucks, all of them badly overloaded, and most of them so decrepit and worn-out that MacGonigal realized the truth of Maldonado's claim that these particular trucks were the best available.

About three o'clock, Maldonado returned, the back of his truck heaped with tires, some nearly new, others showing almost as much wear as those already on the trucks. MacGonigal looked them over, one at a time. Several of them were holed, but there were patched innertubes for these. Maldonado was defensive.

"Hey, man, it was the best they had. I got everything in the place."

MacGonigal just shook his head and went on with his inspection. There were three or four cases of oil, of mixed vintages and weights, and a collection of tools that might have been sold to a museum. Thankfully the collection included an ancient scissors jack, as well as a hefty four-way lug wrench and several broad tire irons.

"Well," he said, "let's get the best of the tires on them, fill the crankcases, and get on the road."

Maldonado translated, and was rewarded with the now-customary voluble protest. After a full five minutes of arm-waving protest, he turned back to MacGonigal.

"They say the tires they have still have air in them, so why change them?"

Struck by the irrefutable logic of this argument, MacGonigal yielded. "Just check the oil, gas and water, and let's get on the road."

After another twenty minutes of discussion, they were finally ready. One after another, four of their five trucks were coaxed into life. The ancient skeleton was recalcitrant at first, but a push by *Tigre Volante* finally got its engine started, and although it rattled and clattered alarmingly, with occasional backfires that shot flames two or three feet into the air, its driver beamed proudly and climbed aboard, seating himself on a wooden box lashed to the frame with wire, and pulled the vehicle out onto the road.

Maldonado took the lead in the first jeep and led them a short distance down the cracked and potholed blacktop, then turned off into a narrow, brush-lined lane. They followed that for several miles, taking what appeared to be random twists and turns, and passing through several small villages, clusters of thatched or tiled huts that hugged the dusty road as closely as the jungle.

After an hour or so, almost at dusk, they came to a collection of huts and shanties made of corrugated iron, cardboard and other scrap materials. A few potbellied kids and scrawny dogs occupied the rutted street—at risk of their lives, it seemed, as the convoy bore down on the shanties. Maldonado brought his jeep to a halt in the middle of the street, and the trucks, with much screeching of brakes and skidding in the dust, managed somehow to stop without ramming him or each other. As the dust settled, an unmistakably American face appeared at the window of the jeep.

"Jeeze, I thought you guys weren't gonna make it today. I was startin' to get worried."

# IX.

Grunting and sweating, they made their slow way through the swamp. Each step was an effort, as their feet sank into the almost bottomless ooze which held them captive until they managed to drag the next foot out of the sucking mud. Burdened with over a hundred pounds of weapons, ammunition, and equipment apiece, even the ragged, cheerful Indians who made up the bulk of the column were suffering. Sweat dripped into their eyes and saturated their mud-encrusted clothing, attracting clouds of mosquitoes, doctor flies and dozens of other biting, bloodsucking insects which swarmed in clouds around them.

MacGonigal waved a temporary hole in the cloud of insects that seemed to be trying to crowd into his eyes, and looked the column over. They were making progress, but slowly. The men with the heavy Zodiacs and the big twenty-man rafts seemed to be getting the worst of it, along with the men who carried the big 75-horse outboards slung between them on bamboo poles. He motioned to Tomás to have them spelled, and they gratefully turned over their burdens to another set of porters.

They had left the trucks just north of Caño el Diós, less than five miles from the border, offloading their mountain of gear into the brush that formed a narrow margin between the road and the water-logged, swampy, poisonous ground that bordered the Rio Frio. The trucks and a skeleton crew under Samuels' control had gone on to Los Chiles, a settlement almost too small to dignify with the name of "town," where they pretended to carry on a picture-taking safari. Los Chiles would serve as the rendezvous point for the returning raiders.

In the meantime, the rest of them squelched and sucked their way through the swamp. They reached the river—less than a mile away—only after two hours of hard slogging. It took them two trips to move everything, and then they had the problem of inflating and loading the boats.

MacGonigal watched them as they fitted the transom on the first Zodiac and bolted on the motor. "Willie, are you *sure* that damn thing's gonna start?"

Faith was offended. "Of course I'm sure. What do you think, Mac—I can't fix a damn outboard motor, for chrissake?"

MacGonigal rubbed his beard. The flesh beneath it was lumpy with bites and he itched abominably. "No,

Willie, I know you can fix damn near anything—but an outboard that's been under water . . . well, it's been my experience that the damn things hold a grudge for a long time."

"Well, don't worry about it. She's gonna run. You can count on it."

He slurped away to supervise a group of men setting up a temporary equipment dump. They had spread out one of the twenty-man rafts and partially inflated it. It provided the only dry spot where they could dump their burdens while they went back for a second load of equipment.

They worked all through the evening, hauling weapons, ammunition, communications equipment and other gear through the swamp. The pile of gear in the raft grew, and soon they had to unpack and inflate the second raft.

By dark, they were all exhausted, but they couldn't stop. The second Zodiac was broken out and moved to the riverbank—actually, there was no true bank, but as they approached the river, the swamp gradually became deeper and more treacherous. When they could no longer maintain their footing, they inflated the Zodiac, loading its motor into it, and worked the two inflatables out a little farther, until finally they found enough water to lower the motors without burying the props in the muddy bottom. They anchored them with poles, jammed deep into the mud, fore and aft.

They formed a chain, passing equipment from the big, unpowered rafts to the Zodiacs, until they managed to lighten one of the rafts enough to bring it forward. Once it was afloat, it served as a receptacle for more gear, until they could float the other one forward.

It seemed to take forever, but at last both rafts were loaded, the equipment properly sorted and the men aboard. With the rafts in tow, they started the Zodiacs and moved slowly down the current of the Río Frío.

Within a couple of miles, they could see the yellow glow of a kerosene lamp in the little village of Los Chiles. They cut the engines and drifted, fending off now and then as the river made its way through sluggish, hairpin bends above the town.

They ghosted along in the current, eyes on the banks, full of tension, lest they be discovered so close to the border. As they approached the village, they could make out the stark outlines of their four trucks—the ancient one had finally given up the ghost, and they had left it outside San Miguel, after paying its driver enough to change his protests and complaints to voluble thanks.

As they drew even with Los Chiles, they could hear the amplified voice of a popular narrator of nature films. Their decoy operation seemed to be working, with the skeleton crew showing movies on an outdoor screen, giving the population an example of the sort of work they claimed to be doing.

Once clear of the village, they dared to start the motors again for the next leg of their trip. Within twenty minutes, they crossed an invisible line, the border between Nicaragua and Costa Rica.

"We're in bandit country now, boys," said Collins. He had the Dragunov sniper rifle assembled, with the lamp and battery pack, and he was scanning both sides of the river through the scope.

"There's a house over there, Mac."

MacGonigal took the weapon and looked through the scope. In the flat green light of the night sight, he could see a small, thatched building about four-hundred yards away. It seemed perched exactly on the border. He examined it carefully. There was no light or movement. He handed the weapon back to Collins.

"Keep your eye on it, D.W. It could be nothing, and then again . . ."

They passed the house and continued on downstream. In less than a mile, the river made a tight bend, turning almost a full circle in a few-hundred yards. They slowed the lead Zodiac, and MacGonigal took the painter ashore. Collins covered him with the Dragunov while Lawrence, Watson, and one of the other locally recruited mercenaries provided backup from the second Zodiac, training the RPD machine gun on the shore, ready to fire.

The ground was firmer here, mostly thick, almost impenetrable scrub, not much higher than a man's head. MacGonigal forced his way through, following a compass course, while Collins trailed him, sniper rifle at the ready.

They made a quick cloverleaf, going into the brush at an angle, turning 120 degrees, moving the same distance, then turning 120 degrees again to bring them back to their starting point.

"It looks secure. Let's get the stuff ashore."

They spilled out of the rafts, moving quickly and efficiently. Watson and his fellow mercenaries moved out to set up security posts up- and downstream while the unloading took place. In the distance, a dog barked and was answered by another animal on the other side of the river. A tiny light glowed in a window about a mile downstream, but there was no other sign of human presence.

The men began to shuttle equipment ashore, forming a human chain to pass weapons and ammunition up the bank. Lawrence commandeered the 60mm mortar and set it up, laying out a few rounds so that he could provide fire quickly.

In a remarkably short time, the equipment was ashore and arranged in packs and bundles for the next stage of the trip. The inflatables were out of the water and being rolled up preparatory to being slung between carrying poles.

When he was satisfied that things were going well, MacGonigal took the first group forward, leading them through the thick undergrowth, while Lawrence supervised the rest in packing up.

In less than a mile, they were back in the swamp again, struggling through the sucking mud, enduring the mosquitoes and other insects. It seemed worse this time, although the journey was shorter.

The little Rio Boca Ancha was a miserable slough. Less than three feet deep anywhere, it was a mere channel through the swamp, with a tiny cluster of fishing huts perched on the beach where it flowed into Lake Nicaragua. They inflated the boats again, this time launching a cheap, lightweight two-man raft along with the other boats. While the rest of the men went back under Watson's leadership, Maldonado and Faith set up a security post.

MacGonigal waited until he was sure that things were going as smoothly as possible, then he and Collins paddled the little boat silently downstream, landing just above the mouth of the Boca Ancha and cautiously approaching the fishing huts.

There was no light from the huts, no boats pulled up on the shore, no sign of a dog or any other evidence of occupation. They lay in the scrub, straining their ears, but there was no sound—at least none they could hear above the constant buzzing and whining of the insect cloud that seemed to totally envelop them. Collins put the big Dragunov to his shoulder, switching on the sight and scanning the area slowly.

"Not a damn thing moving, Mac."

MacGonigal didn't answer at once. He took the rifle and searched the surrounding area himself, sweeping the sight slowly across the near ground, the middle ground, and finally the background. It was as Collins had said—nothing was moving.

"Okay. I'll go in and check. You keep me covered."
He paused a moment. "And for God's sake, don't
shoot unless you have to."

Collins was insulted. "What do you take me for, a
fuckin' amateur? I ain't bustin' a cap without good
reason."

MacGonigal grunted, slapped him on the shoulder
and slipped away, moving off to the left, out of his
line of fire. He moved slowly and cautiously, his
AK-47 held across his chest, his right thumb hooked
in the clumsy safety.

There was no one in the first hut. He entered it
through the open doorway and searched it quickly
but thoroughly, finding nothing but a little trash and
a few fishing floats. Once he had searched it, he
moved along the wall, hugging it for cover, until he
was as close as he could get to the second hut, then
ghosted across the intervening space to the doorway.

He crouched there by the doorway, listening and
waiting. There was no sound, but this doorway,
unlike the first hut, was blocked by a hanging blanket.
He stretched himself full length on the ground and
tried to peer under the blanket, without success. It
was simply too dark in the hut.

He pushed the muzzle of the AK-47 under the
blanket and lifted it slightly. Still too dark. He wriggled forward until his face was even with the opening. He pulled back the opening, then froze.
Something was moving inside.

He listened, eyes aching with strain as he sought to

peer through the velvet-black interior of the hut. Someone was coughing, hacking up phlegm. He heard someone spit, then cough again. He slowly lowered the corner of the blanket and wormed backward, the AK-47 trained on the doorway.

There was more noise, a rustling sound. He pressed downward and inward on the safety, trying to push it off with as little noise as possible. The muted clicks sounded impossibly loud in his ears. He pushed again, checking to be sure the safety was all the way down, on semiautomatic. *Careful Francis. You don't want to rip off a whole magazine.*

The blanket was lifted aside. A short, bowlegged man with a drooping mustache and a huge belly stood a moment in the opening. MacGonigal covered him with the assault rifle from only a yard away. *Christ, I don't want to shoot this bastard!*

The man stood there, scratching, hawking and spitting. He was dressed in a torn singlet and a pair of wrinkled pants. His belly hung far out over his belt. He reached back into the hut and took something from the wall by the door. At first, MacGonigal couldn't see what it was, but when the man buckled it around his waist, he realized that it had to be a pistol. *And that means he's some kind of a guard, me boyo.*

The man shifted the holster around slightly, then stepped past MacGonigal, who held his breath as the man passed him. He walked across the space that separated the two huts. Standing beside the vacant hut, he opened his fly and leaned one hand against the wall. MacGonigal cautiously slithered backward, keeping the weapon trained on the man. He watched the man shiver, shake himself, then turn back to his hut. At the door, he hawked and spit again. A gray-green glob landed inches from MacGonigal's nose. He went inside again, dropping the curtain into place behind him.

MacGonigal waited. He could hear more sounds inside the hut, and then quiet. He backed away, keeping the weapon trained on the doorway, then melted back into the brush.

"What was all that about? You acted like you found something."

"Yeah. A security type of some kind. Probably a policeman. He came out to take a leak and almost stepped on me."

Collins made a snorting noise, a suppressed bark of laughter. "You're lucky—he could have pissed on you."

"He almost did," said MacGonigal. "Come on. Let's get back to the boats. I don't think we'll have a problem here, if we take it easy."

By the time they returned, the two Zodiacs and their companion rafts were almost loaded. The men climbed aboard and took up paddles and shoved out into the shallow, stagnant stream. It was only a little over a mile to the mouth, and they paddled well out onto the foreshore flat, sounding with their paddles until they could find no bottom.

"We should be safe now, Mac. We're about a mile offshore."

MacGonigal lowered the binoculars. He could see a few dim lights a few miles to the north, the village of San Carlos at the mouth of the Friwo. Behind him, to the east, there was no light at all. In fact, there was probably nothing at all back there—except one pot-bellied policeman.

"Okay, start her up."

Faith coaxed the motor to life, and as soon as it steadied down, they could hear the motor of the second Zodiac purring away a hundred yards to the north of them. MacGonigal risked a couple of flashes with a red-shielded penlight, and Lawrence, in command of the other Zodiac, replied.

They settled down on course, heading west, almost parallel to the shore, for the Punta del Diablo, a trio of low rocks that barely broke the surface, some eight miles away. Under their heavy loads, the Zodiacs were sluggish, and the loaded rafts behind them did nothing to improve their performance.

MacGonigal threw a small chunk of wood over the side, timing its passage down the side of the Zodiac with his watch. He did a quick calculation in his head. Eleven miles an hour. He pulled a poncho over himself, tucking the edges under so no light would show, and checked the chart with the little two-lens penlight. He figured on the margin of the chart with a stub of a pencil. *Forty-two minutes, give or take a bit.* He snapped the little light off and emerged from the poncho.

"Hold your heading, Willie. Keep it right on 272 degrees."

Faith nodded, but made no reply. He sat motionless, his eyes fixed on the boat compass in front of him, his hand on the tiller of the motor.

They droned on through the night, plowing their way across Lake Nicaragua. The dim lights of San Carlos sank out of sight, and there was nothing else, no lights, no sign that the lakeshore or any of the islands were inhabited, or that they ever had been.

To the north and slightly behind, Lawrence's raft with its ungainly tow kept pace with them. It was a dark shape against the almost palpable blackness of the night, and there was only the purring sound of its engine, counterpointing their own, to assure them that it wasn't some illusion that hung just off their starboard quarter.

"Cut the engine, Willie. I want to listen a minute."

Faith cut the motor, and the raft quickly lost way, its load and the tow dragging it to a stop. Off the quarter, Lawrence imitated them, killing his motor as well. They sat there, bobbing in the swell, while MacGonigal listened.

"You hear it, Willie?"

Faith cupped his hands behind his ears. "Yeah, I hear it, Mac. Off to port."

"What is it, Mac?" Susan had her chin almost resting on his shoulder as she tried to hear whatever it was.

"Waves. Breaking over the Punta del Diablo." He

sighted through his hand compass, then pulled the poncho over him again, checking the chart.

"Steer about 340 degrees, Willie."

They turned almost north, and MacGonigal trained his binoculars on the horizon. He could see an irregular lump, the Isla Zapote, rising dimly in the distance.

"Steer a little right, Willie. About 350 degrees. We want to keep the big island between us and Zapotillo. There's supposed to be a radio tower and a transmitter there."

Faith corrected the course slightly. The raft behind them swept slowly outward, then in again, to trail behind them. Lawrence's Zodiac slowed slightly, and then moved away a little, keeping its station relative to the lead Zodiac.

The Zodiacs moved slowly across the water, with the loaded rafts holding them back. Their engines labored, and they plowed into the waves rather than skimming over them.

"They aren't made for this kind of shit," muttered Faith.

"Don't worry, Willie. We'll make it—easy."

"Yeah, we'll make it, Mac. But these high-speed engines weren't made for towing such a load. It's putting a hell of a strain on them."

"So long as they make this one roundtrip, that's all I ask . . . Hold it! What's that?"

Faith looked in the direction MacGonigal was pointing. A dim red light was visible far off in the darkness. He pulled the pair of 7×50 night glasses out from under the dodger and focused them on the light. At first, the tossing of the laboring boat made it difficult to find the tiny light, but at last he caught it in the binoculars. He hissed between his teeth.

"It's a boat, Mac. And it's on a collision course."

MacGonigal reached for the binoculars, adjusted them carefully and looked. He could see the red light plainly through the glass, and next to it was a fainter green light.

"Running lights!" he said. He grabbed his hooded flashlight and aimed it at the other Zodiac, a mere blur in the darkness behind him.

"Damn! They're not answering." He flashed the light again cautiously. "Come on, Cal. Get your head out of your ass and look this way."

He flashed again, and this time he was rewarded with an answering flash, a single tiny red dot of light. He held the light as steady as he could and signaled for a 90-degree change of course. He peered into the darkness, then relaxed as the answering flashes came back.

The two Zodiacs turned together, tracing a wide quarter circle of wake, with the clumsy rafts swinging outboard of the circle, turning wide. They settled down on the new course, and MacGonigal looked off to port, searching for the running lights. They were still there, the green light plainly visible now. *Shit! Whoever he is, he's really moving.*

The lumbering rafts strained, but the outboards

could make no better headway. Their high-speed propellers were designed to drive light boats over the surface at speed, not to horse sluggish craft through the waves.

"Son of a bitch, Mac, he's getting awful close. Do you think he's spotted us?"

MacGonigal grunted. "Just hold this course. I'm going to signal Cal to cut his engine. When he does, you cut ours."

The far Zodiac responded immediately. Even before the confirming pinpoints of light were seen, the heavy boat was visibly slowing, digging into the waves and losing way. Behind him, MacGonigal heard the noise of their own engine suddenly die away. They sat there, rocking in the waves, watching the approaching red and green lights.

MacGonigal could feel the tension in the boat. Behind him, the men in the raft were deathly quiet. Nothing moved. There was no sound except the lapping of the waves against the sides of the boats. By straining his ears, he could hear the growl of the engine of the approaching vessel.

As it drew nearer, he sighted on it with a small compass. "Shit! 'Bearing constant, range decreasing' —classic collision situation."

A hand closed on his arm. "Are we going to make it, Mac?"

He put his hand over Sue's. "We'll make it, honey —I hope."

They could see the hull of the approaching vessel

now, a black bulk in the darkness. It came on at a fair rate of speed, growing more distinct all the time. In the raft behind them, the men crouched down, huddling instinctively in the bottom of the craft.

They watched it as it bore down on them. At a distance of twenty yards, the green light blinked out, screened by the vessel's superstructure. MacGonigal breathed a sigh of relief and closed his hand over Sue's, squeezing reassuringly.

The patrol boat swept past. It was about forty feet long, apparently a Russian model. They could see a greenish glow on its bridge, the reflected light of its instrument console. On the bow, the massive KPV 14.5mm heavy machine gun pointed skyward, its distinctive long conical flash hider unmistakable.

They held their breath while the boat passed them, rocking in its wake as it swept past. MacGonigal watched it as it motored on, the greenish glow from the bridge showing distinctly from astern. He watched it go, then turned back to Faith.

"Let's get started, Willie."

Off to the right, he could hear Lawrence's engine. As he watched, the Zodiac, lying dead in the water until then, came to life and surged ahead. The towline to the raft came taut and, with a jerk, it settled down to resume its slow tacking behind the Zodiac. He watched as it swept through a slow circle to resume their former course.

"Mac!" The whisper was hoarse, strained. "It won't start!"

He whirled around. Faith was staring at him through the darkness. "I can't get it to crank!"

"Damn!" He fumbled for his flashlight again, and signaled frantically to Lawrence's boat.

"Come *on*, Cal. Look over this way," he pleaded as he flashed the light, playing it around to be sure that the signal was visible over a wide arc.

"Mac! Mac, they've altered course. I think they've heard us."

He turned to see the altered outline of the patrol boat. The last time he had seen it, the bridge and stern lights were showing clearly. Now it showed only its red portside light. It had clearly altered course. As he watched, it swept through its turn, and the green sidelight came into view as well. It was well and truly on a collision course now!

They stared at it as it bore down on them, a bone in its teeth. MacGonigal looked around. Cal's boat was almost invisible in the darkness, heading away. Either it had not seen the patrol boat alter course, or else it had, and was doing the only sensible thing, getting the hell out of there!

MacGonigal began to strip off his camouflage fatigues. He sorted through his gear and took his knife, a few grenades, and his revolver, rolling an olive-green life jacket around them, forming a bundle.

Suddenly Faith noticed what he was doing. "You're not going in that water! There are sharks in there!"

MacGonigal paused a moment. "Sharks? In a *lake*?"

"He's right, Mac," said Collins. "We checked it out when we were planning this phase of the operation. They run up to two-hundred pounds."

"Then they better think twice before they tangle with a two-hundred-and-ten-pound Irishman!" said MacGonigal as he slipped into the water.

He let himself down, sinking so that only his head and the bundle remained above the surface. The patrol boat was nearer now, heading straight for them. He looked over the gunnel of the Zodiac. "I don't know exactly what I can do, but whenever I do it, you all be ready."

Without waiting for a reply, he pushed off, swimming away from the Zodiac, pushing the bundle in front of him.

Suddenly, a dazzling spear of light darted out from the bows of the oncoming patrol boat. It swept over the surface of the lake, swinging from left to right. MacGonigal ignored it and swam on, trying to put distance between himself and the Zodiac.

The light passed over the raft, then hesitated and swept back. The men in the raft were huddling helplessly, their knees drawn up, their faces down. The light steadied on the raft, and the note of the patrol vessel's engine changed, slowing to a throb as it approached its find.

MacGonigal watched as the patrol boat ghosted down on them, its engines barely turning over as it made its final approach. The KPV heavy machine gun no longer pointed skyward. It was manned and trained forward, menacing the raft that bobbed in the waves a few yards ahead of it. As the patrol boat closed with its quarry, it passed in front of MacGonigal, obscuring his view of the raft and the Zodiac.

He could hear a voice, apparently the vessel's captain, on a bullhorn. He strained his ears as he swam toward the vessel, but could hear no reply.

There was a platform on the stern of the patrol boat, he saw, apparently so that divers or boarding crews could get aboard. He grasped its rail and hoisted himself out of the water, dragging his bundle with him, and slithered over the stern rail.

There was no one to challenge him. The patrol boat's crew was clustered forward, attracted by their find. He could hear a babble of voices up there, apparently an argument of some kind. *Sounds like somebody's come up with a cover story. I hope it keeps 'em busy for another minute or two.*

There were two men on the bridge, apparently the helmsman and the navigator. He could see both of them peering through the glass windscreen, absorbed in what was going on forward. He opened his bundle, slipping on the jacket and hanging grenades from its tie strings. He padded forward, knife in one fist, revolver in the other.

The bridge companionway was open and unguarded. In the bow, the arguments and discussions continued unabated, occasionally reinforced by shouting over the bullhorn. No one onboard seemed to have the slightest idea that there might be danger anywhere near.

MacGonigal halted by the bridge companionway. He stuffed his weapons into the life jacket and worked one of the grenades loose. He bent the pin more or less straight, forcing the spread ends back together, and eased it silently out. Taking a deep breath, he transferred the grenade to his left hand, holding the safety lever down. Taking a second grenade, he repeated the process, pulling the pin with the thumb of his left hand. He took one more quick glance around, then released both safety levers simultaneously.

The sudden double *pop* as the strikers struck the priming caps went unnoticed. He forced himself to count steadily, *one thousand, two thousand, three thousand*, as the grenades cooked off. Then he threw them, lobbing one backhanded into the bridge house, and bowling the other up the deck, toward the knot of men gathered in the bow.

As he threw, he dove for the deck, flattening himself behind a locker on the afterdeck. He had barely touched the rough, nonskid surface when he heard the first of the two grenades go off, the second adding its thump to the sound of the first even before it had registered in his brain.

He didn't bother to get to his feet, but simply slithered around the corner of the locker, the revolver held in front of him with both fists. The searchlight had gone out, as had the instrument panel lights.

There was a dark, tangled mass in the bow, and he fired into the midst of it, the muzzle flash and side spray of the revolver shockingly bright in the darkness.

He could hear shooting from up ahead now. He couldn't tell who it was, so he ducked back behind the locker as he fired his last shot. He had one grenade left, so he pulled the pin and let it cook off, then rolled it out onto the deck. He heard it rattle and bounce a moment in the scuppers, and then there was the familiar thump again as it went off. He heard the tiny wire fragments sing overhead and splatter into the superstructure of the boat.

He groped for ammunition, then realized that he had failed to bring any. Cursing, he got to his feet, leaving the revolver lying on the deck. The door to the bridge hung open, swaying as the vessel rocked in the swell, and thin, acrid smoke was coming out of the door. He went in, knife held in front of him.

The two bodies that lay crumpled on the deck plates were of no interest to him, save to make him pause a moment to ensure that they were truly out of action. He searched the bridge quickly, hoping to find a weapon of some kind, but there was nothing. He stepped out on deck again, feeling the sticky, slick blood under his bare feet.

He looked around the corner of the bridge. The shooting had stopped. The barrel of the KPV machine gun pointed skyward again. There was some low moaning, but otherwise everything was quiet. He held the knife in front of him and moved slowly forward.

Something lay on the deck in front of him. He picked it up, feeling for it in the dark. His fingers closed around a pistol grip, and he hefted it hopefully, but it was only the bullhorn. Its bell was dented, and there were several tiny holes in it, obviously from grenade fragments.

"Mac! Mac! Are you okay?"

He flattened himself against the side of the vessel. The shout was repeated. This time he answered.

"Yeah, I'm okay, D.W. How are things with you?"

"We're all okay here, Mac. I'm coming aboard."

There was a scuffing sound, and D.W.'s head appeared above the gunnel. He laid an AK-47 on the deck. "Give me a hand, will you, Mac?"

MacGonigal pulled him aboard, and together they searched the vessel. The entire crew was either dead or dying. When the first grenade had gone off, they had been thickly clustered in the bow, and it had apparently rolled into the midst of them. The shooting MacGonigal had heard was Collins, who had whipped up his AK-47 and fired into the midst of the crew at point-blank range as soon as the grenade exploded.

"Well, what now?"

Collins scratched his head. "I could rig a time fuse real easy. Set the charge next to the fuel tanks. This baby would go sky-high."

"And take us with it. Unless we can get that engine

started, we're adrift." MacGonigal walked over to the rail and looked down. Faith had the cover off the outboard and was laboring over its innards. Susan held a shielded flashlight for him.

"What's it look like, Willie?"

"If you can find a twelve-volt battery, I think I can get it started."

"Then we're in business," said Collins. "Pass me up an adjustable wrench."

He disappeared below, diving into the little engine room, and came up a few minutes later carrying a black object. "Try this—it seems charged up."

Faith reached up for the battery and lowered it gently to the floorboards of the Zodiac. He opened the plastic battery box and disconnected the cables, reconnecting them to the battery Collins had given him.

"Cross your fingers. Here we go."

The 75-horsepower outboard surged into life. "That's got it," said Faith. He took the old battery out of the box and dropped it over the side, then stowed the new one in the waterproof box.

"Let's go, D.W."

"You go ahead, Mac. I'll be there in a minute."

Soon he came tumbling over the rail. "Let's get out of here!"

The Zodiac swung away, its companion raft at first balking, then following more or less obediently. Collins took the binoculars and focused them on the patrol boat, watching it slowly recede.

"I hope to God you didn't set a fireworks display in that thing. The last thing we need now is to attract more attention to ourselves."

He lowered the glasses. "Don't worry, Mac. I just put a couple of charges beside the keel. You won't even notice it when they go off."

MacGonigal took the binoculars from him and readjusted them. Through the night glasses, the patrol boat stood out clearly, a black silhouette on the water. As he watched, a tremor seemed to run through the boat, blurring its outlines in the glass. A low rumble came from deep in the vessel's bowels.

For a long time, nothing more happened, but through the glasses, it seemed that the patrol boat was riding lower in the water. As he watched, it seemed to wearily lower its head to the water until the bow was awash. Now and then he could see something floating near the bow as a wave crested near the vessel. It wasn't easy to see, but imagination supplied details, and it seemed to be a man, floating facedown in the water.

The boat was visibly lower in the water now. Even without binoculars they could tell that. They were all watching it, and suddenly it was gone. They stared a moment at the spot where it had been, but there was nothing there. Through the glasses, MacGonigal could see a little disturbance in the water and some debris on the surface.

Faith opened the throttle a little, and the Zodiac gained a little way, straining at the towline. The raft behind them protested at the increase in speed, tacking back and forth at the end of the line and making it difficult to steer a straight course.

"Slack off a little, Willie. We've got plenty of time."

Faith made no reply, but stared straight ahead. He pointed, and MacGonigal turned. A shape loomed out of the darkness, bearing straight down on them.

# X.

MacGonigal jerked the binoculars up, but everything was a blur. The oncoming vessel was so close that the binoculars were out of focus. A shot cracked past his head. He dropped the binoculars and dove for the floorboards. Someone in the raft behind the Zodiac was firing at the looming shape. The first shot was followed by a second and third. Green tracers streamed past, reaching out toward the unknown vessel. Spouts of water jumped, shining fluorescently in the dark. Some of them hit so close that they splashed water into the Zodiac.

*Christ*, thought MacGonigal, *it's a hell of a thing to be shot in the back by your own people!*

Susan and Faith were both perfectly flat on the floorboards. Collins lay hunched over, trying to untangle an AK-47 from the spray dodger. A steady stream of green tracers was flying overhead now, all of them apparently coming from the raft behind

276

them, and most of them, it seemed, just barely skimming the side tubes of the Zodiac.

"Cease fire, goddammit! It's us! Cease fire!"

Behind him, MacGonigal could hear a commotion as Watson or one of the other mercenaries tried to stop the firing. There were a few more shots—mostly straight up, as weapons were wrested away from excited men—and then there was silence.

He scooped up the binoculars and focused them. The shape of the Zodiac showed plainly, and he even thought he could recognize Lawrence huddling in the bow.

"Are you okay, Cal? Anybody hit?"

"I don't think so, but Jesus Christ, you scared the shit out of us!"

"How about the guys you're towing? Have somebody check them."

"Yeah. Okay," said Lawrence. "In the meantime, have somebody check the crazy bastards in the raft *you're* towing."

"It's quite all right. Everything here is under control." There was a pause. "Frightfully sorry, old boy."

There was a long silence. The reply, when it came, was loaded with sarcasm. "Quite all right, old boy."

MacGonigal leaned over to Faith. "Let's go Willie. If nobody's hurt, there's no point in staying around here."

Faith put the outboard back in gear and swung the Zodiac around, maneuvering carefully to keep from fouling the prop in either his own tow rope or that of the other Zodiac.

"What's the course, Mac?"

"Shit," said MacGonigal, "let me check." He pulled the poncho over himself again while the two Zodiacs chugged slowly forward, about twenty yards apart.

"Steer due north for about five minutes, then steer 315 degrees. That ought to clear the tip of Zapote far enough out to hide us from the installation on Zapotillo. Our next checkpoint is Isla Chichicaste. We ought to see it in about twelve minutes."

He thought a minute. "The island's pretty low in the water. D.W., have you got enough juice in that battery to keep a lookout with the night sight?"

For an answer, Collins poked the big Dragunov over the bow of the Zodiac, steadying it with the bow tube. He flicked the switch on, then off. "Looks okay. I think it'll be fine if we conserve the battery. Tell me when we should be getting close, and I'll switch it back on."

MacGonigal checked his watch, pressing the night-light button from time to time, shielding the glow with his hand. In between, he took the binoculars and scanned the horizon. There was nothing out there—at least nothing the 7×50s could pick up. And if there was another patrol boat, he hoped they'd hear it before it got close enough for the Dragunov's infrared sight.

The minutes went by slowly. At last, near the end of their estimated-time run, he heard a sound like waves breaking.

"Okay, D.W. Switch on, and see if you can pick anything up."

Collins braced the rifle and scanned the water in front of them.

"Yeah, I think that's it. Looks like a pretty fair-sized island."

"Should be about a quarter of a mile long, maybe a hundred yards or more on the side facing us."

They continued at reduced speed, the breaking waves off to the port quarter now.

"There! Ahead of us. Looks like a big sucker."

MacGonigal searched with the binoculars. He could see something rising up out of the water ahead of them. He ducked back under the poncho.

"Yeah. There's a little sandbar just south of Chichicaste. That must be it to our left, and Chichicaste itself is directly ahead."

He turned to Faith. "Once we clear Chichicaste, come a little more left, say 305 degrees. That'll put us on the south end of La Venada. I'd like to land just west of the isthmus connecting La Venada with La Venadita."

They moved slowly shoreward, almost holding their breath. To the left rose up the heights of La Venada, a large hilly island in the southern part of Lake Nicaragua. To their right was the smaller, triangular-shaped La Venadita, joined to the larger mass by a narrow strip of an isthmus, its separate name justified by its isolated, almost detached existence. Crowning the low hill that dominated La

Venadita was Cesare Prison, a massive, sprawling structure of concrete and steel.

They ran the Zodiacs ashore at the base of the cliffs that form the southern point of La Venada proper. The men, cramped and seasick from their long trip across the southern part of the lake, moved stiffly out of the rafts, their weapons held awkwardly. Here and there, one of the mercs or one of MacGonigal's crew helped one who seemed particularly stricken. The unloading of the rafts proceeded with agonizing slowness.

In the meantime, MacGonigal, Collins and Lawrence climbed the low cliff that backed the beach while Susan followed them, plugging gamely in their tracks.

Once on the high ground, they could look down to the little village of Punta Gruesa to the northwest, and Cesare Prison to the west, about a mile away. MacGonigal surveyed the scene through his glasses, then took the sniper rifle from Collins.

"Certainly looks peaceful. Looks like they don't have the slightest inkling that we're here."

Lawrence took the glasses and scanned the area. Two patrol boats were tied up at the quay in the little harbor between the village of Punta Gruesa and the point itself.

"That must be the way they bring prisoners in," he said, indicating the quay and the miscellaneous collection of small craft that snuggled up to the patrol boats. "If they knew we were coming, they wouldn't have those boats tied up—they'd be out looking for us."

"I think you're right, Cal." He took the glasses back. "I'll tell you what—you stay here until we can get a party up to relieve you. We'll leave them here as security while we get into position."

He swept the glasses over the low-lying isthmus again. "Put an ambush team on the narrow neck —just in case somebody from the main island wants to crash the party—and set up your support group at the base of the hill."

Lawrence looked toward the frowning concrete mass that crowned the hill. "Okay. That's good. I can support you when you go into the prison, and still provide support for the ambush team, if anyone tries to get across the isthmus."

Susan slipped up beside them, and MacGonigal handed her the glasses. She scanned the area. "My God, Mac, that thing looks like a fortress. We'll never be able to break into that!"

He grinned at her in the darkness. "You just watch, beautiful. We'll crack that thing like an egg."

He looked over at Collins. "Let's get back down and tend to business." He clapped a hand on Lawrence's shoulder, and the three of them slipped away, back down the steep bluff to the beach. As they came down, plunging and sliding the last few feet, they saw a scene of orderly confusion. The men unloading the rafts had sorted and assembled their equipment and gathered in three separate groups—one to be led by

Lawrence, one by Watson, and the largest by MacGonigal himself. MacGonigal sent two men up the cliff to relieve Lawrence, then beckoned the leaders to assemble.

Without preamble, he launched into his assault plan. "Okay—Cal will provide support with the 60mm mortar and other heavy weapons from the base of the hill. He'll also put out an ambush to block enemy reinforcements coming from the direction of Punta Gruesa. Tomás and I will take the assault party forward as soon as Cal is set up. We'll blast the front gate while Collins takes out any opposition. Once we're through, we'll fan out and begin the search. If anybody tries to stop us, deal with them quickly. Use lots of firepower, and blast your way through. Don't take any risks that you don't have to take.

"As soon as we have the main yard secure, Watson will bring his group up. They'll be responsible for the actual rescue—they'll break open the cell blocks, collect the prisoners, furnish carrying parties for those too weak to walk. Tomás will stick with me. Bring anyone who even looks like he has some information to us. Remember—we're looking for an American named Nichols, but we'll take everyone we can.

"I want us in and out in half an hour. No sideshows, no excursions, no souvenir hunting. Got it?"

There was a round of affirmative grunts and nods.

"Let's move, then!"

The leaders quickly dispersed to their respective

groups. There were hurried, muffled discussions as they gave their orders, and men began to shoulder their burdens. Within a minute or two, Lawrence's group began to move out, a lightly armed party —apparently the men he had picked for the ambush —leading the way, and the more heavily burdened mortarmen following.

A faint trail led from the base of the cliff across the isthmus, and they followed that, moving out in a long column. At the base of the hill, the lead party turned aside, crossing the narrow isthmus and moving back in the direction they had come, seeking a good sport with cover and a killing ground for their part of the operation. The support party following them eased their burdens to the ground. There was some rattling and thumping as they set the little mortar up. The rest of the column halted while Lawrence checked the mounting azimuth with the Chinese compass and positioned his machine guns.

Once the support group was ready, the assault party moved past them, climbing the hill toward the gate. The huge, grim concrete walls loomed over them, and they halted a little short of the arched gateway.

"What do you see, D.W.?"

"Nothin' much," muttered Collins, his eye glued to the night sight of his sniper rifle. "Nobody in sight. No guards that I can see."

He paused a moment. "There's a machine gun up there in the gatehouse. Nobody manning it, though."

"Well, you keep it covered, anyway," said MacGonigal. He turned to Maldonado. "You got that thing ready, Tomás?"

Maldonado grinned back at him in the darkness. "*Sí, jefe.*"

"Okay, let's go," said MacGonigal, rising to his feet. He gripped the carrying handle of the forty-pound breaching charge while Maldonado took the tool kit, and the two of them went forward at a shuffling trot, crouching low.

They reached the massive gate of the fortress without incident, and MacGonigal heaved the breaching charge up against the structure. Maldonado drew a heavy hammer and a pair of large spikes from the kit and nailed the charge in place, driving the spikes through the flanges of the charge. The hammer blows sounded hollowly through the prison yard, and there was a sudden undecipherable babble above them.

MacGonigal checked the charge. It was securely fastened to the gate. He pulled the two blasting caps from the bandolier that hung across his chest while Maldonado drove the point of a priming tool deep into the explosive. They inserted the caps and sealed the wound in the plastic. Above them, a voice called out threateningly.

There was a sudden, shocking boom from behind them. They both flinched, then flinched again as the sound was repeated. Glancing back, MacGonigal saw a flash as the big Dragunov fired again. There were two or three weapons firing now, just a few shots here and there as the prison guards attempted to man positions on the wall.

Maldonado was already moving away, running parallel to the wall, hugging the concrete, trailing the wires behind him. MacGonigal followed him, and together they crouched at the base of the wall while they fitted the firing devices to the wires. MacGonigal pulled the safety wire away from his clacker and looked at Maldonado, who nodded back at him in the darkness, then covered his ears. MacGonigal squeezed the clacker, and there was a tremendous roar from the gatehouse. The flash of the explosion was almost blinding, and MacGonigal got only a dim impression of flying stone and concrete.

The fragments hadn't stopped falling before the assault group was up and running, heading for the gaping hole where the gate had been in a single, concerted rush. MacGonigal and Maldonado came running back along the wall and joined them as the first men poured through.

The interior of the prison was a paved square, perhaps two-hundred yards on a side. Across this open space were the cell blocks, separate concrete buildings arrayed in a regular pattern, like city blocks. Nearer the gatehouse were other structures that seemed to be barracks for guards, armories and administrative offices. From some of these came shots—not many, just a feeble show of resistance. MacGonigal's men replied with restrained shooting and an occasional grenade, while he led the bulk of them straight across the open yard toward the first cell block.

As they approached the rough-finished concrete buildings, they could hear shouts and cheers. Prisoners, aroused by the sounds of combat, were awakening to the fact that a rescue operation was in progress. MacGonigal led his men beyond the first row of cell blocks and formed a rough perimeter. Behind him, Watson's party came up, laden with stretchers, explosives and breaching tools. MacGonigal watched as they blew the door off the first cell block and went in. He could hear muffled thumps as they set off small charges at the intersecting grilles, and in a moment a stream of ragged men began to come out of the building.

To their left, there was the sound of firing. Some of the men moved in that direction, as what appeared to be a brisk firefight developed in one section of the prison. In a moment, Collins came scurrying to MacGonigal.

"There's a bunch of the bastards holed up along the north wall. I don't think we can get to 'em without a lot of casualties."

"All right," said MacGonigal. "See if you can contain them—keep 'em from making too much trouble until we're ready to pull out."

Collins hurried away, the Dragunov slung across his shoulder. MacGonigal turned to see Maldonado leading a scrawny, ragged man forward, one of the released prisoners.

"I think we've got something here, Mac. He says there's a special cell block in the back." He pointed down the street between the cell blocks. "He says he's heard that there are some *norteamericanos* there."

"Okay. Let's head in that direction. Tell Watson to follow us, then pass the word to D.W." He turned to Susan. "How about it, beautiful? This enough excitement for you?"

She squeezed his arm. Her eyes were shining. "Mac, I wouldn't have missed this for the world!"

They moved out, scattering along the sides of the street, keeping to the sides, ducking from locked door to locked door as they made their way toward the special cell block. There was quite a bit of fire now, as small groups of guards and soldiers coalesced into points of resistance. Looking back down the street, MacGonigal could see Watson's party moving up. He raised his fist, pumping it up and down, signaling them to hurry.

The assault party was strung along the street now, taking cover wherever they could find it, and returning fire. Small groups of two or three men moved out, expanding their perimeter, pushing the still-disorganized guards and soldiers back, providing a safe route for Watson's men as they ran crouching down the street toward the special cell block.

The first of them reached the cell block and paused only a moment at the door, then leaped aside. With a thump, the steel door was blasted off its hinges, and they went in. MacGonigal heard a few shots fired from inside the cell block, then silence.

"Come on, beautiful, let's go in there and I'll introduce you to my old buddy Steve."

They went in through the still-smoking doorway, stepping over the body of a guard who had been foolish enough to resist Watson's men. In a small lighted room next to the door were several uniformed men standing with their faces to the wall while a Miskito Indian covered them with an AK-47.

At the first grille, they caught up with Watson. He was overseeing a group of men who were busy with sledgehammers and bolt cutters, opening cells. He looked up at MacGonigal.

· "Hello, old boy. Bit of a mess here—bitched up the opening mechanism when we blasted the grille, have to open the cells here one by one."

MacGonigal nodded. "Found any Americans yet?"

"Ah. I was wondering when you'd get around to that. I believe your man's over there."

MacGonigal looked in the direction indicated and saw a cell with its door gaping open. There were three men on stretchers on the floor there, and several armed Indians around them. He went into the cell and looked down at the emaciated, disfigured men. One of them looked vaguely familiar.

"Steve? Is that you, old buddy?"

The figure on the stretcher moved and seemed to be trying to speak. MacGonigal squatted down next to him, bending low to hear.

"You fuckin' Mick bastard! They told me, but I didn't believe . . ."

MacGonigal looked down into the scarred, one-eyed face. He could think of nothing to say.

Suddenly there was commotion outside.

"Mac! Mac, you better get the hell back outside. D.W. says we've got trouble—maybe more than we can handle!"

The lights of the trucks sliced through the night. Lawrence counted them as they came down the hill, highballing it along the one-lane road that led through the scrub across the isthmus. There were twelve of them. *Jesus! There must be a couple hundred of the bastards! I hope the boys down there don't get overeager.*

He had barely formed the thought when there was a bright flash behind the second truck. Someone had fired a Claymore—someone with a little sense, because he had let the first couple of trucks through before detonating the directional mine. The column was cut in two now, as the third and fourth trucks caught the full force of the blast, slewing sideways in the narrow roadway, one of them turning over.

The next two trucks, following too closely, slammed into the wreckage. There was a long burst of fire as someone raked the twisted mass of metal with an RPD machine gun. The rattle of the RPD was punctuated by another blinding flash as a second Claymore went off, this time blasting its shotgunlike cone of fragments into the closely packed trucks in the rear of the column as they sat bumper-to-bumper, immobilized.

There was more firing down there now, and someone fired a third Claymore. Grenades began to go off, and there was the shattering *whoosh* of an RPG-7. The antitank warhead detonated in the middle of the jammed-together trucks, and was followed in a split second by a spectacular ball of roiling flame as one of the gas tanks went up. The convoy seemed to shake itself apart as the explosions spread, running up and down the packed mass of machines, as one gas tank after another went up.

The two trucks that had made it through halted a hundred yards from the mortar position, as if their drivers were uncertain as to what they should do. Suddenly the nearest of them lurched forward, accelerating rapidly, obviously making a run form the prison gate. Lawrence brought his AK-47 to his shoulder, but before he could get a round off, several shots hit the truck. He saw them thump into the door on the passenger side, and the windshield shattered. The truck swerved, swayed dangerously, somehow righted itself, and plunged down the beach, heading into the water, throwing up a huge wave as it plowed into the lake. He watched fascinated as it surged on, its momentum carrying it forward until it finally came to a stop with just its canvas top showing above the surface. A few heads were bobbing around it, and splashes erupted around them as bullets slapped into the water.

He turned his attention back to the remaining truck. It sat forlornly where it had stopped, its shot-out front tires causing it to sag in the front, like a kneeling camel. Steam poured from the punctured radiator, and there were bodies scattered around, but no sign of life.

As Lawrence surveyed the results of the ambush, something struck the ground violently beside him. He jumped back, startled, and heard the crack of a bullet overhead. Diving for cover, he was aware of a sudden rattle of fire from his men, while more shots cracked overhead.

One of his men was horsing the little mortar around—it had been trained on the isthmus road to back up the ambush party. He crawled up to sit as more shots slapped into the ground or snapped overhead.

It was clear by now that the shooting was coming from the prison gatehouse. *Shit* he thought. *They've got Mac bottled up now*.

He checked the sights on the little mortar and grabbed a shell, pulling the charge bags off and ripping out the safety pin. He made one last check, then dropped the round down the muzzle. The round rose from the stubby barrel, a soaring red spark, and traced a lazy parabola, arching high up in the air, then suddenly plunging down. He watched it all the way, following it as it crashed into the ground just short of the gatehouse. He spun the elevating wheel and shoved another down the muzzle.

That one was lost—he couldn't tell where it landed. *Must have gone over the gatehouse*, he muttered to himself as he backed off the wheel a half turn and dropped a third round down the muzzle. This time he was rewarded by a flash on the facade of the gatehouse.

"Willie!" he yelled back over his shoulder. "You better tell Mac to get his ass back out here! I don't know how long we can handle this bunch."

Someone—a member of the mortar crew—was unpacking rounds, cutting the charges, pulling the pins and passing the little shells to him. He dropped them down the muzzle in a steady rhythm, watching them rise high over the scene of the fighting, then accelerate rapidly downward into the gatehouse. Big chunks of concrete were beginning to flake away from the structure now, revealing the tangle of reinforcing rod beneath. He was aware of an increase in the intensity of the enemy's fire, through, and realized that they had pushed a platoon-size force through the gate, deploying in a half-moon around it. His own men had spread out as well, taking positions to contain the enemy, and a hot firefight was in progress. He spun the wheel back another half turn, searching for the enemy riflemen who had gone to ground only a hundred yards away.

Someone was tugging at his sleeve and shouting in his ear. Half deaf from the muzzle blast of the little mortar, he strained to hear. It was Faith, his face full of concern.

"Cal! Cal! We're out of commo with Mac! He's not answering the radio!"

They had formed a rough barricade across the street, heaping sections of pavement, chunks of concrete, cell furniture, and the blasted remains of steel cell doors to provide them with some shelter from the almost solid stream of tracers that came down the street. Susan sheltered at the base of the barricade, unable to bring herself to move as the storm of fire swept over her head. Lying beside her, not an arm's length away, was a dead man, his head blasted open, his blood and brains forming a puddle in front of her face.

"I've had about enough of this horse shit!"

She turned to look in MacGonigal's direction and gave a surprised gasp. Collins turned to see him stripping off his camouflage pants. For a moment, he stood there, naked from the waist to the knees. He rummaged in his rucksack, drawing out first his kilt, then the box containing his bagpipes.

"Oh, shit, Mac! You're not gonna do *that* again, are you?"

MacGonigal made no answer as the fitted the drones of his bagpipes together.

Collins turned to Sue. "You'd better find yourself a safe place, honey. When he gets bare-assed like that, it means there's gonna be one hell of a fight."

MacGonigal had the pipes assembled now, and was wrapping the seven yards of saffron wool around his waist. He attached the leather sporran, then buckled on his web pistol belt. He was standing upright, and tracers zipped closely overhead.

"Get down, Mac! Please!"

A flare burst high over the position and bathed it in a sickly, greenish light. They all instinctively cowered, and a stream of tracer came flying down the street, ricocheting off the walls and filling the air with chunks of metal and stone. MacGonigal stood erect, legs spread apart, the drones thrust over his left shoulder, and inflated the bag, one huge breath after another.

"Shit! There's nothing we can do now but follow the crazy Irish bastard."

MacGonigal struck in his drones. The light of the flare had died down now, and the firing with it. In the silence, there was only the sound of the moans of the wounded and the deep bass hum of the drones. MacGonigal began to counterpoint those sounds with the thin, high wail of the pipes.

Watson crouched in the ruins of the special cell block with his charges. Outside he could hear the rattle of small-arms fire, punctuated by the occasional whump of a mortar round—or perhaps some other form of ordnance, he couldn't tell from his position.

He looked back along the walkway. There were at least fifty men back there, half of them crippled in one way or another. He didn't have enough healthy men to get the others down to the boats even if there were no battle going on just outside. He crawled up to the cell-block door and looked outside. He could barely make out a couple of men from the assault party flattened against the pavement, close up against the walls. Neither of them moved, and he wondered if they were dead, abandoned by the others.

He shook his head sadly. *I should have known better . . . bloody Yanks!* he thought to himself. It seemed clear that they had been abandoned—if anyone in the assault or covering parties survived to abandon them.

*Well,* he consoled himself, *I suppose I'd do the same in their place.*

One of his men came forward, as if asking for instructions. Watson motioned him back. *No point in letting these poor beggars know . . . they'll find out soon enough.*

Another flare burst above the central complex, and he ducked back instinctively. He could hear firing from ahead and see an occasional tracer ricochet off the pavement in front of his position.

The sound of firing seemed to die away with the flare. In the almost supernatural quiet that followed, he could hear a faintly familiar sound. He shook his head. *I must be hallucinating,* he thought. He could see the Gurkha pipers in his mind, marching at quick time to the sound of their pipes.

He shook his head again disbelievingly. This wasn't typical Gurkha quick march, somehow conjured out of his memory. It was measured, disciplined Celtic playing. He listened, wondering.

A sudden burst of fire intruded; drowning out the sound of the pipes. There was a ripple of mortar fire, then the sound of small arms, punctuated by some measured, heavy-toned weapon. There were more explosions, and a glow appeared in the direction of the main gate. Then the sound of firing died away again.

*Well, I suppose that's it. They're either out and gone, or else they've all bought it. Either way . . .*

He couldn't quite bring himself to finish the thought. He drew his pistol and checked the magazine. Eleven rounds. He reinserted the magazine and pumped one into the chamber. There wasn't much he could do with a pistol, but it was just as well to be ready.

As he returned the pistol to its holster, he saw a flicker of movement out of the corner of his eye. He drew the weapon again and motioned to the men behind him. One or two came up, crawling forward with their weapons cradled in their arms. Wordlessly he pointed to where the figure had gone to ground.

Suddenly the figure burst out of hiding, running full tilt diagonally across the open space, legs pumping madly. An AK-47 went off next to Watson's ear, half stunning him. The bullet knocked sparks off the pavement just behind the running figure. The man collapsed, rolling himself into a ball, and trumbled to the ground.

"Stop the goddamn shooting, man! It's me, Tomás!" A string of unintelligible shouts followed, which Watson could only speculate where Spanish curses. He knocked aside one of the AK-47s.

"Terribly sorry, old boy, but we didn't know it was you."

The response was another string of cursing as

Tomás pried himself off the pavement and came running toward them.

"We got to get out of here, man. MacGonigal is trying for a breakout but I don't know how long he can hold an opening for us."

"I see," said Watson. "Sent you back for us, did he? Seems I've misjudged the chap."

He signaled to the men behind him while the two riflemen with him moved out across the open area and took up positions at the entrance to the next street. He stayed long enough to make sure that those who couldn't walk under their own power were being helped, then he and Tomás set off across the open space.

They joined the two riflemen on the opposite side and looked down the now-silent street. There seemed to be nothing moving there. A glance back over his shoulder showed Watson that the released prisoners were following, some walking, some hobbling, some leaning on others, and a few being carried. The group carrying the American, Nichols, was near the head of the column.

"Right. Let's get to where MacGonigal is and see what's what."

He led out, with Tomás beside him. His two rifle-men hung back a little, hugging the walls on each side of the street. There was an almost eerie quiet as they moved down the littered pavement, stepping on expended cartridge cases, fragments of glass and chunks of broken concrete.

They reached the next corner without incident.

Watson halted to check on the progress of the column of prisoners. They seemed to be keeping up, and his few remaining riflemen were well-dispersed, providing them with a little protection.

"All right, chaps. Let's move on."

They moved out cautiously, the two men hanging back under cover as before, while Watson and Tomás took the lead. They had crossed the first ten yards of open space when the shooting started, a single, prolonged burst of automatic fire.

"I'm hit, man! I'm hit! Son of a bitch! My legs . . . " Tomás rolled in the street while Watson sprinted for cover, clawing at his holster. Behind him, his two riflemen began to fire, slow, single shots, evenly spaced.

MacGonigal climbed up over the barricade in front of him, the drones thrust over his shoulder, his fingers flying over the chanter.

> *"On, ev'ry mountaineer,*
> *strangers to flight or fear,*
> *flock to the standard of dauntless Red Hugh.*

> *"Bonnach and gallowglass,*
> *sprung from each mountain pass,*
> *on for old Erin! O'Donnell Abu!"*

He was marching straight down the middle of the street now, fully exposed, his kilt swaying. One after another, his men left their positions and crept along the sides of the street, sheltering in the doorways, trying to stay even with him. So far, not a shot had been fired. They had covered half the distance to the machine gun.

*"Many a heart shall quail,*
*under the coat of mail.*
*Deeply his cruelties the foeman shall rue,*

*"When on his ears shall ring,*
*borne on the breeze's wing,*
*Tyrconnel's dread war cry, O'Donnell Abu!"*

"Christ! It makes the hackles rise, don't it?" Watson said to no one in particular.

Lawrence paused, a mortar shell in his hand, poised over the muzzle of the little weapon.

"Do I hear what I think I hear?"

Faith cocked his head, listening for a moment. "I hear it! That crazy fuckin' bastard is *attacking!*"

They stood frozen a moment. There was no firing, nothing. The high, clear skirling of the pipes cut through the darkness.

*"Son of a bitch!* Son of a *bitch!* Those bastards are giving it to them! That fuckin' MacGonigal is feeding 'em the bayonet!"

"Jesus," said Faith, "we got to support them!"

Lawrence reacted as if hit with a douche of cold water. He looked down. There were ten mortar shells left. He ripped the safety pins out of them, cut the charges, and slammed them all down the muzzle, one after the other. They rose into the sky to fall in a rippling splatter on the Sandinista position. Before the first one landed, however, he was out of the mortar position, AK-47 in hand, running straight toward the enemy.

"Get off your asses! Let's kill these bastards!"

His action caught both the enemy and his own men by surprise, but Faith got the men off the ground and into motion. For a long moment, the enemy's reaction was one of shock, as if they were unable to believe that Lawrence and his men would charge out into the open. This paralysis lasted only a moment, however, and a few uncertain shots were fired from the enemy position. This tentative action was followed by a blast of fire that caught the leading men in the middle of the open space. Out of the corner of his eye, Lawrence saw two of his men crumple to the ground.

*Jesus, they'll cut us apart!* he thought, even as he continued across the narrowing gap between himself and the enemy position. The air in front of him was laced with flying green tracers that seemed to reach out for them.

Then the mortar shells began to fall, plunging into the Sandinistas in an almost continuous roar. By now, Lawrence was so close to the position that the fragments whizzed all around him, clanging off the sheet-metal roofs on both sides of him. As the last round impacted, he leaped into the midst of the enemy. Several Sandinistas lay huddled on the ground—wounded, dead, or merely overcome with the sudden violence of the mortar barrage, he couldn't tell. He fired quickly, one shot into each, and plunged on.

Behind him, he could hear his men screaming, a high, ululating cry that in its own way was as unnerving as the pipes. It seemed to paralyze the Sandinista troops, because they made no effective resistance as his men slashed through the position.

He could hear firing ahead of him now, uncertain and tentative at first, then building to a crackling roar. *Christ! Mac has really tied into it!*

He reached the high stone wall of the prison. The heavy wooden gate gaped ajar, blasted and hanging on a single hinge. As he approached it, he heard an engine start. Suddenly the shattered gate was filled with a huge, black hulk.

*Goddamn! A BTR!*

The eight-wheeled armored vehicle lumbered through the gate, its turret-mounted machine gun marking it as a BTR 60PB. It moved forward slowly, traversing its turret and firing long bursts. The slow, measured klunk, klunk of the Soviet 14.5 mm KPV seemed to fill his head. He fired at the vehicle's vision blocks, hoping to blind it before it could roll into the midst of his men.

There was a sudden blast near him, an explosion that left his ears ringing. Before he could assimilate what was happening, there was a bright flash on the front slope of the BTR between the forward view ports. The vehicle slewed around and came to a stop, smoke pouring from the vision ports. Faith ran past him, inserting another round into the muzzle of the RPG-7. He dropped to one knee just in front of Lawrence.

"Get the shit out of the way, man! That bastard isn't dead yet!"

Lawrence dove out of the back-blast area of the weapon just as Faith fired again. He saw the rocket-propelled grenade describe an arc through the air and detonate against the turret of the BTR. The turret hatch blew off, spinning end over end, making a lazy parabola before clattering to the pavement.

His ears ringing, Lawrence covered the smoking vehicle with his AK-47 as Faith reloaded the RPG-7. Two of his men came up and joined Faith. The three of them cautiously approached the BTR. There was no movement from within the vehicle. One of the men clambered up its sloped side and dropped a grenade inside the now-open hatch, then jumped back down, covering his head with his hands.

There was a dull thump from inside the BTR, followed by a rumble.

"Get away from it, man! It's gonna blow!"

The man who had thrown the grenade scrambled for cover while the rest of them turned and ran. Lawrence could feel a sudden wave of heat wash over him, followed by a gigantic shove that almost knocked him off his feet.

*Goddamn! The son of a bitch must have been full of ammo!*

He turned back to see the BTR burning brightly, a

huge torch blocking the gateway. Faith and his co-horts approached it cautiously, holding their arms in front of them to shield themselves from the heat. In a moment, Faith stepped back, the RPG-7 at the ready.

"What is it, Willie?"

Faith looked at him briefly, the flames of the burning BTR giving a ruddy glow to his face.

"I'm not sure, Cal. I thought I heard another engine somewhere."

They edged past the burning hulk. The interior of the prison complex was lit up by the flames. A hundred yards or so away, almost directly across from them, a dark shape lurked against a corner of one of the cell blocks. As they watched, it moved, detaching itself from the shelter of the building.

"Another BTR! How many of these damn things do they have?"

Instead of answering, Faith leveled the RPG-7 and tracked the slowly moving vehicle. Lawrence ducked, clapping his hands over both ears as the concussion of firing lifted the short hairs on the back of his neck. The projectile streaked across the open space and detonated on the lower edge of the turret, just where it joined the hull.

Men were pushing past them now, streaming into the prison complex, fanning out to cover the streets between each cell block. Lawrence could hear iso-lated shots as they mopped up the remnants of the enemy. In the distance, deep inside the prison com-plex, he could hear more concentrated shooting.

\* \* \*

The machine gunner seemed to awaken from a dream. He swung the gun around and tried to bring it to bear on MacGonigal. An AK-47 barked from a doorway, and he was flung backward. There was a sudden rush past the piper, and a flurry of shooting. Men sprung up from the Sandinista positions and took to their heels. MacGonigal's men cut them down as they ran.

As the knot of men surged forward, a dark object came flying from the crowd of Sandinista troops, tumbling end over end. MacGonigal shrugged off the pipes and threw up his arm just in time, batting the object away. He turned his head and there was an explosion that sent fragments into his arm and side. The shock of the impact seemed to paralyze his arm. Another object came flying in his direction, bouncing off the wall next to him. He looked down in horror and recognized it as an RG-42 grenade, obsolete, underpowered and unreliable, but deadly for all of that. He kicked it away, and it went skittering. It must have been a dud—at least, he didn't see or hear it explode.

With his left arm almost useless, he groped for his revolver, dragging it out of the holster. He was in the midst of the fight now, too close to shoot, unless he had a clear target. He struck out with the revolver, clubbing one Sandinista down with the heavy barrel of the Python, and then the weapon was knocked from his grasp. He kicked out desperately and drew his knife, lunging at a figure that loomed in front of him, thrusting home with all the weight of his body, turning to his right to get more force into the blow. But in doing so, he exposed his right shoulder and side. He felt his knife grate against bone, and he drove the full weight of his body forward and felt the point penetrate deeply. Then he took a blow under the ribs that drove the breath from his body. He lost his grip on the knife and fell to his knees. Vaguely he sensed the men to his left and right step beyond him and close ranks. He dimly heard the noise of the fight as his men drove their attack home. A heavy body fell with a rattle and clatter of equipment, but who or what it was, he couldn't tell.

He couldn't catch his breath, and he felt suddenly thirsty. He couldn't focus his eyes. He scrabbled with his one good hand and found his knife, slippery with blood. With a huge effort, he got his knees under him and tried to push himself to his feet. A dark figure suddenly loomed over him and by instinct he grappled with the figure. Somehow, he managed to get his feet under him, half leaning on, half wrestling with his opponent. His enemy dragged him erect, pulling him around as he sought to force the knife out of his hand, but he jerked free, then fell forward in an attempt to thrust home.

He clinched with his opponent, clinging tightly while the man struck again and again with his fist and the butt of an empty pistol. The blows fell thickly and MacGonigal had no choice but to endure them. He scrabbled at his enemy's face, feeling for the eyes. The man stepped back, hauling on MacGonigal's knife hand as he did so. MacGonigal was almost jerked off his feet. He thudded into the man, and somehow they both went down, with MacGonigal on top.

He could hardly think straight, but he realized that he had a momentary advantage and had to use it. He clawed at the man's face again, and the man snapped at him. He felt teeth rip into his flesh, but he clawed again. His fingers located the eye sockets and he dug deeply into them. They resisted him, the eyeballs moving back under pressure. The man bucked convulsively underneath him. Desperate, he drove his thumb into the inner corner of his enemy's right eye. He could feel the eyeball slide sideways, and the thumb drove deeper. The connective tissue began to tear, and he plunged the thumb in to the last joint, then crooked it and ripped outward.

His opponent's reaction was electric. He heaved MacGonigal off of his chest with a mighty surge. MacGonigal fell, rolling over on his side, with his left arm pinned underneath him. He saw the bulky figure rise swayingly to his feet, the head hanging and wobbling from side to side. The man flailed about with his hands and seized a castaway machete. With a roar, he turned back to MacGonigal heaved the machete back over his head for a full blow. The man's face was a mask of blood, and the eyeball hung down on the right cheek. MacGonigal tried to roll out of the way, but his left arm was underneath him and prevented him.

The machete blade flashed down and buried itself in the ground beside his head. The man seemed unable to coordinate his movements with only one eye. Somehow, MacGonigal managed to work his arm out from under his body and slither out of range. His opponent bellowed and started forward. MacGonigal tried to move again, but he wasn't fast enough. The descending machete blade struck his forehead a glancing blow and laid it open to the bone, neatly peeling back a flap of skin. He couldn't see. Blood gushed from the wound and filled his eyes.

He rolled over, trying to clear his eyes of blood with his right hand. His left hand still wouldn't obey him. His vision was blurred and double. Dim, fuzzy figures seemed to dance in the gloom all about him, but he could make nothing of them. He knew that he had to keep moving, and he rolled over. There was a ringing in his ears, and over it he could hear the clatter and banging of the battle. Something stung his fingers. He had grasped the blade of a knife or machete lying on the ground. He slithered a few feet more, dragging the weapon with him, lacerating his fingers as he pulled it forward, sliding his hand up the blade to locate the hilt. He wrapped his fingers around it and swung it in desperation, slicing wide arcs through the air, cutting horizontally, the blade just inches off the ground.

He felt the blade sink into some solid substance with a meaty thunk. He swung again and again, making contact each time. The darkness grew, and there was a heavy weight on top of him. He pushed at it and his fingers encountered blood and other things.

He tried to heave the body off of him, but it was too much for him. He lay exhausted and nearly blind while the fight raged around him. He suddenly felt cool and relaxed. It was a delicious feeling, and he surrendered himself to it.

He woke feeling as if he had been beaten by clubs. It was still difficult to see, but by closing one eye, he could make out Sue's concerned features.

"Can you see me now?"

MacGonigal groaned. She swam in his vision, but he forced himself to concentrate on the face. He had difficulty focussing his eyes—they seemed to want to look in different directions.

"Thank God, you're alive." She said. "I know you feel like hell now, but you're alive."

She passed a pungent-smelling cloth over his face. MacGonigal sputtered and tried to pull it off. He could barely breathe, and the cloth was cutting off his air supply. She gently replaced the cloth, being careful to keep it clear of his mouth this time.

She inspected the dressings on MacGonigal's hands. "You're cut up pretty bad, Mac, but I think you'll come out of it all right." She paused a moment. "Better than some, anyway."

MacGonigal waited for her to go on, but she lapsed into silence. "How many did we lose?"

She looked at him. "Not as many as we would have if you weren't such a crazy bastard. We had four or five killed, and we've got another twelve wounded

—one or two of those won't last the night."

She passed the cloth over his forehead again.

"How is he?"

She turned to the speaker. "He's conscious now, Willie."

Faith leaned over him. "Jesus, Mac, I'm glad to see that you're all right. That was a hell of a fight. We thought it was just a matter of them mopping us up, until we heard the pipes. Then we knew that you were coming, and we came out to meet you. They weren't ready for that, and we caught 'em between us."

"You mean we won?"

"Oh, yeah. We won. We won big. You and your group about wiped out their main force, and we did for the last bunch, and that was the end of it. There were a few hiding here and there, but we mopped them up."

A wave of nauseating pain swept over MacGonigal. He couldn't seem to think straight. "Now . . . now what?"

"Well, Cal's taken over. He's got two patrol boats rounded up, along with several smaller craft, and we're loading wounded now, and as soon as we get the wounded on board, we'll start loading everyone else."

"What about the enemy? Did any escape? Are there any groups of them hiding out anywhere in town?"

Faith's expression was grim. "There weren't any who escaped us. Every last maggot is accounted for."

"What about Steve? How's he making it?"

Faith shook his head. "They really worked Steve over—I'm about half-convinced there's some internal damage. He's alive, and we can keep him that way, but I'm not too sure about anything else."

"Where is he now?"

"We've got him on board now. I just came back to see how you were. There's a stretcher party coming for you any minute now."

"How about the rest of our people?"

"Cal's set up his command post on one of the patrol boats. He's in contact with Samuels—he's got a reception committee set up for us, with transportation and medical aid for the wounded, once we reach the south shore of the lake. Tomás is wounded —nothing bad, but he's out of action temporarily. Watson is supervising getting everyone to the boats. D.W. is out with a crew booby-trapping and mining everything he can find—it's going to look like the Fourth of July when we pull out of here."

A small group of men came up with a stretcher, and they rolled MacGonigal onto it and started down to the quay.

"This isn't necessary, you know. I can walk . . . I think."

A small cool hand pressed him down. "You just lie back and behave yourself." She looked at him a moment, and then said threateningly, "If you try to get out of that stretcher, I'll put you back in it."

He grinned weakly. "Yes, ma'am," he said.

"If you want to do something worthwhile, hold these." She thrust something into his hands.

"What is it?"

"Your pipes. I picked them up when you dropped them, and I'm tired of carrying them."

He could think of nothing to say. He ran his bandaged hands along the bundle, but could feel nothing. She put her hand on his arm and walked alongside the stretcher.

At the quay, dozens of emaciated men were being loaded into a miscellaneous collection of boats. Calvin Lawrence appeared on the bridge of one of the patrol boats, giving orders through a bullhorn, sorting out a situation that continually threatened to degenerate into chaos. He stopped a moment when he saw the party come down with MacGonigal.

"Come on up here, Mac. We'll be ready to cast off as soon as D.W. and his boys get back."

They carried him aboard and laid his stretcher down on the port side of the boat, next to another loaded stretcher. MacGonigal looked over at it.

"Hi, Mac. Long time no see." The voice was strangely familiar. He puzzled over it.

"Steve? Is that you?"

"Yeah, it's me, all right." He paused a long moment. "You certainly took your time getting here."

"Yeah, I know," said MacGonigal. "You just can't seem to get good help these days."

Below him, he could feel vibration as the patrol-boat's engines came to life. Someone stepped over his legs, paying out a towline to the smaller craft. Craning his neck, MacGonigal could see several figures running through the darkness toward the quay. He watched them pound down the quay and clamber aboard.

"That's the last of us, Cal."

Lawrence waved an acknowledgment to Collins, then directed the men standing in the bow to cast off. The patrol boat slowly chugged away from the quay, taking a string of smaller craft with it, and straightened out on course across the lake.

As the boat gathered way, Collins made his way back to the stern. "How you doin', Mac?"

"Okay, I reckon. Did we get everybody off?"

"Every last one of 'em. And left our hosts a little going-away present. You just keep your eye on that building next to the quay. In about ten minutes, you're gonna see a fireworks display like you *never* saw before."

He glanced at the figure lying next to MacGonigal. "How's Steve? He gonna make it?"

MacGonigal turned his head. Nichols was asleep, his face relaxed, although showing deep lines and a gray pallor. "I think so. All we've got to do now is get him home."

They sat silent for a few minutes as the boat throbbed its way across the lake. In its wake the smaller craft bobbed and heaved. Collins grinned and pointed aft toward one of the boats. MacGonigal could see what looked like someone hanging his head over the side of the craft. "I'll bet some of those boys are . . . *Holy Jesus!*"

A fountain of fire erupted from the island, spewing flame and sparks high into the air. A ruddy glow played over the faces of the men in the boats as they turned to watch it. In a moment, there was another explosion, and then another. Flames and smoke seemed to engulf the prison, which shook with one blast after another, a rolling drumfire of explosions.

"Sure an' that's a beautiful sight," MacGonigal said as he put one bandaged hand on Collins' shoulder. "D.W., you do good work."

The boat droned steadily on in the growing dawn, heading for the far shore. In the distance, MacGonigal could see a little smudge on the horizon, all that remained of the prison island. As the sun rose, even that became indistinct. It was a brilliant, cloudless day, a fine day for a boat ride, he thought.

"How do you feel, Mac?"

He looked up to see Sue kneeling down beside him. She had a thick mug in one hand, a damp cloth in the other. She passed him the mug and began to sponge him down as he sipped. He put the mug down on the deck beside him and grinned up at her. As she leaned over him, her blouse gaped, and he could see her part breasts peeking at him. In spite of himself, he felt aroused.

"I feel pretty good. I feel like I could do almost anything now."

She looked down at the growing bulge under his

kilt. "My God, Mac! Don't you ever think of anything else?"

"I have to do *something* to compensate," he said. He held up his bandaged hand. "Because I can't even play me pipes now."

She slipped a hand under his kilts. "Don't worry, Mac. I'll play your pipes for you."